PENGUIN BOOKS

CHEESE DONUTS ARE MOST DEFINITELY NOT SUBPAR

Melly Sutjitro is a Chinese Indonesian author who lives in Jakarta with her husband and two teenage kids. She spent a few years living in San Francisco while completing her master's degree. After spending a decade in corporate offices, she decides to pursue her love of storytelling through writing. She has nine Picture Books and three romance novels published under the pen name mellyberry. When she's not stressing over the plot in her manuscripts, she enjoys reading all sorts of books (as long as they're not horror) and documenting her thoughts on her Instagram page. Occasionally, she would spend her time cooking, doing Pilates, and watching re-runs of *Friends* and *The Big Bang Theory*.

PRAISE FOR *CHEESE DONUTS ARE MOST DEFINITELY NOT SUBPAR*

'Featuring fiercely loyal characters you can't help falling for, *Cheese Donuts Are Most Definitely Not Subpar* serves up sparkling banter and plenty of rom-com shenanigans. While the best donut might be up for debate, there's no question Melly Sutjitro's debut is a winner!'
—Melonie Johnson, USA Today Bestselling author of *Too Good to Be Real* and *Too Wrong to Be Right*

'Joyful, warm, and written with a wicked sense of humour, *Cheese Donuts Are Most Definitely Not Subpar* is a heartwarming ride with lots of fun-filled banter between the leads. An entertaining read!'
—Ivy Ngeow, *The Straits Times* Bestselling author of *The American Boyfriend*

'Melly Sutjitro's *Cheese Donuts Are Most Definitely Not Subpar* is a fascinating look into life as a strong independent woman in Indonesia. From meddling aunties to major career shifts to natural girl body problems, *Cheese Donuts* delves deep into the problems that a modern Asian woman has to deal with in a very traditional Asian society. It's not every day you see a Romance that directly deals with PMS, which is what I loved the most about Melly's book! *Cheese Donuts* is simply . . . delectable!'
—Mica De Leon, author of *Love on the Second Read* and *Winds of War*

'Intensely readable! Had me hooked beginning to end.'
—Nona Uppal, author of *Fool Me Twice*

'A sharp, sassy, and deliciously funny tale of simmering attraction and unexpected pairings that leaves you cheering for more.'
—Claire Betita de Guzman, author of *Sudden Superstar* and *Huê' City*

'*Cheese Donuts Are Most Definitely Not Subpar* delivers an irresistibly entertaining journey with delightful banter between its charming characters.'
—Durjoy Datta, author of nineteen bestselling romance novels

'Just as its title promises, *Cheese Donuts Are Most Definitely Not Subpar* is sweet, a bit salty, and good till the last bite. Readers are sure to fall in love with this swoony, yet relatable romance set in Indonesia.'
—Tanya Guerrero, author of *Adrift, All You Knead is Love,* and *How to Make Friends with the Sea*

'What a fantastic debut! *Cheese Donuts Are Most Definitely Not Subpar* is the reluctant-allies-to-lovers romance novel of my dreams. Melly Sutjitro effortlessly combines the crackling tension of forced proximity with the soft emotion of two people who choose each other despite their rocky start. Ellie and Dion will be in your heart long after you've finished reading.'
—Swati Hegde, author of *Match Me If You Can*

Cheese Donuts Are Most Definitely Not Subpar

Melly Sutjitro

PENGUIN BOOKS

An imprint of Penguin Random House

PENGUIN BOOKS

Penguin Books is an imprint of the Penguin Random House group of
companies whose addresses can be found at
global.penguinrandomhouse.com

Published by Penguin Random House SEA Pte Ltd
40 Penjuru Lane, #03-12, Block 2
Singapore 609216

First published in Penguin Books by Penguin Random House SEA 2024

ISBN 9789815204988

Typeset in Garamond by MAP Systems, Bengaluru, India

www.penguin.sg

Deli,
you were the closest thing to a big sister I've ever had,
I miss you dearly every day

Playlist

As It Was	Harry Styles
At My Worst	Pink Sweat$
Cruel Summer	Taylor Swift
Fallin' All in You	Shawn Mendes
Hate You	Jungkook
It'll Be Okay	Shawn Mendes
It's My Life	Bon Jovi
Kiss Me	Sixpence None The Richer
Manusia Biasa	Yovie & Nuno
Perahu Kertas	Maudy Ayunda
Running	Gaho
Style	Taylor Swift
Whenever, Wherever	Roy Kim

January

Chapter 1

Ellie

This is the Mondayest Monday in the history of all my Mondays. I've been staring at the plate number of the car in front of me for the last half hour. The clock ticks, ticks, ticks without a care in the world, and we're not moving. Not even an inch.

Ashley bangs her tiny fists against her own thighs. 'C'mon, c'mon. We're late!'

Chuckling and shaking his head a little, our driver gestures towards the unmoving cars before ours. 'We're stuck, Ash.'

I glance at the digital clock in the middle of the car's dashboard. 'We still have ten minutes,' I tell my ten-year-old niece in what I hope is a collected voice despite my jiggling knees. 'I can already see the school gates from here.'

'Where? Where?' Aureli's head appears between the two second row seats. My younger niece stretches her neck to get a better view of the school. She leans back and grins at me. 'I can't see it, Auntie Ellie.'

'You will.' It's impossible not to smile at her cheerful, innocent face.

'Nine minutes.' Ashley's tight reply brings my attention back to her.

'Relax.' I pat Ashley's arm, acting like an adult who has her shit together in the early hours. 'They're not gonna flunk you. Worst case? They'll send you to the principal's office.'

Ashley's horrified face makes me wish I could take back my words. The driver, whose name I didn't get and who's been working for my sister's family for years, catches my eyes in the rear-view mirror. He blames me for this morning mess, I can tell. He's not wrong. The whole thing *is* my fault. The distance between my sister's house and the school is, theoretically, ten minutes by car. I didn't take into account the morning rush when hundreds of students depart for school at relatively the same time in their private cars. The queue snakes a few kilometres long, spilling into the streets and everywhere else. The driver tells me that the original ten-minutes' drive often turns into forty-five in the morning drop off. I should've listened to the housekeeper when she woke me up an hour earlier than my usual time.

The driver clears his throat. 'Miss. It's faster if you walk.'

My eyes bulge. 'Here?' The narrow street leading up to the main gates has no proper sidewalk. Plus, it's January, the heaviest rainy season of the year. Though it's not raining now, it definitely was last night, if the wet asphalt is any indication. The small water puddles don't look inviting.

The driver's eyes find mine again in the mirror. 'This won't move until eight.'

Jesus. By that time, my nieces will be thirty minutes late. Without consulting me, Ashley gathers her stuff and opens the car door. My heart drops.

'Ash! Shit, shit!' If anything happens to her, Lyla will skin me alive, and I would humbly let her.

Aureli giggles from the car's third row. 'You said bad words, Auntie Ellie.'

In another time, I'd respond by saying a few more harmless curse words. I grab my bag and jump out of the car, puddles on the street be damned. The moment I'm out, the air hits my face with its signature tropical humidity. I appreciate the warmth, especially since the car's AC has been blasting directly to the right side of my face. I wish I could tilt my head up and bask in the sunshine a little bit more. Instead, my eyes dart between Ashley's swinging ponytail and Aureli's grinning face in the back seat. I hesitate. Aureli is tiny. I wonder if the distance from here to the class would be too much for her and her seven-year-old feet. Unfortunately, Ashley has left us no choice.

'Come, Aur. We'll walk.'

Run is more like it.

The driver calls me from behind the wheel, shoving his thumbs-up in the air. 'I'll text you when I reach the parking lot, Miss.'

Aureli slips her hand into mine and jogs to keep up with my strides. 'Is your first day fun, Auntie Ellie?'

I grin at her as I manoeuvre her in between the queueing cars and the wired fence with red *Private Property* signs on our left. When my bag gets caught in the metal fence, I pull at it so hard to release it from the hook, I accidentally swing it to the right. It slaps against the passenger's window of someone else's car. The driver honks angrily at me. I don't stop to apologize or investigate because *I have no time*. I wave my hand in the air and hope whoever honked understands my universal attempt at saying sorry.

I glimpse Ashley's blue backpack ahead. 'Ash! Hey! Wait up!'

After zigzagging between other students and cars, Aureli and I manage to catch up with Ashley. 'Six minutes and fifty-one seconds,' Ashley moans while glancing at her Casio watch.

'You turned on the timer?' I shouldn't smile. Not when my heart is in my throat from an involuntary jog at 7.23 a.m.

The sunshine I adored a moment ago starts to irritate my skin. Too hot, too dry, too sticky. I envy the driver who I picture is sitting comfortably in the air-conditioned car, probably whistling to the tune of the radio.

The gates loom in our distant left, like time machine portals in sci-fi movies. The moment we reach them, I'm immediately relieved. We're safe inside the campus. There are security guards everywhere. There's a proper sidewalk under our feet. I ignore the speck of dirt on my sandals, but I can't ignore the long line of cars that rolls so ever slowly towards what I assume is the drop-off lobby. I've seen worse traffic, but I'm not ready to see the length *and* the numbers of luxurious cars queuing bumper-to-bumper this early.

Aureli's forehead is sweaty, and her chubby cheeks look like mini red apples. 'I can carry you,' I say between laboured breaths, to which she giggles and shakes her head. She makes me feel like maybe I'm not a bad aunt.

We skip past a few hallways, gardens, and a basketball court. Finally, we arrive at a huge open space. Two towering brick buildings with shades of crimson and yellow stand behind a pair of maroon steel gates. The well-groomed patch of grass that fills up the outer side of the area offers a nice balance to the matted grey stone floor. There's a lot of commotion with many kids running around.

'Is that it?' I ask the girls.

Aureli nods, one of her pigtails looped lower than the other. Ashley glances over her shoulder, her expression tight. 'Two minutes and fifty-seven seconds.' She sounds like she's already crying. 'Aur. *Faster.*'

'Oh . . . kay . . .' Aureli pants.

My heart squeezes. Ashley could've run and left her sister behind. But despite her clear panic, she slows down and waits for the wheezing Aureli. I resist the urge to ruffle her hair and tell her what a wonderful sister she is.

I take off Aureli's bag from her back and sling it over my shoulder. Without the extra weight, Aureli bounces up closer to her big sister. I grab the girls' hands—Aureli on my left and Ashley on my right—and we fly across the lobby like super girls. We're close, we're close. At last, we're *there*. I let go of the girls' hands, pass over the bag to Aureli, and watch them sail into the building through the towering maroon gates. So many gates. Makes sense since this is a school, but still. I've seen too many of these metal doors in the last nine minutes and I'm slightly traumatized. Aureli turns and waves at me, showing her whole teeth. Ashley doesn't bother, and it's fine.

At precisely 7.30 a.m., the bell chimes. Like a knife, it cuts time into before and after, between punctual students and tardy ones, between a clean record and well, a not-so-clean one. The look on the students' faces raises my sympathy. I don't go to school anymore, but my heartbeat races just the same watching them sprint towards the gates like it's their only goal in life.

Ten minutes later, the lobby is completely deserted. The rows of cars slowly disperse as they leave the drop-off zone and line back out of the complex, no doubt creating another round of congestion around the campus. I walk towards the edge of the lobby and fish out my phone from my bag. The driver hasn't called so I assume he's still outside. I open Lyla's Google Docs. She's shared pages of instructions on how to manage the girls' wellbeing. I click on today's date. The first thing I see is *Sex Education for Parents.*

Bubbling laughter rushes to the surface. The word 'sex' manages to clear my brain fog faster than any coffee would. Yes, I might as well be a teenager with how I'm giggling. Yes, I'm amused at my own thought because why on Earth would there be a workshop on sex education for *parents? Sex* is the reason they're parents. Not only have they mastered the art, they're also aware of its consequences, which normally arrive nine months after they've had it.

I read the rest of the information.

Room A-2001

Monday, 8.30 - 9.30 a.m.

I suck in my cheeks and weigh my options. The workshop's still some time away and if I choose to attend it, I'll have forty-five minutes to kill. I can always go home, but I doubt I'll find the motivation to leave my room once I rest my ass on my bed and doom-scroll TikTok. There's also this thing about my resume. My chest pinches in a way that feels suspiciously like guilt. Lyla asked me to polish it to perfection before she left because she plans to pass it to a couple of her high-profile friends who might help me finally land a job. She instructed me—quite sternly—'Impress them, Ellie.'

I'm not worried about impressing other people. I'm worried about impressing my sister.

I should head back and work on my resume, probably browse a few property contractors as well, just in case the jobs Lyla's friends find for me are not a match for my architecture degree.

Yes, I should do that. It concerns my future. It's important.

Should, should, should.

The thing about *should* is that it indicates another option that's either easier or more appealing. Also, *should* has no place in the present. Lyla is not here, so I don't see why I need to spend the morning agonizing over my resume. It's decided then. I'll attend the sex-ed workshop. Never mind that I'm not a parent. I'm here in the capacity of one, and to me, that's pretty much the same thing.

I take a moment surveying my surroundings. I knew beforehand that the campus is huge, but the reality of it still manages to steal my breath. The junior lobby is roughly the size of four tennis courts. I can easily visualize the size of their senior lobby, or the hugeness of the whole entire school, from the imposing black iron gates to the sprawling gardens, koi ponds, Olympic-sized pool, multiple running tracks, a soccer field, and horse tracks in the back. My old school looks like a cramped studio apartment compared to this.

Shortly after Lyla asked me to babysit for her, I googled Spring International Academy. Spring, as their community calls it, is one of the most prestigious, trilingual international schools in Indonesia. Using English, Mandarin, and Bahasa Indonesia as their teaching languages, its reputation and certification are at par with other international schools around the world. This institution ranked on the list of Top Fifty Private Schools in Asia. Located in the suburb, just a twenty-minute drive from the capital city of Jakarta, Spring stands on twenty hectares of land. I guess rich people love their space, which is exactly what Spring is: a rich people's school. One must have an enormous bank account to be able to put their kids here. I made the mistake of clicking on the page about their tuition fee, and my eyes hurt from counting the zeros that lined up like trains after a number. Back in my day, we didn't have these fancy schools, at least from what I know. Plus, even if they existed, my parents wouldn't have been able to afford it.

With Lyla and her husband, Ferdinan, away in London, I'm their daughters' guardian from now until June, or until they're back—whichever is sooner. This means I get to experience Spring up close and personal for the next six months.

'Don't let this disrupt your plan, Ellie,' Lyla said when we met over lunch a month ago.

She'd laid out her itinerary and the girls' timetable for me, so I could think it over. Lyla loves all kinds of plans: the ones she makes for herself, for her girls, for me, and for other people who aren't family. The only thing she didn't plan beforehand was getting pregnant with Ashley while in college. I often wonder if Lyla's obsession with planning has something to do with the fact that she didn't get the chance to execute her own when she was younger.

'If you can't do this, I'll ask Mama,' Lyla said.

I've been between plans since my graduation last October. 'I'll do it. You don't need to pay me.'

She waved her arm like money was no object. For her, it was no object. 'You can save it for the down payment of your first house'—at my *not this again* face, she wagged a finger in front of me—'I don't mean *now*. Someday in the near future.'

The *future* seems to be the only topic my family is interested in discussing. It's also the only topic I don't know much about. Every time I say 'I don't know' or 'I don't have a plan yet', I'm met with shocked faces. 'How can you not know?' I'd reply with 'I don't know' again, and the cycle would continue.

I ask a security guard for directions to Room A-2001. I have no idea what he's describing, but I walk in the general direction he's shown me. On my way, I stop by an outdoor café. The moment I see it, I feel like I'm strolling the streets of Paris. Spring Academy as a whole is designed like an eighteenth-century European castle with its classical columns and perfect symmetry. This old-world feel is juxtaposed by their minimalist modern decor. Colourful posters hang in certain corners of the school. Splashes of Spring colours can be spotted nearly everywhere—maroon, navy, and yellow. The doors and windows of the classrooms are in the colour of warm wood, a soothing contrast to the stone-grey floor. The architect in me, who has been in love with the beauty of lines and colours since I was a kid, approved of their design.

The café I'm about to enter is located in the open space in front of the school library. Small round tables are set in front of the counter. The green patio umbrellas that tower over each table remind me of Starbucks. The smell of coffee and sweet pastries makes my stomach stir in a joyful dance. I haven't gotten any food in me since I opened my eyes this morning, not even a sip of water. I'd never thought a school morning rush would be this . . . well, *rushed.*

A woman who looks about Lyla's age stands from her seat and smiles at me. 'Are you Lyla's sister?'

'Yes.' I offer her a handshake. 'Hi, I'm Ellie.'

She takes my hand; her grip is loose, but her wide smile makes up for it. For a moment, she just beams at me. 'Oh my God, you two look so alike.'

I laugh politely at her enthusiasm. Lyla and I get most of our genes from our mother: wavy black hair, high cheekbones, full lips, light golden skin, and medium height with round hips—too round for my liking but my mother and Lyla swear big hips help in childbirth, something I haven't experienced, and may never.

'I'm Tara,' she introduces herself. 'Has Lyla told you about me?'

No. Lyla never mentioned any of her friends. When the two of us meet, we talk about her daughters, her husband, our parents, and my studies. Sometimes we talk about how exasperated she is with my lack of future plans, which in turn, frustrates me too. I know Lyla as a sister, a daughter, a mother, and a wife. I have no idea who Lyla is as a friend. Judging from the warmth in Tara's gesture, I guess my sister is quite a nice friend.

'Are you waiting for the workshop?' Tara asks when I don't respond.

'The sex-ed one?' I grin. 'Yeah. Is it good?'

Tara shoots me a cheeky look I can't interpret. 'It's *Dion*.'

'Sorry?'

Just then, a group of women walk into the café and Tara squeals. For the next few minutes, I'm in the middle of their loud banter, giggles, and air-kisses. I amusedly try to picture Lyla with them. It takes a while for the image to come.

Tara turns to me. 'I'll save you a seat over there.'

'Wait. I'll come with you.' In a rush to stand, I knock my coffee cup over. Yelping, I grab my phone to save it from the spill. When I'm done wiping the table with the napkins, I find the hallway empty. No sign of Tara and her friends. With a sigh, I drop my ass back to the seat. I guess I'll have to find my way to the meeting room myself.

Chapter 2

Ellie

After taking a few wrong turns, I finally arrive at room A-2001 with only a few minutes to spare. Mothers crowd the reception desks as they wait for their turn to be let inside. When I reach the front, I'm greeted by a cheerful woman in Spring uniform. I like her instantly. She looks like she's in her early forties. Her pepper-coloured hair is tied up in a simple low ponytail. She has soft, natural lipstick on her face. She reminds me of my mom, not because of her age, but because of the calming effect she has on me. Though her whole appearance seems kind and maternal, it also radiates the no-nonsense energy I assume one must have when they work in a school. I can't imagine the amount of shit these adults have to endure from the kids.

'Which grade level?' the lady asks.

'Primary two and five.'

She aggressively skims the papers. 'Which two and five? We have multiple classes per grade level. 5A, 5B, 5C, and so on.'

Lyla must've listed this information down in the docs. I plunge my hand into my bag and frantically search for my phone. I love my tent-sized bag, but it never behaves when I urgently need to find something inside.

'What are the students' names?' she asks after surveying me for a moment.

'Ashley Belinda and Aureli Bianca. Last name Kurnia.' I always thought my nieces' names were pretentious, but I quickly learned that millennial parents purposely name their kids this way. The harder and the longer it is, the better.

The woman freezes. Her sudden change of body language alarms me. Does she think I'm an impostor? Is she about to throw me out of the meeting room? I don't blame her. I didn't exactly dress for a workshop. I'm the aunt who takes her nieces to school on her first day in a pair of khaki shorts, a black Ghostbusters T-shirt that's seen better days, a pair of green beach slippers, and a beige canvas bag that's in dire need of a wash by a professional laundrette.

I clear my throat and bring forth my most formal voice. 'I'm Ellie, Lyla's sister. I'm her children's guardian until she's back from her trip.'

The staff's expression changes from frozen-surprise to ecstatic. If anything, the mood swings alarm me more. If she was already helpful before, now she acts like I'm the Queen of England. She bows (bows!). At me (me!).

'Ibu Ellie. It's so nice to meet you.' She pronounces my name with such deep respect, I nearly fold myself into my bag. It feels weird to be formally addressed as 'ma'am'. The other staff who's been guarding the adjacent station perks up at hearing my sister's name. Now both of them beam at me like I just saved their lives. They swiftly take care of the paperwork without me having to lift a finger. A good thing too as my hand is still stuck inside my bag. The woman who reminds me of my mother ushers me into the meeting room. The moment I step inside, two things knock the breath out of my chest.

First, the space. I expected a regular room, not a hotel ballroom that can easily fit hundreds of people. Plush cream-coloured carpet underneath my feet, warm, intimate lights above my head, full blown air-conditioning that makes me momentarily forget I live in a tropical country, and state-of-the-art presentation equipment—three big screens on the right, centre, and left side of the stage. I recognize Yiruma's music from the speakers. Burgundy chairs like the ones I see in hotel conference rooms are lined up perfectly row after row as far as my eyes can see. And they are full. It's a *full house*. I'm not the only one who likes to hear people talk about sex, then.

The second thing that catches my eye—and my heart—is the buffet selection. Two long, rectangular tables are stationed at the back of the room. They're impossible to miss because they're full of food. I'm not joining a workshop; I'm attending a wedding at a five-star hotel. My heart blooms because, honestly, I'm easy. Give me free food and I'm in love with whoever you are forever. By forever, I mean as long as the free food lasts.

I catalogue the variety of food and drinks as I walk past the tables. From choices of beverages such as water, tea, coffee, juices, milk; to bite-sized snacks like crackers, pastries, bread, donuts, cereal, traditional sweets; to porridge and soups. If this is how they do workshops, I will attend every single one of them. Free five-star breakfast? Count me in. I make a mental note to check Lyla's docs for the upcoming ones.

As we approach the middle of the room, a tightness that's akin to panic starts forming in my chest. *Please don't make me sit at the front.* If I do, I will have no choice but to pretend to be attentive the whole time. What if it gets boring? What if I suddenly need to pee? What if people who sit behind me finish all the food on the tables without me knowing—and I can't possibly know if I have to keep my face forward—and all that's left is a plastic fork? The thought is horrifying.

'Ellie!'

I turn my head to the direction of the voice and see Tara patting an empty chair next to her.

The staff notices it too. 'You've met Ibu Tara.'

'Yes,' I say, feeling grateful for Lyla's friend. 'I'm going to sit with her.'

The staff bows again. It's merely a head dip this time, but it makes me uncomfortable just the same. Before she walks away, she asks, 'What do you like, Ibu? Tea, coffee, pastel, donut? We have chicken porridge and soup, if you prefer something warm. I'll have to check what the soup of the day is, but I think it's Miso.'

Oh my God! How to say, 'I want them all,' without sounding too grabby?

'I don't want to be a bother, Ibu . . . err . . .'

'Agatha,' she answers promptly. 'I work in the management office. And it's no bother, Ibu Ellie.'

Well, if she insists. 'Tea and donuts sound great,' I say with a grin. I hope they have cheese donuts; they're my favourite.

'Chocolate, cheese, hazelnut, strawberry, mochaccino, glazed?'

She mentioned cheese. Yay! Also, she can't keep shooting menu selections at my face. My tongue will start lolling and I'll drool and pant like a golden retriever. I swallow a lump of saliva down my throat. 'I'd love some cheese donuts, Ibu Agatha.' I brace myself for the next question, on how I'd take my tea, but to my relief, she nods and walks—as efficiently as before—towards the back of the room.

I begin sliding down the row to reach Tara, mumbling, 'Excuse me,' to a few other parents before I reach my seat. Tara excitedly holds my left arm and addresses everyone around us. 'Ladies. This is Lyla's sister.'

I say hello to everyone. It's like meeting old friends who I know nothing about. They seem very curious. Guess Lyla never shared much about me with her friends either.

'I'm so jealous of Lyla,' the mother who sits in front of Tara says. She twists in her seat to face me. 'Shopping in London every day for the next six months. Can you imagine? *Six. Months.*'

'Actually, she attends meetings a lot,' I answer.

'*London*. She has meetings in *London*.' She holds her cup with her pinky sticking out. 'I wish I could take off—'she snaps her fingers—'just like that.'

Lyla did not technically take off—*snaps*—just like that. She'd been planning this trip for a long time and nearly cancelled because the thought of being away for six months from her young daughters was too much.

'I wish I had a sister who'd take care of my kids when I'm on holiday,' the other woman chips in, giving me an appreciative once over.

Well, Lyla is not on holiday. And I'm not her nanny. Everyone carries on lamenting about their less-than-ideal situation, which is being stuck here in this grand meeting room and not in London. I find their staged disappointment endearing. These people whine like it's an art. Everyone tries to outmatch the other by painting themselves as the most unfortunate person, secretly wishing to be consoled.

'There's a big age difference between you and Lyla, no?' the mother on my diagonal left says.

'Eleven years.'

Due to that age gap, I always felt like I had two mothers growing up. Especially since it's only me and Lyla in this town while our parents live in a smaller city two hours away by plane. Both women in my life love to meddle. Though it's not always a bad thing—I'm not an ungrateful child—it can be suffocating sometimes.

One mother does a quick calculation with her fingers. 'She's the same age as Dion!'

The lady behind me taps my shoulder. She has a twinkle in her smokey green eye-shadowed eyes when she says, 'You and Dion should be friends. You'll love him.'

Before I can ask who Dion is, a girl in Spring uniform appears at the end of my row. She carries a cup and a paper plate in her hands. The cup and the plate are then transferred from hand to hand until they land on my lap. I inhale the sharp aroma of jasmine tea and the sugar from the cheese and chocolate donuts.

'Thank you,' I tell her.

The girl clasps both hands together like a prayer and bows. I'm still overwhelmed by the attention I'm getting from the school staff.

Tara pinches my left arm hard. '*Look*. It's Dion.'

Standing at the bottom of the stage is a young man dressed in a white doctor's coat. I squint to get a better look at his face, but he's currently looking down and fiddling with the laptop. For sure, he's tall, the white coat fits his broad shoulders. He wears a white dress shirt inside and a pale blue tie, and a pair of black pants. I wonder if he's an OBGYN or a child psychologist. Those two are the closest disciplines suited for this sex-ed talk.

He brings the mic to his mouth and the speakers crackle to life. 'Good morning, parents.' His voice is warm like my smoking hot cup of tea and smooth like melting honey. 'Welcome to our first workshop of this year. For those who don't know me . . .'

At this, the room explodes into giggles. Seriously, *giggles*. He waits until the noise subsides. This guy knows how to dance with his all-female audience. 'My name is Dion Saputra.'

The three monitors in front of the room blink to life and his face appears from the left, the middle, and the right. I'm not ready for it. My mouth drops and some air leaves my lungs.

Now I know why every single uterus in this room swoons and ovulates at the sight of him. Why Tara giggled every time she mentioned his name. Why this workshop is a full house. I've seen plenty of beautiful people before—celebrities, models, influencers—but my breath still lodges in my throat when I see his *three* faces for the first time.

God, he's *juicy*.

Juicy like a piece of meat. Like a piece of hot gossip. Like a forbidden sin. There's really no other way to describe him.

Thick, wavy black hair sits artistically on top of his head. It looks like miniature ocean waves that crash against the shore at night. The bangs fall more on the left side of his forehead. He has a masculine, square jaw that could be used as a ruler, and a set of full lips. Those attributes make him look like he could be the love child of Julia Roberts and Daniel Henley. I'm conflicted about whether I should feel envious of his good looks, or squeeze his mouth and make myself a glass of *juicy* apple juice.

Tara playfully elbows me. Her smirk tells an inside joke I have no idea about. Perhaps this is what she does with Lyla.

Oh my God! Lyla.

Does my sister lust over some *young meat* too? See him as an overripe mango she can eat with her bare hands? I quickly terminate the image before it spirals into something horrifying, like the picture of my sister licking her fingers while mango juice drips down her chin. There's no way Lyla would think like this. The sister I know always appears composed and perfectly put together. Lyla would see him as nothing but a young doctor. She won't objectify a person, and I should stop doing that too. Soon.

I narrow my eyes at the monitors. He's what, nineteen, twenty tops? He looks so boyish, even the stubbly hair on his chin appears to be confused. Like it's not yet sure how to grow properly on his face. He clearly doesn't look like someone who's capable to talk about sex to a bunch of seasoned mothers. I cross my legs, careful not to topple the plate on my lap, and take the first bite of the donut. Good Lord in heaven. Why did I waste minutes thinking about McJuicy when I have these donuts in my possession? The cream, the shaved cheese, and the softness of the dough, all blend together nicely inside my mouth.

'Isn't he the smartest?' Tara whispers. The awe in her voice is amusing to hear. 'He's Mr Goh's nephew.'

'Who's Mr Goh?'

She arches one of her groomed eyebrows. I envy people who can do that. My eyebrows always do things together. If I arch or lower them, they both move at the same time.

'He's the Principal. Lyla didn't tell you?'

I shake my head. Lyla didn't *tell* me much. Lyla sent me pages of Google Docs, which I haven't bothered to read yet. I look back at the front of the room. Things begin to make sense now. Dion is Spring's Principal's nephew. He works here.

'What does he teach?' I jerk my chin towards Dion.

'He's not a teacher.'

'He's a parent?' I frown.

'Don't be ridiculous. He's not married. As a matter of fact, we've been trying to find him a girlfriend.' Tara suddenly eyes me with a new interest. 'Do you have a boyfriend?'

I suppress the urge to roll my eyes.

'He's such a sweet kid. The best student Spring has ever had,' Tara explains without really explaining. 'Look at him now. *A doctor.* We're so proud of him.'

That statement only leads to *more* questions.

'We're so grateful that he agrees to help our community in his spare time,' Tara adds.

Community work that brings a *full house*. No kidding. I'm sure his looks have *nothing* to do with it. Dion says something, which I miss entirely because the room swallows up his words in a roar of laughter. He fiddles with the clicker in his hand. His face disappears from the screens and a slide appears. I squint to read the words. The same laugh that bubbled up in me when I stood in the lobby comes back. The title of today's event is so misleading. *Sex Education for Parents* is a workshop that *informs* the parents of what the school will do when they integrate sex-education into their curriculum this year. There's no steamy content other than basic science and lots of timelines. Still, the number of mothers who show up to hear a young med student outline the topic of sex-education is mind-blowing. An email would have sufficed. Then I think about the buffet tables. An email wouldn't bring me donuts.

A few minutes later, I decide I no longer have any reason, nor the will, to listen to the hot doctor talk. I excuse myself and head towards the buffet table in the back. I don't care that I'm the only one who's standing and munching on food while everyone else is absorbed in the presentation.

One salted-egg croissant, one pastel, and a glass of OJ later, I wipe my hands on a napkin, then silently exit. One foot is already out of the door when I hear my sister's name being mentioned. I pause. There's a heated conversation going on and Lyla's name is on everyone's lips. If it's about Lyla, I must pay attention. I make my way back to my seat. The moment I reach my row, Tara excitedly points at me. 'There she is! That's Lyla's sister!'

Chapter 3

Dion

That's the girl from the street earlier. I recognize her monstrous-sized bag. A slap from it cracked the glass film on the passenger side's window of my car. What does she put in there? Her whole house?

The room falls silent as all eyes zoom in on her. She's currently suspended between standing and slipping back into her row. She must've realized how absurd she looks, crouching like a tiny mouse, because immediately—and inelegantly—she pulls her spine up. Smiling, she does a 360-degree wave like she's some kind of a celebrity. The room remains mute. No smiles, no waving back. All gawking. Me included.

I dip my chin to my chest and make a face at my shoes. Growing up in Spring, I'm familiar with this type; I can smell them from miles away. These are the super-rich, out-of-this-world entitled, spoiled brats. I bet my medical degree that she's the kind of person who doesn't take responsibility seriously. I bet she runs to her big sister every time she faces even a teeny-weeny problem. I got burned once by *this* type of person, and believe me, once is already one time too many.

'Ellie is perfect for the job,' Ibu Tara states. 'She knows Lyla's schedule better than any of us.'

I can't believe Ibu Lyla's BFF is suggesting we replace our chairwoman with some new girl who walks around Spring in her pyjamas.

Ibu Agatha, rushing to stand next to me from her seat, speaks into the mic. 'If Ibu Ellie agrees to sit on the committee, then we can proceed as planned.'

'Whoa, whoa.' Ellie holds out her palms in front of her. 'Hold on. What committee?' She's alarmed, and she should be. I slide my hands into my pants pockets and enjoy the impromptu entertainment. I'm glad there's something to prevent me from snoring while standing up. I'm feeling the effect of last night's hospital shift in my bones.

Ibu Agatha promptly gestures at the three mega screens behind us. My eyes follow and read the words I know by heart.

Musical Gala Fundraising
In honour of the 50th Anniversary of Spring International Academy
June 1ˢᵗ, Sunday, 07.30 p.m.
Nusantara multi-purpose hall

Under the person-in-charge section, Ellie's sister's name pops up like mushrooms on a forest ground on a rainy day.

Lyla Soraya Kurnia - PTA chairwoman

I turn around and watch Ellie. An understanding dawns on her face. I wonder if she knew that her sister is the most powerful PTA chairperson in the history of this school. Even the Board and my uncle are slightly intimidated by her.

Ellie bursts out cackling. She sounds so much like a happy child, the corners of my own mouth quirk up. 'Oh nonononono. I'm only here to babysit my nieces, people. I won't be part of your . . .' she gestures towards the screens '. . . committee.'

People. She calls Spring mothers 'people.' Against my judgement, my mouth curves up higher. She's funny; she also spells disaster. I hate that my first instinct is to rescue her. I shouldn't get involved in the PTA business. I bring the mic up. 'Duly noted, Ibu Ellie.'

She's surprised to hear my voice coming out of the speakers. We hold eye contact for about two seconds. She nods at me as a gesture of thanks. My tone might lack warmth, but she gets that I'm trying to get her out of this situation.

'Why can't one of us *here* chair it? It doesn't have to be Lyla or her inexperienced family.'

Next to me, Ibu Agatha freezes. We recognize the speaker's voice. Ellie's head swings around until she locates the woman who spoke. Now all eyes and ears are tuned in to this mother. If there's one person who can challenge Ibu Lyla head on, it would be Ibu Bernadet. These two women are equally head-strong and dominating, no wonder they hate each other's guts.

'As the head of Spring Administration Office, I can confidently say that the school wishes nothing but to move forward,' Ibu Agatha says diplomatically. 'We should've run this before the Christmas break. We can't afford to spend any more time on organizational changes.'

'That's why Ellie is perfect for the job. We change nothing,' Ibu Tara insists. She waves her phone in the air. 'If anyone wants to remove Lyla from the PTA, I suggest you call her.'

'Of course we don't want to remove Lyla. She's our leader,' a mother shouts from one row down.

'But is she *here* now?' Ibu Bernadet challenges. The mothers who sit next to her support her cold statement by nodding and clapping. 'We need a *present* leader who can lead.'

'Lyla can lead from anywhere.'

One mother on the left row stands. Two more follow. And before long, everyone speaks all at once. This is so different from the giddy atmosphere during my presentation an hour ago. It's now a boiling pot of pasta. I wipe my dry forehead and exhale a sigh.

The PTA, for crying out loud! Always PTA. Always the fight for (more) power.

In the middle of the verbal chaos, the girl's arm jerks upward, like she's about to punch a hole in the ceiling. In a clear voice, she shouts, 'I'll do it. I'll sit in on behalf of Lyla.'

The room falls into absolute stillness.

My eyes widen. What the hell is she doing? PTA is her sister's problem, not hers. Judging from the wild look on her face, she clearly has no idea either.

Ibu Tara breaks the unnatural silence by taunting everyone. 'Well? Anyone disagrees?'

And we're back at chaos. The volume rises so high, I swear I can hear the glasses and cups tremble. At that moment, surrounded by feminine shrieks from all sides, I realize that *none* of them dare to call Ibu Lyla. I sympathize. Let's just say there are reasons why every teacher and staff at Spring bows to her.

The screens behind me give out a loud beep, then they go dark. Ibu Agatha crouches over the laptop. From the corner of my eye, I spot Spring technicians hurry forward to fix the technical error, but Ibu Agatha stops them. Instead, she waves me closer. I stand next to her and look at the laptop. She has turned off the connection between the computer and the screens on purpose. Her fingers fly through the keyboard as she types a sentence in a newly opened Microsoft Word document.

do something. there will be pta wars if you don't step in.

I find myself parroting Ellie in my head. *Nonononono.* I've agreed to contribute my time in the musical production as a trainer and a performer because working with the students always brings me joy, but handling PTA is a separate job entirely. This is a league where the rules are only clear to whoever is playing the game. Anyone who is stupid enough to enter the arena uninformed will be dead before they can even say hello.

No. Nope. Hell nu-uh!

dion you're the only neutral party here. HURRY!!! BEFORE THEY RUIN THE MUSICAL!!!

The caps lock pushes me into an action, albeit a stupid one. She's right. PTA plays an important role in assisting the musical both through groundwork and monetary donations. Chaos on that level will affect everything. The gala is important to the school, and by extension, to my uncle, as the Principal of Spring Academy. I won't let anyone ruin what would've been the greatest legacy of his career.

Ibu Agatha still doesn't look at me, but she must have felt my resolve because her shoulders drop from where they'd risen to her ears, and she quickly deletes the document before connecting the laptop back to the screens.

I know what I need to do. I've spent almost my whole life with these kinds of demanding people, I can salsa with them without hurting myself. My voice cuts through the room like cool water splashing on a raging fire. I pace in front of the monitors. 'Mothers, if I may, please?'

The level of noise is down to a buzz now—as if a swarm of bees just flew in. Ellie uses this opportunity to slide into her seat. I notice Ibu Tara giving the girl's arm a squeeze.

'As Ibu Agatha explained, we're pressed for time. We should've started the training in November last year. I appreciate Ibu Tara's suggestion to have everyone remain as they are, so we won't waste any more time re-organizing.' I pause and let the room hold its breath, clinging to my every word. '*But* Ibu Bernadet is also right. This is such an important event for our school. A *fifty-year* milestone. The board has invested so much in this.' I make eye contact with the audience, sweeping everyone from left to right. 'In my humble opinion, it's too risky to chance it to an inexperienced girl who, God help us I don't mean to offend, may not take things seriously, no matter how fast she can reach our chairwoman. We can't afford unnecessary mistakes that would cause delay.'

My eyes skirt to Ellie before moving away in the next second. I don't need a pair of binoculars to notice how thunderous her expression is. I feel bad that I have to make a point to these mothers at her expense. If I had more time to prepare, I would've come up with a grander scenario. But this is all I've got this Monday morning. Ibu Agatha and I exchange a quick glance. She gives me a subtle nod. I face the audience and say, 'With your permission, I'll be sitting on behalf of Ibu Lyla too.'

My heart races after I utter those words. I expect some protest from Ibu Lyla's loyalists, but to my astonishment, there's nothing from the audience. Knowing these mothers, they *will* protest. The question is *when*. Ibu Agatha must have sensed that too because she deftly, professionally, and smartly wraps up our meeting before the momentum is ruined by another set of arguments. 'It's settled then. Ibu Ellie *and* Pak Dion will co-chair the PTA on behalf of Ibu Lyla until she returns. They'll be the sole PTA representatives for the musical.' She smiles at the audience, her voice softens. 'I personally think this is the best solution. Everyone is familiar with Pak Dion. Ibu Ellie will be the bridge between us and Ibu Lyla. This way, we'll hit the ground running.'

What she didn't say is: The reason I'm the perfect candidate to hold the PTA front while the incumbent is away is because I don't belong to any group of mothers. I'm not technically a staff; the school doesn't pay me. I'm a volunteer who happens to be a Spring alumnus. My job is similar to that of a post office. I pass information between the school and the parents. I decentralize jobs from top to bottom and monitor progress. I have no use of PTA power for myself. At the end of the day, the school wins. My already tight schedule between the ER and the afternoon trainings will kill me, but it's nothing I can't handle. If the school needs my help, I'll help. If *my uncle* needs my help, I'll help.

* * *

'Sorry, Dion. I panicked.' Ibu Agatha speaks from the corner of her mouth as we tidy up our stuff. 'I kept thinking about *that* PTA war.'

I inwardly groan. Who can forget the worst PTA war that went down here seven years ago—during my senior year? People were being held hostage in separate rooms by conflicted parties until their demands were met. If that wasn't scary enough, the school was hit by lawsuits by the ousted PTA chairwoman, for failing to conduct a safe and democratic environment for its community. Lots of memes were floating around afterwards. Nearly all my friends made crass jokes about the incident. All I can remember is how frail and grey my uncle had become in those months.

I smile at Ibu Agatha as I fold my doctor's coat and push it into my backpack. Over the years, I've regarded her more like my aunt than a senior school personnel. 'It won't be a war. Trust me.'

She turns to me. 'You don't have to do this if you're busy. We'll find another way.'

I'm always busy. 'No worries, Ibu. I just hope she's not difficult to work with.'

'Who? Ellie?' Ibu Agatha thinks for a moment. 'Maybe she'll quit. It's not impossible.'

My mood brightens exponentially at the possibility of me holding the PTA front by myself. It will do my mental health good. There'll be fewer people to worry about, or worse, to please.

'Let's hope you're right.' I cross my fingers and Ibu Agatha snorts.

Most mothers leave the room after visiting the breakfast tables. Thinking about food makes my stomach growl. I haven't eaten anything since last night. My stamina was already at the lowest level before I listened to these mothers bickering about PTA. If I don't chew on something soon, I'll faint.

I stack mochaccino donuts on my plate and make my way back to the front of the room. From the corner of my eye, I spot Ellie standing at the edge of her row. Her eyes are trained unapologetically on me, but she looks rather uncertain. I slow my steps, feeling slightly uncertain myself. Do I greet her or pretend I don't notice her? Chivalry demands me to properly introduce myself and engage in chit-chat, but I'm tired and I really want to eat my carbs in peace.

For some reason, the memory that occupies my head is that of her gargantuan size bag slapping my car window. She could've said sorry when that happened, but nope. I'm annoyed again. She wipes her hand on her shorts, and I'm gripped by a sense of dread. Please don't shake my hand. My fingers are all sticky from the donuts. I don't want to make her hand dirty. I don't want to wipe mine on my pants either. To my relief, she looks like she's having a second thought about the handshake.

'Hi,' she says. Her hands remain by her sides.

I stare at her Ghostbuster printed shirt. Pieces of dry cheese stick to the front of her shirt, making the bald Ghostbuster's ghost look like he's sporting a buzzcut. She slowly crosses her arms in front of her chest, her cheeks turning an angry shade of pink.

Ah, shit. She thought I was checking out her boobs? I drag my eyes up, so high that I glimpse a speaker in the corner of the ceiling. In an effort to explain why my eyes were on her chest, I summon what I think is my most monotonous, neutral tone. 'You've got cheese on your ghost.'

She's startled. 'My what?' She looks down at her shirt. '*Oh.*' She plucks them off using her thumb and index finger, then plops them into her mouth. What the heck? Those cheese bits must taste like toothpicks, not to mention how unsanitary that is. My frown deepens until I can feel my pointed forehead slice my face in two. Of course I have to co-chair the most pretentious organization in this school with a girl who apparently loves cheese donuts so much, she eats the bits out of her shirt.

I take a big bite of my donut and chew it slowly. 'You should try mochaccino. It's the best donut. The cheese is . . .' I pause for a second. From the corner of my mouth, I cough out, '. . . subpar.'

I quickly walk away before she can say anything back, but apparently not fast enough to not catch her muttering, 'pompous ass,' behind my back. The grin that splits my face is as wild as it's unexpected. If she regards me as an ass, she'll refuse to work with me, right? She'll quit on her own and make my life at Spring simpler. I wolf down two mochaccinos in three big bites. I'm feeling hopeful. What do you know? The first day of school might *not* suck.

Chapter 4

Ellie

'I can't believe you didn't tell me about PTA.' I shoot Lyla a glare the moment her face appears on my phone screen. I'm stretched out on the living room couch with the TV muted in front of me. 'And here you write down Ashley and Aureli's doctors' contact numbers, their tutor schedules, and their weekly fruit intake. In colourful highlights and bullet points, no less.'

Lyla laughs so hard, she has tears in her eyes. 'Oh my God.' She fans her cheek with her hand. 'I'd pay millions of bucks to see everyone's faces.'

'*Who* are you? Why does everyone in school kowtow every time they hear your name?' An idea strikes, and I gasp at its ridiculousness as well as at its possibility. 'Do you own the school? My god, you do, don't you? You're the owner of Spring.'

She rolls her eyes. 'I don't know if you learned accounting back in your school days,' she says, 'but sadly, I can't afford to buy Spring.'

'If you're not their boss, why are they scared of you?'

'No, not scared.' She smiles fondly at me. 'It's more like mutual respect. I worked on many programmes that benefit Spring community. Just last year, I successfully proposed to Ferdinan's management to give Spring students and staff a special discounted rate at their hospital.'

'Wow. Lucky them.' Ferdinan's hospital is one of the best in the country.

Lyla ticks off her fingers. 'My team and I brought in a healthier menu in our canteen, instead of junk food and soda. We raised funds to bring awareness to issues of mental health prevalent in young children. We launched initiatives with the local government to aid the under-privileged communities around Spring. Have I shown you the TV clip about that? The governor came to our school, Ellie.'

'You're amazing, Lyla.' I bring my face closer to the screen and bat my eyelashes at her. 'Now, please get me out of this. Appoint Tara to replace you.'

'Oh God. Tara.' Lyla sighs. 'No wonder my inbox exploded this morning. Haven't gotten the time to read the messages.'

'I can imagine,' I say dryly. 'So, you'll deal with it, yes?'

'But you agreed to it. In front of the whole school.'

'I was protecting *you*!' I realize how silly that sounds. Me protecting Lyla? Ha! Ha! My big sister doesn't need protection from anyone.

'You'll quit before you start?' She makes the familiar soft click with her tongue. I know that sound and what it means so, so well.

Aur, don't play with your food. Click.

Ashley. Sit straight. Click.

Ellie. Where do you spend all your savings? Click.

'It's your job, Lyla. I quit nothing,' I say.

She regards me fondly. 'You said Dion will co-chair? Then you'll be fine.'

His juicy/grumpy face appears in front of me, momentarily blocking Lyla's. To be honest, I'm terrified of him: his size, his looks, his coldness, his charisma when he handled the screaming mothers, and the obvious sign that he doesn't like me. I have no idea what his problem with cheese donuts is, but that too adds to the list of why I'm apprehensive about him.

'Dion is the sweetest kid,' Lyla says. 'Aside from my own and you, of course. Hey. Let me see my girls. We'll talk more about this tomorrow.'

'Tomorrow?' I screech. 'No way. Sort this out *first*. Then I'll call the girls.'

'You're holding my daughters hostage?' Lyla laughs. I doubt this is the version she shows to the people of Spring. This grinning Lyla doesn't command waist bows and blind fear. 'Where are they, by the way?' Lyla stretches her neck like she expects the girls to jump out from the back of the sofa and surprise her.

'In their rooms,' I lie.

'Homework?' Lyla asks.

No, the girls are currently watching Disney+ in their parents' bedroom. One of Lyla's Google Docs specifically states that TV on school nights is prohibited. I figure what Lyla doesn't know won't hurt me and the girls.

'I didn't tell you about PTA because I thought I could carry on from here,' she says.

'You can?' I perk up. 'Yes, Lyla. Of course you can!'

'I was wrong. I clearly underestimated the meetings I have to attend with Ferdinan. The school is right to appoint you as my ground person. Think about it, Ellie. It'll be good for you. Get a chance to know people. Practice your organization skills, learn to lead—'

I sink my face into my hands and muffle-scream. 'LYLA!'

'It'll work. Trust me.'

'You don't pay me enough for this shit.'

'*Word*,' Lyla admonishes. 'I'll double your allowance.'

I'm not the sort of person who takes money from my sister like it's my inheritance, no matter how loaded her husband is. But being her relative has its perks. While the rich work hard day and night, their families benefit from their wealth simply by being related to them: their spouse, children, grandchildren, *me*. I'm family.

'Listen, Ellie.' Lyla turns serious. 'I've been running PTA for two years and I'm running for a third term. There are initiatives

I want to launch urgently because I know those will benefit the students. *I know* it, El.'

I believe her. My sister is the opposite of me. While I don't know a lot, Lyla knows everything. Whatever Lyla puts her attention on, she drives it to success. Ferdinan's rise to stardom wouldn't have happened without Lyla by his side. He alone is a talented neurosurgeon. Together with Lyla, he's a renowned, respected, highly sought-after doctor in the country.

'The school's regulations on PTA are pretty loose. Everything is fair game. So, *Ellie*,' she stresses my name. My stomach rolls a little because whenever she uses this tone, she won't accept *no* as an answer. 'Don't let anyone fucking steal it from under your nose. Especially not Bernadet and her pals.'

'You said a bad word.'

'I'm thirty-four. I'm allowed.'

'What should I do?' I ask, a lot more deflated than before. The fact that I have to co-chair PTA with a person who looks down on me feels like momentous work.

'Just show up. Some people will use my absence as a chance to insert their own interest. Or worse, spend the parents' money on irresponsible things. Hold down the agenda and *do not* change anything.'

'Why can't Tara do it? She told me you two are like this.' I link my index and middle fingers together.

Lyla gives a little head shake. 'A leader cannot be everyone's best friend. As a leader, you will have to make decisions that will piss people off. The other mothers won't listen to Tara. But you . . . *you* have a different weight.'

I mentally groan because she always manages to turn a simple conversation into a lecture. I throw my arm above my head. 'I can't go around pissing people off, Lyla. Besides, Tara defended you in the meeting.'

'Everyone feels brave when they're in a large group. But when cornered, a lot of them will choose to avoid conflict.

Bernadet and Netty have been trying to sabotage my programmes for years.'

I need to find out which one Netty is. They all look the same to me.

Trying my best to deflect, I tell her, 'You could appoint Tara and you'd achieve the same result. There are other urgent matters outside Spring. The school is not everything, you know.'

'Of course,' Lyla says, 'but I'm not a member in those outside groups. I volunteer at Spring because my girls are there and I want this place to be the best place any kid could have. In order to achieve that, I have to get involved however I can. This is the job of *a community.*'

The dynamic in Spring is puzzling to me. In my time, my old school managed the operation. Students followed the rules. Parents paid the tuition fee. Simple. I'm afraid to ask who she means by community. Wealthy parents? Is wealthy parents trumping the school board a trend in this day and age? Possible, if their clients are influential figures with deep pockets.

I regard my sister for a moment. Lyla may live in her own bubble, but she's good at what she does. Besides, I won't let anyone stab my sister behind her back, no matter what the excuse is. My life rule is fairly straightforward: Touch my family, you die.

'Fine. I'll be your puppet doll.'

'Not the name I would use. This is *my sister* we're talking about. I know she has a brain or two. Be confident in your power, Ellie. *Believe* in it.'

These pep talks start making my brain hurt. 'Lyla. I don't have any power. I'm twenty-three.'

'Joan of Arc was nineteen.'

I gape at my sister. 'She was executed!'

'You won't get executed. You have *me.*'

Oh, to have that level of confidence.

I look at my sister's face on the screen. I get why the people in Spring bow when they hear her name, why nobody in the audience dares to call her directly and ask her to step down as the chairwoman. I get why Bernadet prefers to challenge her from behind. My sister intimidates the shit out of people. Not because she's loud. It's because she's a smart, stubborn as hell, no-nonsense kind of woman. My flare of irritation is softened by my love for her. Lyla is my centre. I can't tell which way is North without her. 'Remind me again why you have to be away for six months?'

Her expression turns tender. 'Because I love my husband?'

I smile. Her answer doesn't cover the whole picture. Like any other genius man in history, Ferdinan is completely useless in other aspects of life outside his work. He can't remember his daughters' age. On some days, he forgets his tie, his glasses, or his wallet. His bosses recognize his strengths and shortcomings. When a joint venture with a renowned hospital in the UK came up, they had to send their best, and their best was Ferdinan *and* his wife. What my brother-in-law lacks, my sister makes up for in abundance. The hospital begged Lyla to come along to help secure the partnership between two hospitals. They dangled a huge compensation in front of Lyla's nose. Amazing what that woman can do *without* a college diploma.

I'm deep in my own thoughts when Lyla speaks again. 'Our job as PTA this year is to support the musical. We'll help with whatever the school needs. The other job is to set up a proposal for next year's PTA program. *This* is my bread and butter, Ellie. I'll email the proposal to you later. All you need to do is get the principal's approval.'

'What if Dion doesn't agree with your proposal?'

Since we're co-chairing the PTA in Lyla's absence, we're required to sign off on everything as a team. Ibu Agatha has stressed this to both me and Dion in an official email she sent not long after our meeting this morning.

Lyla's killer stare makes me want to slide down the couch and hide under the table. Or bow my head like the Spring people do. Anything to escape *those eyes*.

After what feels like forever, she says, 'Then you *make* him agree.'

Chapter 5

Dion

In my years of working as a volunteer at Spring, I was always the first to arrive at every meeting, sometimes as early as the technicians who prepared the room. I don't expect my clean record to be broken this morning.

Ellie doesn't look up when I come in. The reason she didn't hear me is because she's *asleep*. Her head dips low, her phone is on the table in front of her. Blurred images of people dancing stare up at me upside down. My eyes spot the cup of untouched tea and a plate of . . . cheese donuts? *Again?* Don't they taste horrible? I'm a little disappointed. For some strange reason, I'm eager to see her try my mochaccino recommendation and tell me what she thinks of it to my face.

I knock on the table before I pull out a chair. She jerks awake, her body swaying a little at first. She looks up and I startle. She doesn't look like the girl from yesterday *at all*. She's put on a bit of makeup; her hair is in a neat ponytail. She's wearing a navy blazer over a white shirt. She looks so much like her sister—dressed like this—that for a moment I think I'm face-to-face with a younger and curvier Ibu Lyla. If not for her ridiculous bag that lies on the table next to her, I wouldn't have believed that this is the same girl who ate dried cheese straight off her shirt yesterday. This morning, she looks pretty and put together. I might have stared a little too long.

She's checking me out too. Her eyes move down the length of my body. At last, she rests her eyes on my face and grimaces. Well, if she doesn't like what she sees, there's nothing much I can do about it.

'You're early,' I say.

'Can't be late to my first PTA meeting.'

'The first good quality of a leader.'

'That, and we had to leave the house an hour earlier to beat the traffic.' She eyes me, her expression a mix of horror and curiosity. 'How do you guys live with that five days a week, year by year?' She makes an explosive noise. 'Brutal.'

Her eyes captivate me. No matter what emotion her face is showing, her eyes always twinkle, making them look like they're smiling. A complete opposite of her sister's. Ibu Lyla's stare is famous for being sharp and unapologetic. It either inspires people she's conversing with and pushes them to do great things, or gives them the worst stomach ulcer.

'Welcome to Spring.' I drop my ass on the chair opposite her.

Her thumb slides over her phone screen to close the TikTok app. 'What's the second?'

'What?'

'You said the first quality of a leader. What's the second?'

She's been paying attention.

'Having a brain and knowing how to use it.' I lace my fingers in front of my chest and put on my charming smile.

She nods. 'Thank god I have both. You?'

Despite my best effort to squeeze all the juice from my brain cells, the best response I can come up with is, 'I'm a doctor.'

She laughs, sounding like a little kid who enjoys life too much. The corners of her eyes crinkle deeper, making it hard for me to peel my gaze off her face.

'You mean, because you're a doctor, you're automatically smart? I bet my Advanced Math is better than yours.'

I choke, then whistle. 'Advanced Math. You took Physics.' I feel a glimmer of respect for her. Science is a male-dominated field. The composition of female students in universities is usually very low.

'Architecture. Institute of Technology. 3.8 GPA,' she confirms.

How smug. But she has every right to be. That's one hell of a GPA. And her college sits in the top ten best national universities. It's well known for producing high profile scientists and engineers, just as my uni is famous for producing well-respected doctors.

'My Chemistry is definitely better than yours,' I say. Just as Physics students must take Advanced Math as their compulsory subject, all Biology students must take Chemistry. She's not the only one who can flex her educational background.

'Oh, I'm not sure about that,' she drawls. 'I notice that *your people's chemistry* kinda sucks.'

'Everyone here likes me,' I say, a little too fast for my reply to come off as indifferent. She baited me, and I'm grasping her hook like it's pizza. Idiot.

She twirls the end of her ponytail in one finger. 'I'm *here* and I *don't* like you.'

Against my will, I snort. 'If your GPA is *really* 3.8, you'd be snatched by companies before you even graduated,' I say. 'Why aren't you employed yet? Are you planning to open your own architecture business?' Which is very possible. Rich kids go straight from school to lead their own companies, or work in their parents' businesses. For them, shortcuts are the only way of life.

'I'm in no rush. Life is supposed to be lived leisurely,' she says, shrugging one of her petite shoulders and avoiding my eyes.

Right, of course. These people can live leisurely without worrying about a single thing, namely money. Just like shortcuts, living leisurely is a given for wealthy folks. Though she didn't go to Spring, Ellie would fit right in. I, on the other hand, have spent years in this school and still feel like I'm a charity case. Like I don't belong. Oftentimes, I'm not sure I want to.

'Why here and not an overseas university?' I ask, unable to hide the curiosity in my voice.

'Can't afford it.'

I laugh, then at seeing her *what?* face, I clear my throat. 'Oh, you're serious. But your sister surely—'

'I'm not my sister.'

'Your family—'

'My dad is a regular employee; my mom is a housewife. They're not my sister either.'

'What I mean is—'

'I know what you mean.' She crosses her arms on the table and leans forward. Her sparkling eyes have some menace in them. 'Why do people like you always underestimate Indonesia? You look down on everything we have. Our local talents, our local products, our local education. All bad. Why?'

For crying out loud, I graduated from one of the local universities and I'm proud as hell about it. I lean forward and say quietly, 'People like *me*?'

'Yes, people like you. People who can afford to come here, to Spring.' She gestures around the meeting room.

I open my mouth, ready to shed light on the history of my life, ready to tell her she's wrong in her assumptions, but then I realize I owe her nothing. I bite the inside of my cheek and just stare at her until she exhales and leans back against the fake leather seat.

'Are you a real doctor?' she asks.

'No. I play dress-up.'

'Like Ken and Barbie?' She smiles good-naturedly. 'The reason I asked is because you look too young to be a doctor. How old are you? You can't be more than nineteen.'

'Older than you, *petal.*' The nickname just jumped out of my mouth. I didn't plan it.

'*Petal?*'

I smell a bloodbath. 'Yes. Petal. Like flowers. Easily deterred and blown away by the wind.'

I can tell by the twitch in her hand that she longs to punch the smirk off my face. 7.42 a.m. is too early for a meeting, let alone a duel, but if the situation demands it, I'll entertain her. She can use her oversized bag as a weapon.

'Maybe I'm inexperienced, but I'm not some ridiculous flower,' she says, her voice low.

I did call her inexperienced during my speech yesterday. My irritation revisits me and with that comes this unbearable urgency to make her see sense. '*You are* inexperienced. I understand why Ibu Lyla might have erred in her judgment about you but everyone else sees it. Why do you think I'm here? I'm here to *babysit you*.'

'Go ask your uncle to remove me,' she demands.

I wish things were that simple. 'How do you think the school will explain *that* to *your sister?* You think I want to be here? I'm the only safe choice. Other alternatives beside me would open a war among PTA members. The school will have to intervene. God knows how long the whole thing will take. The musical is only months away, we can't afford any delays.'

Her face is a mosaic of multiple emotions: disbelief, amusement, irritation, and a blind loyalty to her sister.

'I won't allow anyone to treat Lyla with disrespect. Removing her without her consent is rude. Especially if she can't be here to defend herself. And I assure you my sister has not erred in her judgment.'

'You can still support your sister and quit PTA,' I say.

Her eyes narrow. 'What's the difference if I quit or am fired? For the record, I'm not quitting anything.'

'Big difference, petal. If you quit, we can reason with Ibu Lyla that we gave you a chance but you couldn't take it. I'll remain a *neutral* person for PTA. Nobody will have a problem with me being there because I don't belong to any side. Once Ibu Lyla returns, I'll give the crown back to her, though, if I'm being honest, anything can happen in six months. But let's say it stays with Ibu Lyla, then she can do whatever she wants with it and the other mothers can bicker about it like they always do. Everyone's happy.' Tapping my fingers on the table, I summon my doctor's voice—the calm, soothing, and authoritative one. 'Imagine, you don't have to get stuck in the traffic to get to our meetings. You could sleep in, have some me-time in the spa, go out with your boyfriend . . .'

I let her fantasize about it for a minute. Does she have a boyfriend? Not that it's my business anyway. 'It's not too late, petal. Quitting is free.'

'Likewise, doctor.'

I opt for a different voice. It's the one I use whenever I deal with Spring helicopter mothers—submissive, respectful, and with a pinch of begging. 'Please, Ellie. You'll slow us down with your mistakes.'

'I haven't made one yet.'

'You already have,' I say, throwing my hand in the air. 'You chose cheese donuts. *Again.*'

For a split second, she looks like she can't decide if she should throw the plate with the cheese donuts at my face or storm out of the room. In the end, her face opens up like a ray of sunshine and her shoulders tremble with her loud, yet melodious, laughter.

'Well, you're wrong about donuts . . . and chemistry,' she says. 'Anyway, I have *you* now. You'll steer me away from mistakes and blablabla. Right?'

She *did not* just blablabla the most important event in our school history. 'Do you have any clue what you're getting into? Has your sister prepped you yet?'

'Oh, she h-a-a-a-s.'

She's so lying.

'Stop being dramatic. It's only PTA.' She dismisses me with a wave of her hand. 'It's not like we have to meet every day for the rest of our lives.'

'If you quit, you can have *no meeting* for the rest of your life.'

The door opens with a thud. Ibu Agatha and the members of the PTA loudly make their entrance. Tara waves when she spots my co-captain. 'Ellie-e-e-e!'

I look down at my phone. 8.07 a.m. (almost) on time.

* * *

Ellie

The first item in the agenda is musical fundraising, and we have Ibu Agatha to chair it. A stack of papers that lists out the team and their detailed responsibilities has been distributed to every attendant. Ibu Agatha stresses that the board wishes for every stakeholder's involvement, from the staff, the students, all the way to parents, alumni, and the local government. It's an ambitious goal, but one that's expected from an international school of Spring calibre. Lyla as the PTA president naturally has her name mentioned on every page. In a clean, typed document such as this, the *Ellie/Dion* handwriting that was added at the last minute next to Lyla's name begs scrutiny.

My co-captain swivels in his chair, his fingers steepled in front of his chin, his expression calmly attentive. 'Ellie is an architect,' he tells Ibu Agatha in his sweet, sweet voice. 'She'd be a valuable addition to the art and design team, wouldn't she?'

For the second time in two days, he's put me in a hot spot. After being roped into babysitting PTA, the last thing I want is another babysitting job.

I throw my sharpest glare at Dion, hoping he feels the burn from the laser cuts I give him. But he only smiles indulgently at me.

'She graduated with a 3.8 GPA in Architecture. Our Ellie here is the direct descendant of Einstein.'

Oh, please.

The room giggles at his dry joke. Entertaining older mothers should be at the top of his resume. Under the table, I extend my middle finger in his direction. Yesterday it was God; today it's Einstein.

'We *do* need to build giant props,' Ibu Agatha muses, giving me an adorable puppy-eyed look.

Oh, nononono. Not her.

'I don't think my time will allow me.' How do I get out of this without sounding like I'm afraid, lazy, or rude?

'There'll be teams.' Dion is cooing like he's talking to a baby. 'I'm sure it won't interfere with your *leisure time*, Ellie.'

I blister because that pompous ass just used my own words against me. I want to rebel, but I can't come up with a believable excuse. It's rather challenging to appear smart and collected when he tricks me into saying yes to a thing I didn't really want to get involved with in the first place. All while using the information I gave him willingly a few minutes ago.

Those juicy lips twitch. 'But if you think you're not up for it, you can always, you know . . .'

Nice try, asshole.

The pressure of every pair of eyes in this room forces me to act recklessly.

'Sure, I'll do it,' I say firmly, slapping my palm against the desk, the sound reminding me of a gavel coming down to make a pronouncement in the courthouse. Can't believe I'm uttering these words two days in a row. Even Lyla won't be able to dig me out from my grave if I keep agreeing to do things I don't want to do. Or know how to do. I've never built a real thing in my life before—only things on paper and 3D computer software. *No need to panic*, my subconscious calms me, *you can find a tutorial for anything on YouTube and TikTok.*

'Thank you, Ellie,' Ibu Agatha says with so much maternal affection, my cheeks warm. With a smile and a head bow, she wraps up her presentation and leaves the room. She does it so effortlessly, that it's only logical to think that chairing a meeting will be an easy job. My first PTA meeting is going to be a piece of cake.

* * *

My first PTA meeting is the mother of all disasters.

Tara and a few women who sat with us on Monday sit on my side of the table. Bernadet, Dion, and some of the faces I saw sitting on the other row yesterday are opposite us. Once Ibu Agatha is out the door, everyone decides to speak at their loudest volume. At the same time. About everything.

My eyes meet Dion's. He arches one of his eyebrows. I hate that he can do that and I can't. If he's not gonna say anything, then I will. Time to show these mothers who's in charge. A little noise won't make me quit. I quickly chant Lyla's magic word in my head. *Confidence, confidence.* I roll my shoulders and clear my throat.

'Hi, everyone! Hello!' I have to shout to make everyone hear me. The room slowly shushes back into a resemblance of quiet. Suppressed giggles and murmurs bounce from wall to wall.

I can do this.

'If you weren't in the meeting yesterday, I'd like to introduce myself. My name is Ellie. I'm here on Lyla's behalf. Don't worry, she's very much involved in everything; it's as if she's sitting right here with you all. Oh, and she says hi.'

Lyla didn't, but I thought it would be a good ice breaker. Also, because the people who sit facing me are not smiling. I catch Bernadet whisper something to Dion. He smiles with only the corners of his mouth.

'We must resubmit the proposal about homework,' someone on my right says.

Happy that somebody threw me a line, I respond eagerly. 'Sure. What about it?'

'It must be reduced,' the mother answers.

'No. We must increase it,' the other protests. 'My kids do nothing at home after school. They're growing lazier day by day.'

'Agreed. Our national ranking has dropped. We're not even in the top ten anymore.'

I try to keep up while skimming the email Lyla sent me last night. Is homework part of the agenda in Lyla's proposal?

'Finland is the best country for education and their schools don't assign homework,' someone shouts above the noise.

'We're not in Finland,' the mother who sits next to Tara snaps.

'*I'm aware.* What a shame,' comes the retort.

I mentally bring Ibu Agatha into my mind. How did she manage her audience?

Mic. I need a mic. Maybe three.

'Lyla never takes this seriously,' the mother next to Bernadet addresses me.

'That's not true. Lyla takes everything seriously,' Tara answers. I shoot her a grateful smile. Her loyalty to Lyla is loyalty to me.

'Is fee structure part of today's agenda, Ellie?' someone interrupts. She looks nice. At least she doesn't shout. 'We must stop them before they increase the tuition.'

I can't forgive myself for not preparing well enough for today. I've underestimated the audience. I thought I could handle a bunch of mothers. I read the bullet points in Lyla's email and my stomach sinks. No tuition fee and homework policy in her proposal. The debate goes on fiercely without me.

The same mother who asked about the fee, angles her torso towards Dion. 'What does your uncle say?'

I look up from my phone. His eyes flick to me, amusement and confidence blending into one. He turns his head to address the mother. 'Mr Goh will make sure that all inputs from the parents will be presented to the board.'

Okay. He clearly has some experience in dealing with these women. Dion glances at me and one corner of his mouth curls. From that single lip twitch, I know. I know he could easily handle the situation but chooses not to because he's a jerk. He's testing me. Or attempting to make me cry.

The topic grows from homework to many, many different things.

'Teacher quality is a shame.'

'Homework policy is a shame too.'

Oh, we're back at the homework again?

'Traffic is getting worse. We urgently need a solution.'

I give Bernadet a sympathetic nod. I experienced their morning traffic yesterday. Once is enough to know it's a nightmare.

'I thought the most urgent thing right now is the musical?' another woman says.

'Oh my god, can you imagine how grand it's going to be? We're all going to dress up!'

We do? Wait. We're talking about designer dresses now? Salon appointments and photo sessions? Hotel catering, wait staff, and menu? We're discussing *menu*?

In my bewildered state, I accidentally lock eyes with Bernadet. We stare at each other mutely for a few seconds before she breaks eye contact.

'Every single matter we discuss today is urgent.' At the sound of Bernadet's raised voice, the room goes relatively quiet, all excited talk about gowns and makeup ceases. 'Above all, we can't delay the talk about traffic. The school, and by extension our own PTA, has been neglecting it for years. The communities that surround our school and the police must sit together to solve this. What better time to do it than now since everyone wants to look good for the musical?'

'The police?' I hear myself squeak. Involving the police sounds like a big deal to me.

'The traffic we cause is not just our problem, it's everyone's.' Bernadet gives me a once-over and I try not to squirm under her cold glare. 'Yes, my dear. *The police.*'

The room holds its breath—some people still whisper among themselves—but the audience is listening to Bernadet. Her penetrating gaze shifts to Tara. I witness some tense communication there. Without taking her eyes off Tara, Bernadet speaks to the entire room. 'I propose the PTA chairperson to push this matter. What do you say, Dion?'

It doesn't escape my attention that she leaves the other PTA leader's name out. *Mine.*

'Bernadet, listen,' Tara says sweetly. 'There are time and budget constraints. Especially with the musical coming up, we must postpone other big issues until next year.'

'Can you guarantee that these *big* issues will be added to next year's agenda?' Bernadet asks, her face slips into a smooth mask that's projecting contempt and disdain.

My conversation with Lyla creeps back.

Don't change anything. Make them agree. I'm running for a third term.

'A change in leadership is needed,' Bernadet starts, and at once, the room lets out the breath—along with the gasp—it had been holding since Bernadet spoke.

My skin breaks into goosebumps. When Bernadet pauses and holds my gaze, I do not look away. I don't even blink. She's boldly threatening Lyla and the position my sister holds. I may be a silly girl pretending to be a grown up, but nobody touches my family. *Nobody.* I won't allow it.

'I suggested to Mr Goh some time ago that PTA leadership cannot be held by the same person for more than two years. Progress is stagnant, Tara, despite whatever excuses you and Lyla may tell yourselves.'

The clapback is colder than ice. I stiffen in my seat. I need to say something. 'Ibu Bernadet, I'm sure Lyla takes every issue seriously. She has plans to improve things around here.' I recognize my mistake the moment I close my mouth. Her words were bait and I, like a kid, ate it right from her hand. I'm defending my family openly, like a little girl defending her mother.

Dion tilts his head at me, disapproval clear on his face. God, I hate it when he's right; that I don't know what I'm doing, that my sister hasn't prepared me yet, that he's the superior captain between us two. I can't ask for Lyla's help at this very minute. I'm on my own.

Bernadet returns my smile, a little too eager on her end. '*Dear.* You were not here in the past so you *can't possibly be sure.* Can you be a sweetheart and let the people who actually have real stakes in this school talk?'

Some people snort loudly. Dion turns his head towards Bernadet and mutters a few words. He looks a little upset. Bernadet ignores him, because why wouldn't she? She has me trapped like a little mouse in her cheese-covered cage and she's having too much fun watching me die.

Tara clicks her tongue. 'Now, now, Bernadet. Don't be a bitch.'

'Need to be one to get things done around here.'

'*Ibu Tara. Ibu Bernadet.*' Dion sighs, touching his brow with his fingertip. 'Language please.'

'We're all adults here, Dion. What's the matter? You can't handle a little B word?' Bernadet says without taking her eyes off Tara.

'Oh my god, Dion is blushing,' someone points out.

Dion shakes his head a little, not in a mad way, more like he's resigned to how he's being teased. He drags his chair forward, then stiffly rests his arms on the table. It's hard to reconcile the image of this shy-looking guy with the one who *aggressively* pushed me to quit.

'He and Ellie make a cute pair, don't they?' I hear someone say, followed by cackling.

What the . . .? Dion's eyes meet mine, then we look away quickly. How can he still smile? I'm embarrassed. I clear my throat. The noise that comes out, however, makes it sound like I'm gagging.

'Yes, Ellie?' Bernadet asks from across the table.

My skin flushes hot. 'I'll tell Lyla your concerns.' I hate how young I sound.

'You do that. Meanwhile, every PTA member is encouraged to submit recommendations that they deem urgent to be considered for next year's agenda. We're doing that, or—' her pointed eyebrows are directed at me—'we're not allowed to change anything?'

'Bernadet. Stop it. The PTA is not about you, okay?' Tara says.

'Of course not, Tara. We're doing this for the kids.'

That's exactly what Lyla said. She's doing it for the kids. She's running for president to create better things for the Spring community. I wonder if they see how similar they both are to each other.

Dion finally arrives at the scene, addressing the audience with his level-headed attitude. 'Everyone is welcome to submit ideas by the end of March. Ellie and I will review them together.'

I hate that he has to rescue me. It shows everyone that I'm the weak leader. I desperately want to catch his eye, but he's currently staring down at his table and stifling a yawn.

'It'd be good to limit PTA management to two years,' the woman on Bernadet's right murmurs. 'The school cannot play favourites.'

'We tried that, remember?' Tara says in her jovial tone. 'You were the PTA chair once, Netty, and as I recall, your team spent most of the budget on parties.'

My head snaps up. So, this is Netty. And wow. Interesting. This flips the table back in our favour. *Thank you, Tara.*

Netty links her hands on the table in a way that reminds me of a cat sharpening her claws. 'I didn't recall you complaining about the Bali tickets you won from those parties, Tara darling.'

The table flips again. Damn these mothers.

It's pure chaos from that point on. I slip outside while everyone is arguing with everyone else. I walk towards the stairs and down to the empty marketing lobby. I keep walking until I'm out of the building, passing the garden and the massive parking lot. I drop myself onto one of the steps near the security post by the entry gates. Some guards nod at me but I'm too worked up to greet them back. I rest my elbows on my knees, put my head down, and close my eyes. The warmth from the natural air feels good. I no longer feel like I'm being caged inside a cold, noisy freezer with no way out.

I don't know how long I sit like that when I hear familiar chatter behind me. I turn my head in time to see the group of ladies who have been in the meeting with me walk hand-in-hand. They're smiling, giggling, talking. Like, seriously. Like, *normal*. As if what just happened inside the room was only a dream. Even Bernadet and Tara are laughing at something Netty says. When Tara spots me, she separates herself from the group.

'Hey, you,' Tara says. 'I called but you didn't pick up.'

I left my phone in my bag. It's still in the room.

'You guys are . . . done?' I'm so flabbergasted, my voice sounds weird even to my own ears.

'It's ten. They're gonna use the room for another meeting.'

It's so simple, logical, yet totally does not answer my question. Tara carefully dusts off the ground before sitting on the step next to me. I glance back at the throng of chit-chatting mothers. 'What happens now?'

'What do you mean?'

'You agreed on everything?' I'm sceptical about it, but this school has proven me wrong so many times in two days alone. Maybe when I left, they all miraculously hugged it out and solved their disagreements.

Tara laughs. 'No, silly. We'll go with the one Lyla has drafted.'

'And they're okay with that?'

'Who cares? Hey. We're gonna head to the mall for coffee. Wanna come?'

I gape at her. Coffee? There is an abundance of coffee inside! And untouched snacks! They don't need to go to the mall for brunch. 'Err, no thanks. You girls have fun.'

Once the mothers are out of sight, I'm suddenly gripped with the overwhelming feeling of missing my sister; like I'm missing air and I can't breathe. Despite our age difference, Lyla and I share a similar sense of humour, and there was plenty of dark humour in today's meeting.

A pair of sports shoes appear in my peripheral vision. Dion is watching me from the grandness that's his height. His backpack is hoisted over one shoulder. One hand holds the strap, the other is jammed into his jeans pocket.

'They can be too much sometimes,' he opens without pleasantries.

'*Sometimes?*' I squeak.

He chuckles. I refuse to acknowledge how rich that sound is. Like the taste of my favourite palm sugar coffee.

'Don't think too much about what Ibu Bernadet said back there. Believe me, it's not about you. She's just showing off her muscles.'

I'm touched and confused. 'Um . . . sure.'

'You don't have to be a part of any of this,' he says quietly. 'You're free to go. Nobody will blame you.'

I rise to my feet and dust off my pants. 'You can leave too.' I remember the way he was being teased. He and I are not friendly, but he's a *person* and he doesn't have to put up with that. If I were him, I'd walk away.

He releases a long breath. 'I *want* to be here.'

'Why? Do they pay you?'

He stares at some middle distance, pretending not to hear me.

'So,' he says conversationally after a second. 'What do you say? You'll quit?'

He can't stop himself, can he? Our conversation runs in circles, making it impossible to separate its head from its tail.

'How can I? You just added me to the art team.'

'Stay with the art team, but quit PTA.'

'Why the double standard?'

'Art team does isolated work. PTA is more complex and prone to conflicts.'

'I see.' Somewhere in the back of my head, I agree with the logic of his reasoning. 'What would happen to Lyla if I quit?'

'Well, she's not here, is she?'

My eyes narrow. I recognize a veiled threat when I hear one. Getting rid of Lyla will solve a lot of their political problems. He and those mothers are the same: bullies. The blood roars back into my ears. '*In that case*, I'll be here until Lyla is back.' I egg him on with a sneer. 'Go on. Try removing me. See what happens.'

His mouth thins. '*In that case*, I'll dump task after task on you until you're buried underneath them and you run out of the door crying. I know your kind. People of your nature always choose the easiest way out.'

The frosty air between us freezes the beads of sweat that were rolling down under my shirt and blazer.

'*People of my nature?*' I take a step forward. If by that he means I lack purpose and goals, then yes, he's probably correct. My mother often calls me lazy when she's frustrated with me. But Dion is not my mother; he has no right to judge me. I drop my voice. '*In that case*, I'll keep accepting them until I'm buried underneath and screw everything up. Yeah, I'll screw things up so bad, by that time you realize it, it'll be too late for you to fix it.' I poke a finger at his chest. It's like poking a wall. 'I'll sabotage your precious musical in the last minute. Neat, huh?'

He freezes for a moment.

Then a moment more.

'You wouldn't dare,' he says in a quiet, threatening voice.

'Try me, doll-face.' Mentally, I cringe because I just did what the mothers in the meeting did to him. But then I remember why we're in this argument and the last shred of guilt is gone from my consciousness.

'Do you mean it as an insult? Because I take care of my skincare religiously. Doll-face is a compliment.'

'Sure, pimple-face.'

'It would hurt if I actually had pimples.'

'Whatever, donut-face.'

'Ah. Now we're getting somewhere.' He smirks but I notice he doesn't look as confident as before. 'Your sister won't let you wreck things on purpose.'

'Oh, but my sister is not here, is she?'

I hear his sharp intake of breath. He glances at me, dislike imminent in his dark eyes. When he opens his mouth, I brace myself and wait for the punchline. I'm sure it'll blow me to pieces. He looks mad.

'There's plenty of food inside. You look like you could use some sugar in your system.'

'Why do you care?' I snap.

'I can't let my co-captain faint on her first day of duty. It will reflect badly on me and the school.'

His soothing voice—yes, *soothing*, even when it's glazed with venom and spiky nails—and the ray of light behind his head make him appear benevolent and angelic. Is this a peace offering? It must be.

'I thought the room will be used for another meeting,' I say. 'Aren't they cleaning it up already?'

'I asked them to wait for you.'

Oh wow. That sounds awfully thoughtful. And nice. Lyla mentioned that Dion is a good kid. My sister is never—okay, maybe not *never*—rarely wrong.

I pause, feeling unsure but a little hopeful. By default, I don't like confrontations. I avoid them the best I can. To have a friendly face in this new place would be nice. 'Does this mean we're friends?' My life here would s-o-o-o easy if we did. It's ridiculous how hard I cross my fingers behind my back.

I don't know which one is more humiliating, the shock on his face or his booming laughter. Yes, he's laughing his ass off, that mochaccino pompous ass. He's still laughing when he walks away, his back and shoulders trembling with each step. That mocking laughter haunts me all the way to my sleep.

Second day of school sucks.

Chapter 6

Dion

I moved in with my aunt and uncle, who lived in a different city on another island, shortly after my father died. Those early years were a nightmare. Barely ten years old, I found separation from my mother hard, especially after I had already lost one parent. I was gripped by an acute fear that something bad might happen to my mom when I was away. Holidays went by quietly most of the time, but I completely lost it on my mom's birthday. I threw tantrums like the world was ending, screaming and throwing myself on the floor, refusing to go to school, to eat, or to listen to anyone. My aunt and uncle finally devised a plan. Every year on my mom's birthday, we would all celebrate it together at the same time. My mom would choose the type of food she wanted to eat that year—Chinese food, Japanese food, Indonesian food, anything she wanted—and my uncle, aunt, and I would match the restaurant that served the same food my mom had chosen. At the agreed time, my mom would go to the restaurant in Samarinda and we would go to ours in Jakarta. Birthday cakes would be served. We blew the candles together. I felt so much like her normal son despite the

1300 kilometre distance between us. In the early years following my dad's passing, my mother dined alone. No fancy meals, no nice dress, and no laughter. I didn't notice these things because I was too ecstatic to celebrate with her. The fact that we dined in two different restaurants in two different cities didn't bother me. I doubt I even registered it.

As I grew older, I didn't exactly need the shared celebration anymore, but our tradition still holds. In the past few years, my mother has gone to her birthday dinner with her friends and some relatives. The restaurant gets fancier, the clothes get trendier, the calls get louder and merrier with laughter from both sides.

Today is my mother's fifty-fifth birthday, and this year she chooses Manadonese food. Compared to other Indonesian food like Padang or Balinese, Manadonese is less well-known internationally, but not because it's less rich. Their food is famous for its spiciness. It has to, at least, scorch our tongue and burn our stomach. Since Padang and Manadonese are my aunt's favourite Indonesian cuisines, I grew up eating skipjack tuna, hot and spicy chicken rica rica, rendang, and crispy corn critters. *Tinutuan bubur manado*—Manadonese traditional porridge with pumpkin, spinach, sweet corn, cassava, and salted fish—is the comfort food often found in my aunt's kitchen.

I suggest a small mom-pop Manado restaurant near our house for tonight's dinner. My aunt vetoes my suggestion and opts for a bigger, fancier restaurant in the neighbouring complex. It's located next to the highway, about twenty minutes from home by car. 'It's close to your hospital,' she reasons. This is our typical dance. I'd decide things with their comfort in mind; they'd do the same thing with mine. I assure them that the hospital doesn't have a problem with me coming in a little late tonight. My uncle closes the argument by saying, 'If you can be on time, be on time.'

Forever the principal, I see.

I arrive first before 5 p.m. and we have the entire restaurant to ourselves. As soon as my uncle and aunt settle on the table, the waitress hands each of us the menu.

'Ayam rica or telur balado?' My aunt peers over her reading glasses at me.

'I don't mind both chicken and eggs,' I say.

She raises her eyebrows at my uncle.

He sighs. 'Go ahead. I'll eat something else.' As a Singaporean, my uncle has a lower tolerance for spicy food than we do.

'Like what?' my aunt asks.

'Rice and water.'

My aunt laughs. She tells me, 'We must train him harder, Dion.' Once she completes the order, she gets up to go to the restroom.

My uncle beckons me closer. 'The board has approved of my retirement.' He's been talking about it for a few years. He'll be sixty soon and yet, I can't imagine him as anything other than the Spring Principal.

'This year is your last?' I ask.

'Maybe next year. We can't afford drastic changes when there's the big gala on the way.'

So, this fundraising will be his legacy. I'll do whatever I can to ensure its grand success because my uncle is my hero, and he deserves nothing less.

'When is your mandatory internship?' he asks.

Any medical student who wishes to work in Indonesia, or to continue with a specialist study, must complete a government internship program. We're stationed in remote places across Indonesia for a year to help people in underprivileged districts. The government decides the time of service, the place, and the stipend we receive.

'I can check.' I submitted my application last year, so their call can come any time. 'Why do you ask?'

My uncle smiles, a serene expression sweeps across his face. 'I plan to take your aunt to stay in Singapore for a while. You think we could spend some time together before you go to . . . I don't know where? It'd be nice if you could come along.'

'I'd love that.' I smile back at him, fighting against the sting in my throat. He says these things casually, treating me like his own son and not realizing how much it means to me. I can't return the gesture, despite loving him with every inch of my being. I have this urge to pay him back. A part of me always sees myself as my uncle's investment even when I know it isn't his intention at all. This thought has prevented me from accepting him completely as a father. I want to prove myself worthy first.

'How's work?' he asks.

'Hospital, or Spring?'

He looks amused. 'Agatha told me you and some new girl are heading the PTA on behalf of Ibu Lyla? How's that working out for everyone?'

'Surprisingly manageable so far,' I say with a grin. 'She's Ibu Lyla's younger sister. I tried asking her to quit, but she's persistent.'

'Two heads are always better than one, Dion. Unless she's mean to you.'

'Oh, not at all.' I rewind the scenes from this morning. A smile sneaks out of me when I remember Ellie's face during and after our PTA meeting. She looked so damn adorable when she thought we were friends.

My uncle sips his iced tea. 'Well, you know what to do. Maintain your distance and be professional.'

He says these things to me all the time, I'm sure he's not referring to Ruby specifically, but I inwardly cringe nonetheless. Ruby is what happened when I got involved with a privileged kid from a privileged family. These people have the tendency to take pleasure in telling other people who they think are less than them which side of rich vs. poor we belong to. I quickly shake the thought away. Ruby has no place in my mind anymore.

* * *

My phone rings when we're in the middle of our spicier-than-hell dinner. We all have tears running down our faces and sweat rolling down our backs despite sitting in an air-conditioned room. My uncle is faring the worst. His whole face is leaking. He groans every time he spoons food into his mouth, and each bite is followed by a hearty gulp of iced tea.

I press the accept button. The three of us huddle closer to scream at my phone screen. 'Happy birthday!'

My mom looks radiant. And happy. My heart leaps.

'Thank you so much, loves,' she shouts back. Then she notices my uncle. 'Oh my God, Evan! What happened to you?'

My uncle sniffs as he wipes his nose with a napkin. 'These two rascals convinced me that practice makes perfect. I can tell you, Betty, it's all a scam.'

My mom laughs. 'Send them to detention.'

'What's the cake this year?' my aunt asks my mom.

'My friends brought me some fruit cake,' my mom says.

'Fruit cake?' my aunt bellows. 'Dear God. Somebody better get you a chocolate cake! Who eats fruit cake these days?'

The two sisters spend the next few minutes cracking jokes and exchanging gossip, then my aunt hands me back my phone. My mom and I grin at each other.

'Let me see the damage,' she says.

I rotate my phone so my mom can get a glimpse of our meal on the table. Since my uncle didn't contribute much, we still have plenty of food left. Our table looks incredibly appetizing. Red hot ayam rica and telur balado. Big chunks of green chili in the signature cakalang skipjack fish. The stir-fry papaya leaves made us sniff after a few bites. As expected, my aunt didn't half-ass the heat level of our celebratory dinner.

I flip the phone back to face me.

'How's life? Work okay? You're eating right? Sleeping well?' my mom asks. She moves away from the noise in the background. I recognize some of her old work friends on the table behind her. I'm glad to know that my mom will have a great time tonight.

'Yes, everything's good,' I say, wiping the sweat off my forehead with the back of my hand. 'I'll make a wish for you tonight.'

'Oh, Dion.' My mom puts a hand on her chest. 'Thank you, baby.'

'I'd better let you get back to your friends.'

'Sure. I'll talk to you tomorrow?'

'I'll talk you to tomorrow.' I pause. 'Hey, Mami. Have I told you fifty-five looks great on you?'

She bursts out laughing, then points a finger at my face. 'You big flirt! Such a sweet talker.'

'But it's true,' I say.

'Yeah, yeah. Save it for your special someone. By the way, will I ever get to meet your special someone?'

I roll my eyes. A second before she disconnects, I lower my voice because when we say our prayer, we don't shout. We whisper. 'Happiest birthday, Mami. Many, many, *many* happy returns.'

Thanks for being my mother. Thanks for sacrificing so much for my future. I'm sorry I can't be with you tonight. I miss you.

I miss you. I miss you. I miss you. So much it cracks me in two.

Fifteen years.

No more separation anxiety.

Same old guilt.

Chapter 7

Ellie

I've settled into my role as Lyla's house-sitter and her daughters' babysitter more smoothly than I anticipated. It helps that Lyla and Ferdinan have a team of nannies, housekeepers, security guards, gardeners, and drivers at their disposal. It took me a week to familiarize myself with Lyla's neighbourhood. Spring is only a ten-minute drive away. There are a few big malls that can be reached in ten to twenty minutes by car. Rows of hipster cafés and boutiques line up the main streets. We have summer weather almost all year round so these vendors can afford to set up their outdoor seating as long as they like. Sidewalks are sacrificed to make way for more highways that connect Jakarta and other neighbouring suburbs. Tall office buildings fight for more space against public gardens. As is always the case with developing cities, the greens lose to concretes. The suburbs are developing fast like there is no tomorrow.

The routine with my nieces is straightforward. Picking them up from school is fast becoming my favourite thing. They tell me everything about their day. Dinner always starts

at 6 p.m., followed by a video call with Lyla. Ferdinan joins
them occasionally when his schedule allows him to. Afterwards,
I check their homework and bags. When everything is in order,
we watch some TV in Lyla's room from her state-of-the-art
entertainment system. We snack on chips and drink sodas.
I read somewhere in Lyla's numerous instructions that the
girls are not allowed to eat or drink anything sweet before bed,
especially artificial sweets like bottled tea and Cokes, but what
she doesn't know won't kill her. Besides, what is childhood if
you can't snack on junk food once in a while, right? Or break
the no-TV rule? Who wants to live like a soldier? The girls love
me. I nail the cool aunt thing to the T. At 9 p.m., I usher them
to bed. They wash their face and brush their teeth. Then I sit
on their bed and kiss them goodnight.

Tonight, though, seeing as there's no homework, the
three of us huddle together in Lyla's king-sized bed. Time for
some Korean drama (me), Marvel miniseries (Ashley), and
Disney cartoons (Aureli). We decide what we'll watch by playing
rock-paper-scissor.

'How excited are you about the musical?' I ask the girls as we
watch Hawkeye get thrown around by Yelena. Bags of chips are
scattered around us. On the nightstands, we have orange juice for
Aur, iced tea for Ashley, and root beer for me.

'The musical is called *Under the Sea*,' Ashley says. 'Inspired by
the story of *The Little Mermaid*.'

'I'll be Nemo,' Aureli exclaims. 'What are you going to be,
Auntie Ellie?' she asks as I snuggle her tiny frame closer to me.
'Everyone must take part.'

'You mean all students?' I ask.

Both girls nod. Ashley, with a serious expression, adds, 'My
teacher says that students and teachers can audition for cast
members, singers, or dancers. Parents, staff, and other guests can
participate in other supporting roles.'

That's a lot of people. The enormity of the project starts to sink in. No wonder everyone is anxious about it.

'Well, I'll be the one who's clapping the hardest when you're on the stage,' I say.

'Choose one role, Auntie, choose.' Aureli claps.

'It's based on *The Little Mermaid*, you say? Let me think.' I do a thinking pose with a pursed mouth and a finger on my temple. 'I always wanted to be the evil mermaid.'

'Ursula?' Ashley asks.

'That's the one.'

Aureli snickers. 'You're a big kid, Auntie Ellie. You can be anything.'

'You too, baby, once you've reached a certain height,' I say.

'I'm on Ursula's team,' Ashley says.

Aureli bounces to a sitting position so fast, she nearly showers us with her sour cream chips. She looks at Ashley like she's the coolest person on the planet. I bet that's how I look at Lyla. 'You'll be Ursula?'

'No,' Ash answers. 'I'll be Ursula's evil fish-soldier who does the dirty work for her.'

Aureli and I woot. Despite my rocky start with the PTA and Dion, I'm excited about the whole thing. My nieces will play real roles in the musical. Their excitement is my excitement; their success is my success. I would never, in a million years, sabotage the production. My threat was empty. Dion doesn't need to worry unless . . . I swallow thickly, my palm sweats. Unless *I* wreck my responsibilities by accident.

Aureli gets off the bed. 'I want to pee.'

I pick up the empty chip bag from the bed and dust off the sheet to make sure the girls don't leave crumbs everywhere.

'You miss your mom?' I ask Ashley.

She shrugs.

I smile at her. '*I* miss her.'

'Me too,' she admits quietly. 'Mostly at night.' There's a worry line on her forehead. My eldest niece worries a lot, I notice.

'Hey. Guess what? I'll be helping the art team,' I say with extravagant cheerfulness to distract her from missing her parents.

'Will you build the ocean?' Ashley asks.

'I don't know. There'll be meetings to decide what we'll do. Anyway, what does the ocean do in this musical?'

'They'll do battle dances around the ship. That wreckage scene and the fight one in the end. They say it's like a group of kung fu fighters.' Ashley laughs, the worry lines on her young face smoothen making it look like someone has erased pencil marks on her skin. 'It's the first gala in fifty years,' says Ashley, awe in her voice. 'I can't believe we're a part of it, Auntie Ellie.'

Ashley is right. Fifty years' worth of contribution to our country's national education is no joke; not everyone can match Spring's commitment and their sustainable business. They have evolved from a simple one-story building to what they are now. Tara told me that there was a possibility our country's president and his cabinet ministers would attend.

'I'm actually glad that Mom won't be here during the rehearsals,' Ashley says without taking her eyes off the TV. It stops me, my smile hanging in between. I regroup fast. 'She's the late type, isn't she?'

Lyla is very punctual.

Ashley seems to be choosing her next words carefully. While Aureli looks like Lyla and by extension, me, Ashley takes on Ferdinan's facial features: lighter skin, oval-shaped face, deep set of eyes, and a serious expression. With Ashley, I need to pay attention to the unspoken words.

'My teachers are all weird when Mom is around. I don't know if they like me, or they act nice because I'm Mom's daughter. It's so, so weird.'

I rub my nose. For a moment, I debate if I should say something. I stall by calling out to Aureli who's been quiet in the bathroom, 'You okay in there, sweetie?'

'I'm doing number two,' comes Aureli's muffled answer.

I nudge Ashley's knee with my toes. 'Ash. Your mom can't make someone like or not like you. It's all *you*. I bet everyone likes you. You're smart, polite, and not a troublemaker. What's not to like?'

She grins shyly, the way someone does when they're pleased to hear the compliment but are not sure how to respond.

'Your mom has an important job in the PTA. Sometimes being a smart woman can both inspire and intimidate people.'

'How so?' Ashley sounds genuinely curious.

I don't think I'm the right person to tell Ashley about sexism and the stigma against strong women in the real world. But not telling her feels wrong too. These girls will grow up to be strong adults one day. I say, 'Your mother is not afraid to fight for what's important, even when it makes other people uncomfortable. She's inspiring that way, but also intimidating.'

I've experienced first-hand what Lyla's charisma can do to a person.

'The musical is important.' Ashley's eyes spark. 'But I don't do much. My role is not important.'

'Now you listen carefully, young lady,' I say, adding a dramatic finger wag and a stern face. 'Every little fish, every drop of the ocean, every swimming mermaid, every sound system guy, every janitor, every mother who drives their kids to the rehearsals, counts. It's all of you.' I've been listening to Ibu Agatha speak about the musical a lot lately. 'It's what makes it *the* Spring Musical.'

Ashley ponders it for a moment. Then she smiles up at me, causing my heart to simultaneously break and glue itself back together. Is this what it would feel like to have my own kid? I might never know. Every month when the pain hits, I'm convinced that the reproductive option is closed to me forever.

'I can't believe I'm actually excited about going back to school.' I smooth her hair down as I laugh. 'It's going to be fun.'

'Promise?' She offers her pinky to me.

Her grin melts me. I link mine around hers, then cross my heart. This is the easiest promise I've ever made in my entire life.

February

Chapter 8

Ellie

I can hear the music from the parking lot. There are six entrances to the multi-purpose hall and all of them are currently wide open. Teachers and big kids mingle around. Parents and nannies people-watch from the side. For the sake of the rehearsals, Spring has transformed their colossal indoor gym to one gigantic practice studio. My nieces and their younger friends will have their own rehearsals in the junior wing. I promised I'd stop by as soon as the gate opens in thirty minutes.

As I stand on the threshold, a feeling of nostalgia resurfaces. God knows I don't miss going to school, but I do miss the tireless energy these kids seem to have in abundance. They move like they believe they can live forever. That they can live *worry-free* forever. I'd give anything to taste that youthful ignorance one more time. Adulthood—as I learned a little too late—revolves around paying bills and cleaning. Always, always cleaning. Recently, it involves job hunting and resume writing too.

I deposit myself on the floor in a desolate spot near the stage. I sit with my back against the wall, my legs stretched in front of me, my bag draped across my thighs. A group of high school boys are rehearsing close to the stage. The tall one, who looks like their leader, is wearing long black trainers and a tight-fitting black T-shirt while the rest wear PE uniforms. Each boy holds a wooden staff like the ones people used in old kung fu movies. They wield the wood as if they're disciples of Shaolin Temple. Every now and then, they bang the bottom of their stick against the floor and yell some sort of battle cry. The thud adds intensity to their dance. I don't recall a fight scene in *The Little Mermaid* but maybe they're doing some improv and adding scenes to the classic tale. Their leader turns around, and my breath gets stuck in my throat. I already knew that Dion is juicy, tall, and hunky, but muscular? No freaking way. I refuse to accept that he's a doctor, a martial arts guy, a walking thirst trap, a dedicated Spring volunteer, *and* a gym rat.

As he converses with the group, he sports the same smile he blasted everyone during the sex-ed workshop when his face appeared on not one, but three gigantic screens. The *I'll charm the shit out of you* smile. The very same one that brought a full room of mothers to their giggling knees.

The boys break apart from the circle with a loud *Huzzah!* and leave Dion standing by himself. While his teammates wipe their faces and gulp water from their bottles, Dion repeats a certain sequence over and over. If he were my parent's son, my mother would hang a portrait of him as a poster child in each and every room of our house. No wonder he looks down on me. I avoid extra work like the plague; he inhales extra work like it's oxygen. Does Spring pay him? Does he own a clock turner? Does he sleep, eat, or scroll social media? I barely kept up with my classes when I was at college.

Dion slowly edges closer to where I sit. His limbs bend and snap, soft and sharp, like how water and fire dance around each other. Up close, his biceps bulk, straining against the tight sleeves, the sweaty shirt clings to his stomach like cloth sticking to a flat ironing board.

Ugh.

This doesn't do my ego any good but I can't make myself stop looking. The view mesmerizes me. *He* mesmerizes me. He's easy on the eyes as long as he keeps his mouth shut. I'll allow myself to enjoy the show for a few more minutes. On the last try, Dion misses a step and flops on his ass. Somehow, he manages to fall gracefully, using the stick in one hand to balance and the other hand to soften the blow. The word 'shit' slips out of his mouth. I reflexively push off the wall, one hand shooting in front of me like I'm about to catch him. Unfortunately, that's the farthest I'm willing to go to save him. I shouldn't laugh. But he's clearly okay, and he looks adorable sprawled on his ass. His head snaps up at the sound of my laughter. A look of surprise spreads across his face, then it morphs into a look of amusement. Wait, he's pleased to see me? That can't be good.

He pushes himself up, dusts off his bottom, then beckons me to come closer. I shake my head. To my horror, he stalks towards me. I'm ashamed to admit that I'm hugely intimidated by this. I frantically glance behind me, hoping the solid wall would turn into a magic portal like Narnia's wardrobe, swallow me whole, and transport me to a faraway place. When the wall remains solid, I have no choice but to face the intruder in my personal space. The whiff of his scent—sweat, soap or aftershave—passes through me. It's not unpleasant. I might inhale it a little greedily.

'Up, petal,' he instructs as he looms above me like a muscle-y mountain.

Since he's not the boss of me, and since my name is not Petal, I don't move a single limb. His right hand is stiffly extended towards me, all five fingers flexed. If he expects me to grab it so he can haul my ass up, he'll have to extend it until the sun rises again the next morning.

'What's the piece you're performing?' I ask.

'*The Wrecking Sea,*' he says.

So, this is the angry ocean Ashley told me about. It suits him, but I'd rather eat fried chicken with an extra spicy sambal that would annihilate my intestines than admit that out loud.

'Your talent shouldn't be wasted on a nameless sea,' I say with feigned concern. 'You should play Sebastian. You know, the lobster?'

'He's a crab,' he supplies dryly, finally dropping the hand and putting it on his hip instead. 'I can't sing.'

Finally. Something he *can't* do.

'That's perfect, Dion.' I brighten. 'Sebastian has that off-tune voice and irritating personality that matches yours very well. You'll make a believable annoying lobster.'

'Crab.' He massages his nape. Apparently, the height difference between us is a challenge to our necks' mobility. The back of my own neck starts to knot painfully from bending at an odd angle. Looking at him from down here is like looking at a skyscraper. I decide to stand.

As soon as I'm on my feet, he shoves the stick into my face. 'Here.'

I take a step back as I eye it with disgust. Not only does that thing look heavy, it's longer than my body. 'I don't need to prove my masculinity,' I say.

'Only your hand-and-feet coordination. Balance is important.' He raises his eyebrows, eyes glinting. 'If you're not up for it, just say the word.'

'What word?'

'You know it, petal.'

He's so full of himself. I kick my enormous bag to the side. With a theatrical bow, I accept the staff. I'm relieved to learn that it's not as heavy as it looks. He's watching me with a curious spark in his eyes, his arms crossed in front of his chest. I experience a moment of doubt. I work with my hands to *create* art, not to *perform* art. I can barely tell left from right. But I did yoga in my school days. I suppose I can manage a few balancing poses. I hold my breath and get ready in position. I'm gonna improvise the heck out of this shit.

He rolls his eyes, I just know it. I can feel the mocking vibration in the back of my skull.

I breathe dramatically because that's what yoga is about. Then, slowly and deliberately, I settle into the warrior pose, the staff steady in my right hand, the bottom tip resting on the floor. I gotta make sure it won't fall on my head. I block out his low chuckle. After holding the position steady for half a minute, I snap my feet together and smack the end of the staff against the floor. My feet's momentum collides nicely with the *bang*. The sound is so satisfying, I'm tempted to pound it a few more times.

Dion and some of his teammates slow clap. I bow to everyone, then toss the wood back to him. To my dismay and amazement, he grabs it easily, like I just threw him a rag doll.

'Let me teach you our moves.' Dion trails behind me as I walk back to my spot. 'It's as easy as one, two, three.'

I pick up my bag. Time to see my nieces in the junior building. I look over my shoulder and see part of his chest. Sweaty, muscle-y, and expansive. I quickly turn my face forward. 'My hand-and-feet coordination is splendid.'

'Are you afraid I might trick you?'

He's such a bully. His evil laughter when I asked him if we were friends rings loud from inside my head. I immediately put up my defences. 'With *you*? Always.'

'*Always*? We haven't even known each other that long.' He's enjoying himself. His eyes are bright from the exertion and mischief.

I decide to ignore him and his bulking figure, and head towards the doors. He's hot on my heels.

'Why are you following me?' I ask, annoyed.

'Oh, please.' He rolls his eyes so hard I'm afraid they'll disappear in the back of his head. 'I'm heading outside.'

I'm near the doors when someone shouts my name. 'Ellie! Wait up.'

* * *

Dion

Ibu Agatha catches up with me and Ellie. 'Look at you two cuties. Work coming along great, I assume?' She directs her twinkling eyes at me.

I don't need this from Ibu Agatha. Ellie and I are *not* cuties. I admit Ellie is funny, though. The way she did yoga back there. Suppressing my snort, I steal a glance at her. I don't think she realizes her nose scrunches and her eyes light up when she smiles. Without meaning to, I return her smile, which is weird because she is currently smiling at Ibu Agatha and her companions.

All right. Stop smiling at her, with her, just stop.

Ibu Agatha speaks to Ellie. 'I'd like you to meet Ibu Sylvia and Pak Jonas.'

Everyone promptly shakes hands. Since Ellie is related to Spring royalty, the handshakes are followed by solemn head bows.

'Ibu Sylvia is an English teacher by day and the head of our musical by afternoon. She'll oversee every aspect of the production, especially the choreography department,' Ibu Agatha completes the introduction.

Ellie's face transforms into something akin to respect. Though Ibu Sylvia is petite—she's even shorter than Ellie—she exudes such confidence you have no choice but to admire her. Being a woman at the helm is not an easy feat.

'I just told Dion he'd be perfect for Sebastian,' Ellie says.

'A high school teacher will play Sebastian,' Ibu Sylvia tells her, clearly oblivious to our internal joke. 'Pak Roberto has the voice of an angel. No offence, Dion.'

'None taken, Ibu,' I say.

'I always thought Sebastian was a lobster,' Jonas says.

'Oh my god, me too,' Ellie says. Everyone but me laughs.

I tell Ellie, 'He's a crab.' Then to everyone who watches me and Ellie, 'He's a crab.'

'Yeah. Crabby like him.' Ellie speaks from the corner of her mouth while jabbing a thumb in my direction.

I'm ready to list out some more facts about Sebastian the crab when I catch Ibu Agatha's face. With eyes darting between me and Ellie, she has that *aww* look I see so often on my aunt's face when she teases my uncle. I snap my mouth close.

'Pak Jonas here teaches Art,' Ibu Agatha tells Ellie. 'He's also the head of the musical design production and creative team. He leads an amazing group of teachers and art students. And now we have *you*.'

'Thanks for including me in your superb group, Pak Jonas,' Ellie says.

Jonas's ears turn pink. It's growing into a deeper shade of red when Ellie openly does her checking out, like she did to me at the first PTA meeting. She's not leering, more like appreciating what she sees.

Something tangy fills my mouth. I don't like that she's checking out other guys. I suck in a piercing breath. We co-chair PTA together; we're not dating. She's allowed to appreciate Jonas. If she digs a nerd, Jonas has that quality in abundance. He's dressed like any other Spring teacher, but he always adds a little something to the uniform that tells people he's an artist at heart. His white Spring shirt is rolled to the elbows. He wears a maroon vest over his shirt, his tie is perfectly tucked inside, and he's wearing dorky, black-rimmed glasses. His belt buckle is a silver skull, something I would never wear, not even to my grave. He's shorter than me, all bones with a lanky figure. His short beard looks abandoned, like he doesn't bother, or doesn't realize it's there. He's what my mother and aunt would call a charming young man.

'Ibu Agatha says you studied Architecture,' Jonas says a little too formally. Everyone is like this around Ibu Lyla, and by extension, her family.

Ellie nods, blushing, which is cute. Like a rose petal blooming . . .

Okay, that's enough, man!

'3.8 GPA.' Ibu Agatha's eyes crinkle at the corners as she shoots me a knowing grin. I assume she groups us together because my GPA is also 3.8.

'I can't wait to work with your team,' Ellie says. 'What do we do again?'

Ibu Sylvia chuckles, then says, 'The art team will be designing stages and props and whatever the cast needs for the dance.'

Ellie looks excited. I think about my uncle and his upcoming retirement. He told me that excitement from core members is a good thing. I smile at Ellie. She looks suspicious of my sincerity.

After a moment of small talk, the three of them bow to Ellie, then excuse themselves.

'Why do they do that?' Ellie mimics their deep bow.

'They only do it to you and your sister.'

'No, they don't.'

'Yes, they do, petal. They're respectful towards every parent, but they don't do *that*'—I bow to her like a mirror reflection—'to anyone.'

'Well,' she adjusts the bag's strap on her shoulder. 'I gotta run to the junior wing. See you when I see you.' She pauses, smirks, then does an aggravated bow towards me.

Against my will, I laugh. I lean against the door frame, my staff securely tucked inside my elbow, and watch my co-captain sashay her way to the junior lobby.

Someone taps my arm. I almost shit myself. After I swallow my heart, I turn and find a parent standing elegantly next to me.

'Good afternoon, Ibu Netty.' I straighten, my polite mask slides into place.

She nods towards the direction Ellie went. 'She's nowhere near qualified to handle an important job such as PTA, Dion.'

Last month I told my uncle that everything was manageable on the PTA front. I spoke too soon.

'Let's give her some time,' I say. 'She seems qualified to assist Jonas.'

'Oh, I don't mean *that*.' Ibu Netty chuckles and tosses her hair behind her shoulder. 'She can get involved in anything she wants. Just not PTA.'

Of course. These ambitious mothers don't care about other divisions. They care when it's PTA because it's the parents' powerhouse. Everyone wants a piece of it. I loved the work done by PTA in the past, still do, but it doesn't mean I enjoy their drama.

Ellie's threat about sabotaging the musical floats inside my head. My gut feeling says not to buy it, but I'm not entirely certain either. While Ibu Lyla has proven her reputation, I know nothing about her younger sister. She could be the kind of person who walks away from responsibilities without an ounce of guilt because her family would shield her from the consequences. I hope I'm wrong, but I don't want to be completely caught off-guard either.

Ibu Netty smiles up at me. 'Some of us have compiled the list for next year's PTA projects. When can you review it with us?'

'I'll ask Ellie—'

She tuts sharply. 'No need to involve that kid. After *you* read it, you can bring it directly to your uncle.'

My uncle would pass it back to me if he didn't see Ellie's or Ibu Lyla's signature at the bottom. The mothers who side with Ibu Bernadet and Ibu Netty would protest; Ibu Tara and the current PTA members would accuse the school of playing favourites. I don't want to imagine what Ibu Lyla would say if she called my uncle from London about this. There's nothing simple about PTA politics.

'Is tomorrow 3 p.m. okay? We can meet in the canteen before the rehearsal,' she suggests.

Now. *Now* is the perfect time to leave. I move the staff to my right hand. 'If you'll excuse me, I need to get back to practice. I'll email you later? Thank you so much.'

Without waiting for her reply, I retreat.

Maintain my distance. Be professional. Deflect.

Chapter 9

Dion

I'm rounding a corner between the third and second floor in the junior wing when someone crashes into me.

'Jesus!' I grunt as the long, wooden sticks I'm carrying in my arms thud against my forehead at the impact. I rub the spot between my brows.

'Sorry, sorry.'

I push my sweaty hair out of my eyes. It's been a week since I last saw her. Without any greetings, Ellie throws her hands in the air. 'I can't find Ashley. I don't know where she is. Shit.'

Dramatic should've been her first name. I rest the tips of the staff on the floor. I can carry two or three of these with ease, but six? I lean against them slightly. 'I'm sure she's here somewhere. Have you checked the restroom?'

'Not there.'

'Have you asked her teacher?'

'I didn't see any adults in the classroom. I hope they haven't moved the practice again. Last time I had to look in each room of this building.' Beads of sweat dot her hairline and the top of her upper lip.

I hoist the six staffs into my arms. 'Come on. Where's her class?'

She leads me back to the second floor. As we pass many classrooms and groups of parents and nannies, she asks me in a hushed tone, 'What if she was kidnapped?'

'Don't be ridiculous,' I say. 'Though there was a case of kidnapping once.'

She stops walking and clutches her chest. 'Damn it, Dion. You're joking, right?'

I glance at her pale face and immediately feel bad. 'It was the case of divorced parents fighting over their children's custody. It was a mess. The police were called and et cetera, et cetera. It was a long time ago. Nobody is kidnapping anybody today.'

Ellie still looks horrified. 'How do you know? *You* just told me about a kidnapping et cetera, et cetera.' She stops in front of a classroom. After two flights of stairs, we're both breathing hard. 'Here we are. The Ursula team.'

We press our noses against the window until one of the teachers notices us and walks outside the class to meet us. As expected, she greets Ellie with a bow. 'You must be Ashley's aunt. I'm her homeroom teacher, Maria. I was trying to contact you this morning, but I didn't have your number. I called Ibu Lyla instead.'

Ellie's panic shoots through the roof. She gasps, her hand grips the sleeve of my shirt. I don't think she realizes she's doing that. 'What happened? Did she fall? Sick? Kidnapped?'

The teacher takes one long look at her and laughs nervously. 'No, no, no. Everything is fine.' She moves us away from the crowd. We form a small circle, our heads bent close to one another. Ibu Maria's voice lowers to a whisper. 'There are a few openings in King Triton's team. We texted Ibu Lyla this morning and asked if she would want Ashley to join. She said yes.'

Ellie lets go of my shirt.

'King Triton's team is designed for high school students. Ashley is going to be the only primary kid there.' Ibu Maria becomes more animated as excitement takes over.

Understanding washes over me. Everybody is dying to please the most powerful people. Here in Spring Academy, it creates a privileged mini circle within the already privileged community. Doors are opened for these kids without them realizing there are doors in the first place. Surrounded by classmates who owned this special brand of entitlement made me acutely aware of things I didn't have. I didn't come from money. I had to work twice as hard and hold myself to a higher standard than the rest of my friends. I gotta make my own door, even today.

I must bring this situation to my uncle's attention and urge him to stop this practice. Blatant ass-kissing, not to mention subjective evaluation in the face of highly competitive parents, is like signing your own death wish.

'Will more primary students audition for King Triton's team?' Ellie asks.

Ibu Maria blinks. 'I beg your pardon?'

'You said a few openings.' Ellie says. 'I thought every position needs to be auditioned and approved by the head of choreography?'

'There'll be auditions for the high school students for the role of Ariel's sisters. But from primary, it's going to be just Ashley.'

'Wow.' Ellie's pride is brimming on the surface.

To be exclusively chosen is something to be proud of. It means Ashley is truly qualified. The thing is, I bet my annual salary that being qualified has nothing to do with Ashley's selection.

The teacher keeps talking, ' . . . the exception. We only offered it to Ibu Lyla.'

Ellie's smile halts. I can see her brain turning and clicking. *There you go, petal.*

'Can I talk to Ashley?' Ellie says.

Ibu Maria looks momentarily stunned. The expected behaviour from the parent is that they would be jumping with joy, rushing to the practice room to record a few videos, then uploading the said videos to multiple group chats. It isn't real until it's posted on social media and garners a few hundred likes.

The three of us walk further into the hall. Ellie hasn't asked me to leave, so I follow them down the corridor. A few doors later, we arrive at a bigger classroom. The tables and chairs have been stacked in the corners. The dancers are all middle and senior high schoolers. I spot Ashley easily because she's the smallest one in the room. She leans against the far corner wall by herself, far from the noise, the crowd, and the excitement. She might look like any other typical student, but I catch the thinness of her lips and the roundness of her shoulders.

Ellie waves from the window and beckons her niece to come out. Ashley timidly shakes her head. The teacher goes in to fetch Ashley. The moment Ashley is out, Ellie holds her hand and takes her niece into the quieter hallway. The teacher's curious eyes bore holes into their back. I'm stranded in between. Then I slide a step closer to where Ellie and Ashley are.

Ellie kneels in front of her niece. 'You want to be in there?' She tips her chin towards the room.

I guess I'm not the only one who notices Ashley's closed-off expression.

'Mom wanted me there.'

'But do you want to be in King Triton's team?'

Ashley's voice is small when she stubbornly repeats her answer. 'They said Mom wanted me there.'

'Ash,' Ellie says gently, angling her head to catch the girl's eyes. She holds Ashley's upper arms. 'Forget Mom. What do *you* want?'

It's like someone has dropped a bowl of warm water in my stomach. It leaves me with the familiar feeling of comfort, making me nostalgic. Years ago, my mother knelt in front of me on the funeral home floor and asked me the same question.

What do you want, Dion? I hated her for asking me that because wasn't the answer obvious? I'd stay by her side if I had the courage to say so. Why would she make my life difficult by asking me to choose? Why couldn't she decide for me? She was the adult; I was the kid. In the end, I chose to live with my uncle and aunt because I thought that was what my dad would've wanted. I didn't regret it; neither did my mother. As I grew older, I realized how lucky I was to have a mother who put my future, my needs, and choices above hers. Most importantly, how lucky I am to have a mother who listens.

I shift my attention back to Ellie and Ashley. I feel the heaviness of Ashley's silence to the bones. She's only *ten*, the same age as I was when I lost my dad. She shouldn't have to be this conflicted. For the longest moment, she stands there mutely, eyes refusing to meet anyone's.

'Remember what we talked about the other night?' Ellie begins in a soft voice. 'How much you love this musical, and how much you want to make it a success?'

Her niece nods. My chest warms again. I also want to make this musical a success for my uncle. I don't hear Ashley's reason, but it doesn't matter. We might have our own reasons, but we're all heading towards the same goal.

'You're an important part of this, Ash. *You.* What *you* want matters. There's no wrong answer, I promise. Both teams are cool.' Ellie puts a hand on Ashley's shoulder. 'But it will mean more to your team and to *you*, if you're happy.'

The woman in my head doesn't fit this woman who speaks to her niece in the most caring way.

'My friends are all *there*,' Ashley whispers.

'*There* where?' Ellie coaxes her.

'Ursula,' Ashley answers. She looks down at her shoes. 'Will Mom be mad?'

A spark of anger suddenly burns inside me. Ellie shakes her head hard, strands of her hair slapping her cheeks.

'I've already remembered Ursula's routines, Auntie Ellie,' Ashley explains as if she's required to provide us with reasons. Silly girl. She doesn't need reasons. Her choice alone is enough of a reason. It's an indirect answer to her aunt's question, but both Ellie and I nod. We get it. Ellie slaps her palms against her thighs before jumping to her feet. 'What are we waiting for? Go get your things.'

I have the strangest urge to clap.

A flash of light comes into Ashley's eyes. An uncertain smile follows. 'I can move back?'

Ellie's face softens. 'Yes, Ash, you can.'

Ashley runs back to the room without the need to be told twice.

Ellie looks up and our eyes lock. She slowly raises her eyebrows, like she's expecting me to challenge her or something. I don't realize I'm grinning at her until she grins back.

Ellie approaches the teacher. 'I'll take Ashley back to the Ursula team.'

The teacher stutters, 'Are you sure? Ibu Lyla—'

'I'm sure,' Ellie cuts her off firmly but not unkindly. 'So is Ibu Lyla.'

I wonder if Ellie finally understands what her sister's name means to some people in this school. People are especially nice to Ibu Lyla and her daughters—often going all the way to open unforbidden doors—because Lyla's name is power. It's money, influence, and intelligence. We've witnessed Ibu Lyla's steely determination and hot as fire passion. She has a reputation for fighting for what she wants and often stops at nothing to get it. The board recognizes her contributions, both in voluntary work and monetary donations in the seven years she's been here. Ellie's sister is partly responsible for how people react to her. The fear, the wanting to please, the blind adoration, the jealousy. Ibu Lyla is a force to be reckoned with.

They don't bow to just anyone, I told Ellie the other day. They don't offer a prestigious spot in the musical to just any kid. An extra, extra privilege within an already privileged community.

'Ibu Maria,' Ellie says, 'Since I'm Ashley's guardian until Lyla is back, do you mind involving me next time?'

'On what, Ibu?'

'Anything related to the girls.'

Holy shit. Every hair on my body stands on end. If I didn't see this interaction with my own eyes, I would've thought it was Ibu Lyla speaking. Ellie's face is calm; she even shows the teacher a friendly smile that makes her nose crinkle. But her words are sharp, each syllable being given proper weight to convey that she means business. I really, really want to high-five Ellie. And to hug her. And to punch the sky with my fist and scream *woohoo!*

Ibu Maria's face changes. 'Are you sure Ibu Lyla won't be . . . *unhappy?*'

'Ibu Lyla won't, I promise,' Ellie says gently.

There it is again, the tone that indicates finality.

The door behind me clicks. Ashley is standing next to me with her blue backpack slung over her shoulder.

With a flourish, Ellie holds out her hand. 'Ready?'

Ashley's small hand clasps hers. 'Ready, Auntie Ellie.' Her smile is a pop of colour in this greyish hall. Ellie pulls Ashley into a quite uncoordinated sprint, arms swinging, feet thumping, giggling, and squealing all the way back to her old studio. After giving Ibu Maria a genuine sympathetic smile, I follow them down the hall.

* * *

'Your sister would've taken it,' I tell Ellie as we stand side by side outside Ashley's Ursula room. I've lived with this community all my life, I know for certain that nobody will say no to more power and prestige, no matter how small it is. Directly rejecting an exclusive opportunity is unheard of. 'Other moms would've taken pictures and bragged about their kid on Instagram.'

'Lyla would've taken it,' she agrees. 'Ashley too. Between her dominating Mom and the-eager-to-please teacher, what choice does she have?'

From the window, Ashley waves at her aunt. I watch the outline of Ellie's face from the reflection. The window is not a mirror so I'm looking at her blurry image over the people who are on the opposite side of the glass.

'You think I made the wrong decision?' Ellie asks quietly when her eyes find mine in the window. 'What would you do?'

We're doing a little staring contest that feels like she's prying my defences open with her bare hands.

'I don't know. I'm not in fifth grade and I'm not on social media,' I answer. I dip my chin towards her niece. 'But if you ask her, she'll tell you it's the perfect decision.'

Ellie smiles. 'That's what's important, right?'

I've been staring at her mouth the entire time she was talking. It looks soft, almost kissable, and with how she's been amazing with Ashley and the teacher just now, I want to . . . I want to *what*, exactly? My neck and face feel hot. I look away from her lips and confine my eyesight to my own reflection.

'You're right,' I say.

She whips her head. 'You said I was right.' She points to her chest. 'I. Was. Right.'

I ignore her as she cackles.

'All right,' Ellie says, walking away from the classroom. 'Do you know where the storage room is?'

Glad that we don't have to stay here with so many people eavesdropping on our conversation, I walk with her. 'It's behind the . . . you know what, it's easier if I take you.' We make our way back to the stairs. I manoeuvre my way carefully with the heavy set of sticks in my arms. 'Why do you need to go to the storage room?'

'Oh, haven't you heard? You're looking at the lead designer for the 3D Prince Eric ship.' She spreads her arms wide as if presenting the world with the gift that's herself.

'You're welcome, petal,' I say.

'Why?'

'It was *me* who put you in Jonas' team.'

'Pretty sure you put me there because you wanted me to fail.'

'And yet here you are, proving me wrong.'

'Wow! I was right twice in a row? Hallelujah.'

Staring straight ahead, I keep my face blank, which is becoming harder the longer I spend time with her.

'Imagine this is the stage.' She swipes the air with her right hand. 'Visualize the ship in your head. Not the whole ship. Only one-third, because that's the maximum we're going to build.'

'Okay,' I say, not visualizing anything at all.

'We're gonna use the warehouse trolley as the base, and cardboard, a lot of cardboard, as the body.'

Her mood is infectious because now I'm visualizing the ship. 'Is using trolley safe?' I ask.

'You've seen parades, right? The trolley will serve the same function as the car or truck. Then we'll build the 3D ship on top of it. I still need to figure out how to make the small steps inside the ship. They should be sturdy enough for Prince Eric to sing and fight the evil mermaid from up there. Cool, right?' She beams.

'Why can't Jonas get the trolley?' I regret offering to take her to the storage room. It's a long walk and the things in my arms are not getting lighter.

'I volunteered.'

I pant. 'Of course.'

She grins. 'It's called creative energy, Dion. I love working with an amazing team and a leader who doesn't ask me to quit every time we meet.'

What a condescending little architect.

When we arrive at the edge of junior lobby, I rest the staff on the floor and wipe the sweat off my brows.

She studies me, her expression softens. 'You don't have to walk me there. Just point me to the right direction.'

'I'll take you.' I inhale and exhale a few more times before picking up the sticks.

A few mothers I recognize walk pass us. 'Wow, Dion, you are so buff!' One of them playfully squeezes my bicep. I immediately tense, but I remember to smile. Practice makes perfect. I've been donning this facade for almost two decades. I dip my chin. 'Good afternoon, ladies.'

Ellie keeps walking ahead of me. She doesn't even bother to acknowledge the mothers. 'I hate when they do that to you,' she mutters.

'Do what?' I'm annoyed that I'm breathless from this short jog. I used to be able to run ten laps around the soccer field without breaking into a sweat.

'Objectifying you, touching you like that. Doesn't it make you uncomfortable?'

I want to sink into a hole. This is embarrassing enough without her noticing my discomfort. 'I'm used to it. They're harmless,' I say.

'You're not a piece of meat.' She sharply side-eyes me. 'Well, technically, we all are, but you're also a person.'

'What do you suggest? I hang a sign around my neck that says leave me alone?'

'Why not?'

We walk side by side in silence.

'Thanks,' I say quietly. 'Nobody has defended me like that before.'

For the longest time, she doesn't say anything. 'Someone should have,' she finally breaks the silence. 'Someone should be on your team.'

It's not often I'm grasping for words to say. I envy people who have *teams* in their corner. Being an only child, I have zero understanding of the concept of siblings. What does it feel to have someone who watches your back, someone who fights you over food, someone you can pour your guts to when you're down? I went to school where I had classmates but not *friends*. Everyone treated me nicely but watched me from a distance because I didn't fit in with the rich and the famous. I studied very hard when I was in college and didn't have much of a social life. Now I work the graveyard shift and hang out with moms during the day. Not much room for growth there, either. To have someone on my team would be amazing.

Wake up, man.

If it's my fate to feel lonely all the time, then I'll deal with it.

'Hey.' Ellie's voice brings me back to the present.

'What?' I sound grumpier when I'm feeling awkward. It's my go-to coping mechanism.

'Don't worry,' she says, her smiley eyes flickering like a pair of bright lights. 'I'll be on your team. Next time anyone dares to inappropriately touch you, they'll have to go through me first.'

I drop all six wooden staffs to the ground. God, the noise it makes! A few people around us yelp. One of the sticks hits me square in the nose, causing me to slump into a squat as the world around me turns black. I clench my jaw. 'Fuuu . . .' Then I remember I'm at school, and there are parents and students around. '. . . ruuummmm.'

Ellie laughs. 'Frum?'

Through my watery eyes, I see Ellie roll the sticks and group them together. I'll help her once the pain is done wrecking my nervous system and I can open my eyes without crying. I tenderly rub the bridge of my throbbing nose. 'Shithishurts.'

Crouching in front of me, she moves my hand away from my face, grips it tightly, and surveys my nose. 'I hope it won't bruise. What happened? Did you trip?'

'I've been carrying them all the way from the third floor,' I say, my voice thick. 'I'm tired.'

I won't tell her that the reason I lost my balance is because my heart fluttered so hard at her *team* declaration that it was like my entire body was made out of hummingbirds' wings. The adult in me is aware that she most likely didn't mean it, but hearing it is enough to send me over the moon. Also, she's holding my hand. What is actually happening? I like the feel of her soft skin touching mine, but my nose also hurts like a bitch. Both these sensory modes fight for my attention. The pain wins in the end. I drop her hand to clutch my nose.

She looks down at the scattered mess and grimaces. 'Here, I'll help.' She pulls up one stick and holds it with both hands. 'Now. Can you handle those five by yourself?'

* * *

'This is perfect,' Ellie says after we scour the hot and dirty warehouse for half an hour. We're both drenched in sweat—our hands, nails, and palms black with dust. My nose is red, but other than looking like Rudolph the Red-Nosed Reindeer, it's not broken, and the throbbing pain has ebbed. After the incident, we decide it'd probably be best to leave the sticks with security while we check out the warehouse. There's no point carrying them all around campus.

I crouch next to the trolley. 'One of the wheels is broken. Can you pick another one?'

'This one has the perfect width.' She bends to inspect the broken wheel. I get a whiff of her scent, something like vanilla or coconut mixed with her sweat. It's quite intoxicating. I quickly move my head away.

'I'll ask Jonas to fix it.' She climbs to her feet and casts a wide view over the storage ceiling. 'This is more a garbage room than storage.' She pushes her hair out of her face, leaving a line of black smudge on her forehead.

'You have something . . .' I point to her left temple.

'Oh.' She wipes it with her dirty hand, thus expanding the smudge to her entire forehead.

I suck in my cheeks. 'Perfect.'

She's undoing and redoing her ponytail. The blue shirt, which now sports dark patches on her stomach and under arms, rides up, exposing a strip of pale skin above her waist. Her posture adds to her sensuality—her neck exposed, her hands behind her head, and her full chest thrust forward.

Something blinding blurs my eyesight. Every muscle in my body clenches so deliciously, I nearly moan out loud. By default, I'm a very focused person. If I wasn't, I wouldn't have secured my scholarship for eight years and graduated from med school with a high GPA. But Ellie's presence has distracted me lately. I find myself looking for her every time I arrive at the gym for a rehearsal and always feel a little glum if I don't spot her. Our silly conversations have managed to sneak into my head when I'm bored at work in the middle of the night. I quickly avert my eyes before my mind betrays me and starts replaying her gentle voice from when she talked to Ashley, or her fierce declaration about being on my team, or her almost kissable lips and her soft hands.

She's right about one thing, though. This room is the graveyard of all broken things.

'Let's get out of here,' I say.

After filling out some paperwork, we push the trolley out of the door. Ellie squints as the sun attacks her eyes. 'Who'll go first?' she asks.

Puzzled, I look at her. She has a smudge on the back of her neck. I will myself not to stare at it. To my bewilderment, she climbs into the trolley and sits with her feet dangling at the side.

Grinning from ear to ear, she tells me, 'Halfway, then it's your turn. I promise.'

'What?'

'I'll take turns pushing you,' she explains patiently as if I'm an idiot.

My mouth drops. 'You push—you know what? No.'

'Oh.' She sounds disappointed. 'You wanna go first?'

I'm dumbstruck again, but this time I'm also annoyed. 'Are you four?'

'No, but why walk if you can ride this?'

'I . . .' I don't know what to say because her argument is solid. I push her all the way to the gym, trying my best to hide my smile behind my fake frown. My nose throbs as I breathe harder due to exertion while she sits happily on the cart as if it's her royal carriage. As we're nearing the gym, my self-proclaimed teammate looks at me with her broad grin and gives me two thumbs-up.

That's it. I lose the game. I can no longer maintain my phoney grumpy face. I return her smile, just as broad. Broader even. The pain in my nose screams from the muscle stretch, but, dear god, it's so worth it.

March

Chapter 10

Ellie

I notice the signs: sugar cravings, a touch of a headache, and the soreness in my lower stomach that has nothing to do with sit-ups. My period came when I was in the Spring parking lot, about to see the girls' rehearsal and work with my art team. The cramp in my lower belly makes every part of me pulse with pain. The migraine is usually not far behind. People say it'll get better with age, that it won't always feel like my period is gonna kill me.

Spoiler alert: It didn't get any better with age. Not for me anyway. I've dealt with this torture for the past ten years. The cramp would start in my lower stomach, then spread out to my lower back. Without medication, I wouldn't be able to walk with a straight spine on the first two days. Then there's the migraine. One side of my head would belong to the pain and pain only, like someone is hitting multiple nails from behind my eye. I'll be sensitive to light, strong smell, and sharp movement. It's not uncommon if I develop a fever for the first few hours. Painkillers help lessening the pain, but not with the rest of the symptoms. I've survived through school, college, part-time jobs, family dinners, birthdays, drives, anything. Driving in my condition wasn't entirely safe, but sometimes I didn't have a choice. Whenever I could, I'd take a day off. My friends would sympathize but think of it as no big deal. The men—my lecturers mostly—would not care at all. Some of them even deducted my credits because of my monthly absence.

I dread the moment I have to tell my parents about my condition. I don't know which one I'm more afraid of, the worry or the indifference I usually get from people. *Period pain is normal.* But who can say what is normal and what is not, because mine has surely put a stop to my normal life. On these days, my body is a traitor.

I put my sunglasses on and successfully reach the gym without having to talk to anyone. I claim the deserted rows of chairs at the back of the hall as my spot. After carefully stepping around bags and bottles, I prepare four chairs as my makeshift bed, take off my glasses, fold my bag and use it as a pillow.

* * *

'Oh, come on. We're not that boring.' Dion's voice slides into my brain like a bullet. I snap awake, bewildered, not knowing where I am but somehow knowing I'm not supposed to be here. Dion, hovering a few steps away from me, sports a mocking grin on his face. It takes me two blinks to remember. *My nieces.* I sit up so fast, the acid in my mouth shoots through the roof.

'Whoa.' In a blink Dion is there, catching my elbow. He drops his hand as if he's being pricked. I recoil too. Do I smell? Do I look as disgusting as I feel?

He frowns. 'May I?'

Before I know what he means, he touches my forehead. His palm is cool and smooth, and I welcome it by leaning into it.

His expression shifts from neutral to concerned. 'You're warm,' he says.

'I'm fine.' Looks like this month is going to be one of those months with the fever, cramps, *and* migraine. The trifecta of my period hell.

'What time is it?' I make another attempt to stand, and the cramp shoots from my lower stomach to my spine. I sit right back. 'Fuck.'

'Ellie?' He's alarmed.

I want to go lie down. And to be left alone. 'I'm *fine.*'

'You're *not* fine.' He deposits himself next to me. I distract myself by watching the beads of sweat on his neck. He looks masculine in his black muscle tank. It's impressive that my hormones can make me thirst for something while pummelling the inside of my body with a wrecking ball.

'Monthly problem,' I say.

Men tend to run away at the mention of period, blood, and PMS. I'm sure Dion is no different. I see him nod, then get up. Part of me is relieved that he's gone, the other disappointed. There's still fifteen minutes left before I have to leave this gym. I furiously massage my right temple.

Dion reappears with a plastic cup. 'Here.'

I'm too surprised to argue. I gingerly accept the hot tea and inhale the smoke. If only the warmth would travel into my body and ease up all the soreness from within.

'I can find you some painkillers,' he offers. 'What do you usually take?' His head bends low towards my face, his mouth close to my left ear. My face grows hotter, thanks to the hot tea, my embarrassment, and his nearness. I've never talked about my period problem with a guy, not even my dad.

'It's fine. *I'm fine.*' I sound like a broken record.

He releases a long sigh, probably letting me know how disappointed he is with my *fine*. 'Does this happen often?'

'You're a guy,' I mutter. 'Guys don't talk about periods.'

'Do you talk about this with someone who's not a guy then? With your family? With your doctor?'

What to say? We'll share painful stories and get on with our lives.

I avert my gaze to the general direction of the gym. When I'm like this, I can't control my body and emotions. My hormones rule. I'm powerless.

That's the word. *Powerless.* There are many things that might make women feel powerless in this world, but *this*? It's the worst. I'm fighting myself. No matter which direction the fight goes, I will always, always lose. I hate being me sometimes. But when the pain is gone in a few days, I love being in my body again.

The throbbing in my skull sharpens due to my irritation. Without thinking much, I drop my head and grind my left temple against his shoulder. He sways before bracing against me. The pressure helps camouflage the migraine. I don't realize that I've pounded my right temple with my fist until he holds my wrist and brings my hand down to my lap. 'Jesus, Ellie. Stop that.'

Reality hits me like a bucket of cold water. 'Sorry,' I mumble, feeling the heat creeping up my face. He takes the cup from me and puts it on the empty chair next to him. Then he cradles my head and turns me to face him. I blink, disoriented. He's so close, too close, I don't know which part of his face I should stare at. His touch is cool against my feverish skin. His fingers dig into my scalp as he takes over my violent attempt at massaging my head. His thumbs firmly press into the side of my forehead and his second and middle fingers find the hollow spots under my ears. His movements are firm and unyielding, but soft enough to make me unclench my jaw. I don't care about the noises I make. My head lolls in his hands. I surrender all control to him.

'Better?' he asks as his breath warms my nose and his scent envelopes me from everywhere. I register these things, but they feel small compared to the deliciousness of his fingers on my scalp. His hands slide down to the back of my neck. He alternates the work between these two points.

'All medical students know how to do this, huh?'

'Only the ones who suck at math,' he says in his signature dryness, but with a sympathetic gentleness.

I'm not supposed to be this close to him, but having someone who provides comfort, even for the briefest seconds, feels so good. I lean more into him, breathing him in, feeling his warm breath against my hair. He's touching my sweaty nape again. If he's uncomfortable with my clammy skin, he does a great job of not showing it.

I let out a contented sigh. 'Thank you.'

He's steadying my shoulders as he positions me against the side of his body. His thumbs slide down my shoulder blades. Up and down, up and down, the movement is methodical.

'Having periods is natural, petal. You can talk to me.'

I'm embarrassed. I keep my face in the crook of his neck.

'Everything in our body has its purpose. Legs for walking. Lungs for breathing. Spine, kidney, you name it. It's natural for some people to menstruate, just like it's natural for some people to have erections. You know, for reproductive purposes.'

I burst out laughing. When I open my eyes, his signature blank stare fills my sight. Dear Lord, he said erection with a straight face.

He leans back on his seat. Massage time is over. His doctor eyes sweep my features as if looking for cracks. As my laughter fades, I miss the pressure of his fingers. I clear my throat and point to my head.

'What?' he asks. After a few seconds of shooting me a puzzled look, he rolls his eyes. His magic fingers are back, and boy, they're better than any dessert I've ever tasted. Bringing his mouth close to my ear, he rasps, '*Bossy.*'

Despite feeling like my body is being run over by a truck, I manage to sneak a peek at his face. When he catches me looking at him, he looks away. He retracts his arm next. I want to tell him to not stop because his hands are the only things that are helping me breathe like a normal person but I don't utter a word. Instead, I lay my head on his shoulder. He stiffens, his shoulder feels pointy against my cheek, but after a beat, he relaxes.

'Are you planning to be an OBGYN?' It's the most reasonable guess considering how much he loves to talk about reproduction. An uninvited image floats into my mind: Dion in his white coat, sitting on his stool, his face buried in vaginas. I swear every single ounce of discomfort in me is temporarily muted as I'm drenched in embarrassment. Did I imagine him examining his imaginary patient's vagina? Yes. Did I imagine him examining my vagina? Shit. I'm on fire. Literally. I watch my hands and forearms in horror. I'm as red as Sebastian the crab. I can't hide anything. We're too close, too open.

I already forgot about my question when he answers me a few moments later, softly, whispering it into the air like it's a secret. 'Cardiologist.'

'You're gonna fix broken hearts, doctor?' Cheap humour is my go-to mechanism when I'm embarrassed.

'Well, heartbreak is a serious business,' he replies.

He's good with puns. 'How many did you break so far?' I attempt to insert a cheerful tone to my voice.

He looks down at his lap. 'My dad died of a heart attack.'

Oh fuck.

'It was a long time ago.' He smiles at me, a sad one that makes his face mellow. 'One day he was healthy as a bull. The next day my mom and I had to fly here. He was gone before we arrived at the hospital.'

Fuck, fuck, fuck. I can't imagine having my life turned upside down so unexpectedly like that. I reach out without thinking, grasping his hand and squeezing it. Startled, he looks down at his lap. He swallows hard, but then his long fingers close around mine and he squeezes back. I put my head gently on his shoulder again. It's beginning to feel like my spot, a place that fits me perfectly. We don't talk for a while. I will myself not to think about my physical pain because my pain comes and goes. I can bear it. I don't know Dion that well, but I can already see that his pain is not the kind of pain that will go away with time.

Cardiologist. His father is the reason why he wants to be a heart doctor.

'Have you gotten your condition checked?' he asks suddenly. His tone is back to the one I'm used to hear: dry as dying leaves.

Because it's easier to lie, I nod.

His eyes search my face. 'What's the diagnosis?'

'It's private.'

There's a pause. 'Come on. I'll take you home.'

'I promised my nieces.'

'I'm sure they'll understand. It's not like you're going to miss their rehearsals forever.'

'Not only them.' I realize I grip his hand when he grimaces. 'I'll present the ship design today. I worked late last night for this. I'm already here, anyway, might as well finish my job.'

'What are you talking about? Sit down, please.'

'I promised everyone—'

He says my name softly. 'Are you listening to me?'

'You're not listening *to me*.' I'm pleading with my eyes.

'Fine, I'm not,' he snaps. 'I have no idea what you're talking about, but you need rest. I'll make sure the girls are okay and they're doing their practice as they should. I can take them home too, with your permission.'

Rest sounds wonderful. 'And the ship?' I whisper.

'I have no idea what ship that is, but I promise it won't sail without you today.' When I say nothing, he brings his face closer to mine. 'Your wellbeing is more important than anything, Ellie. Are you listening? I can take you home, then pick the girls up.'

'I don't know you.'

Clearly biting back his sarcasm, he decides to play nice. 'Would you like Ibu Tara to do that? I can find her for you.'

In the quietness of my head, the throbbing on the right side of my head sounds like a bell. It's excruciating when I purposely concentrate to catch its ringing. I wish I could bang it against the wall, or curl into myself to minimize the biting stomach pain. Since I don't have a wall available within my reach, I drop my head to Dion's shoulder again, grinding my temple against him and using my arms to hug my middle. For a moment, my migraine slows its pulsing. But I know it's only an illusion. The moment I lift my head, the throb will come back with a roar. The moment I stand, my lower body won't belong to me. But now, right this moment, I get my peace.

'Are you on a break?' I'm stalling. Going home feels like a defeat, and I refuse to be defeated by my own body.

'Technically, no. But someone is using my shoulder as a pillow.' His tone is super dry; I snort despite myself.

'Stop making me laugh.' I reflectively pull my head back. Touching the side of my face, he gently guides me back to his hard shoulder. His palm on my cheek feels like ice. I must be boiling hot.

He spits out a low curse. '*Ellie*. You're clearly in pain and your fever is quite high. The world will not stop because you take a few hours of rest. *Please*.'

'Aren't you needed here?' But even as I say it, I've already surrendered to his idea. I want him to take care of me.

'They can survive ten minutes without me.'

'Twenty minutes roundtrip. Fifteen minutes out of the parking lot. Thirty-five minutes if we're lucky and if the traffic inside Spring is good. Told you I'm good at math.'

His finger makes a soft tap against my right earlobe. When I peek up at him, his eyes envelop me like a thick, fluffy blanket. 'Smart ass,' he mouths with a crooked smile. 'Is that a yes?'

I close my eyes, breathing him in. 'Yes, thank you.'

* * *

We're making a slow trek towards the doors. He leads, I'm a step behind him. Once outside, Dion halts so suddenly, my nose bumps into his back.

'Shit,' he mutters.

Then I see what he sees. The view before us is ugly. It's raining cats and dogs, bumper-to-bumper cars, puddles of water, and the swirling of the wind.

I hunch inward, wrapping my arms around myself. 'Let's go back inside,' I suggest. 'Don't worry about me. I'm used to this.'

My breath stutters at the fierceness in his eyes. Putting one hand at my lower back, he puts his mouth close to my ear, 'I'm gonna find us an umbrella. Wait here.'

As promised, he comes back a few minutes later with one. The umbrella is tiny, fit for only one tiny person, namely kids. It's also bright yellow with a bouncing green dinosaur print. I'd laugh if I wasn't busy wincing against the onslaught of the wind. I watch him shake the umbrella open. It barely fits my head. 'How about you?'

'My car is not far from here.'

I give him a defeated look. 'What does it even mean?'

'You want me to beg you to get some rest?'

'Yes.'

'All right. Consider this begging.'

Holding the umbrella with one hand, he wraps his other arm around my waist and pulls me close until there's no space left between his left side and my right. I whimper but thankfully the roar of the rain hides it from his ears. As we limp into the rain, Dion is immediately soaked. I tilt the umbrella to the right. He pushes it back to the left. After a few games of pushing that leave us both drenched, I give up.

'If you put your head above mine, the umbrella will cover us both,' I say.

'Is that an architect talk?' He looks extra juicy with water sluicing down his face. His thick eyelashes appear thicker, his lips more swollen.

'It's crazy,' I comment about the dead-end traffic, trying to distract myself from the discomfort in my body and the juicy wet guy on my right. It's a jungle of cars—parked cars, queuing cars, it's hard to tell the difference anymore. Smoke from the exhaust pollutes the air around us. 'How do you guys live with this every day?'

'We have to,' Dion says as he keeps his gaze straight ahead. 'Can't fix everything all at once.'

'How does *everything else* trump this?' I'm angry. I'm in pain and seeing this bullshit for the past few weeks has taken a toll on me. Traffic wastes time. It also drags down mental health.

'Homework policy needs to be adjusted,' Dion says. 'Special lessons and tutoring continue right after school. Students come home around dinner time and *still* have homework to finish. They spend more than fourteen hours on schoolwork. It's not healthy.' He stops talking to cross the street. The ghost of his hand on my lower back makes me shiver. *I don't need this, please.* I don't need to be hypersensitive to him.

'But you're right.' He dips his chin towards the line of cars. 'This mess doesn't make sense anymore. It decreases the quality of student's life.'

Not just the students, I correct him mentally. The parents, the chaperones, the people who work in this school. It's hard to imagine that a school this exclusive, with their impressive reputation and curriculum, is powerless against its own traffic jam.

What he says about homework lingers, but I'm afraid he's hit a roadblock with that one. As far as I remember, this is how the education system works in our country. The grades are not made in the classrooms. They come from private tutors outside the school. I won't be surprised if the tutoring business is the real foundation of our education, both in performance and cost. A lot of things have changed ever since I graduated high school. Sadly, a lot of things have remained the same too. Academic excellence is, and has been, the number one goal parents have in mind.

'What can we do?' I ask. This conversation, though bleak and frustrating, somehow distracts me from my own physical hell.

Droplets of rain trickle down his chin. 'We can raise awareness through organizations like the PTA.'

He's speaking about PTA without his usual cynicism. He's speaking like someone who knows about the school intimately, someone who genuinely wants it to get better.

Touching my elbow, he steers me away from the puddle of water on our feet. My insides warm at his protectiveness.

'If you were the Spring Principal, what would you change right away?'

His serious expression melts into a small smile. He side-eyes me. 'If I tell you, I'll have to kill you.'

Oh God. He's *not* flirting. My hormones, though, convince me that he is.

'What would *you* do?' he asks me.

'Same,' I say. 'I'd have to kill you.'

We arrive at a black Honda SUV. He glances at me like he wants to make sure I'm okay. His gaze is full of fondness and something else, something that makes my insides tremble. He holds the door open and waits for me to climb in. By now, both of us are soaked through. The little umbrella has acted more as an

108 Cheese Donuts Are Most Definitely Not Subpar

accessory than a protector against the rain. I have one foot inside the car when a mighty-looking bolt of lightning makes the sky crackle. Deafening thunder booms above our heads, rattling my bones and setting off a lot of car alarms nearby. The explosive sound and the blaring of the sirens shock the shit out of me. I scream and cover my ears in reflex and my already slippery sneakers slip on the wet ground. My back collides with his front. He drops the umbrella to catch me, his arms locked around my waist like steel. I feel his lips brush against the side of my head. 'I got you.' His voice is low, and I barely hear him properly amidst the roaring of multiple sounds around me, but I feel the vibration of his words against my back.

'I'm sorry.'

'Not your fault. Bad, bad thunder.'

We laugh, our bodies mould and gel against each other like perfect puzzle pieces. The sound of his deep chuckle does the worst things to my already non-functioning knees. I'd like to stay within the circle of his arms for a few more minutes but we'll catch a cold if we don't get into his car soon. The deafening alarms finally quiet down with a few clicking sounds. The hold of his arms around me relaxes. I half-turn to peek at him. His hair is plastered to his forehead. Drops of water cling to his eyelashes and the tip of his nose. I'm wrong about him. He's not only juicy, he's intense. And kind. And gentle. And smart and funny. He also carries a broken heart inside him.

My body and mind can't be trusted during this time of the month.

I get into the car and am immediately overwhelmed by the scent of leather and *him*. The car feels very male. I sit with my back straight, not wanting to ruin his seat, which is pointless. My shoes leave dark prints on his carpet.

Dion gets in and carelessly throws his bag and umbrella in the back seat. He leans to the middle and reaches for a box of tissues. He works quickly and methodically, like a doctor who's used to performing under pressure. He offers a few dry sheets to me. I dry my face the best I can. He pulls a few more sheets from the box. Then with a gentleness I would never expect from him, he holds my chin between his thumb and finger and angles me to him. He pouts as he dries my cheeks, nose, and hair—as properly as tissue paper would allow him. I'm beginning to understand why he frowns so often. It's not always a sign of annoyance. Sometimes it's concentration.

In between taking care of me, leaving instructions for his team, and hunting down an umbrella, he hasn't changed out of his tank. I try my best not to stare at his arms, hands, shoulders, chest but they're *right there* in my face.

'You're wet,' I blurt out.

I notice a ghost of a smile. 'I'm aware.'

'You're so nice to me,' I say.

'Why wouldn't I be?' He wipes his own arms with the tissue. My eyes hungrily follow the lines on his defined biceps.

'Because you don't like me.'

When our eyes meet, there's hurt in his.

'What?' I whisper. 'You don't like me. You've been trying to kick me out of this school since the first day we met.'

'Is that so, petal?'

I've heard many varieties of my nickname from his mouth, mostly delivered with a teasing lilt or sarcasm. This is the first time he says it like it means something to him. Like he cares, like it's an intimate word he can't help but say in my presence.

Or maybe it's all in my head, because I'm a giant fucking mess. God, I'd give anything for my head to stop killing me from the inside.

'Why are you sitting like that?' he asks suddenly, his frown deepening.

'Oh. I don't want to get your seat wet.'

'I don't care about the seat.' He gently pushes my shoulder back. 'Seatbelt,' he instructs.

I fasten it across my body.

'You're still sitting like a robot.' Impatience bleeds into his voice.

I gingerly sit back but the forty-five-degree angle position somehow makes the cramp a million times worse. Forgetting about the wet clothes and shoes, I curl myself into a foetal position, or as much of a foetal position as the seat allows. My knees touch my chest, the side of my head is pressed against the seat, my hands clutch the seatbelt in a deathly grip. The coldness from the rain has seeped into my skin, making my teeth rattle. I close my eyes and groan, or maybe I curse, I'm not sure anymore. I let my guard down. I lost today's battle against my pain. I don't care if he sees me like this, I don't. I just wanna curl up and die.

There's a fleeting touch on my wrist, his skin is damp but thankfully it's not shockingly cold. 'It's okay,' he murmurs. He gently pries one of my hands off the seatbelt. When he notices me staring at him, he gives me a small smile. 'Close your eyes,' he says. I obey him. I drift in and out of consciousness during the ride. Sometimes I jolt awake and the first thing I see is this closed-lip smile on his kind face. It relaxes me, making me feel safe, so I close my eyes again. I have no idea how he manages to drive the thirty-five-minute journey to Lyla's house with his hand locked in mine the entire time.

Chapter 11

Dion

I circle the block three times before I park my car just in front of
Ibu Lyla's house. Hard to believe that it was only three hours ago
I dropped off Ellie. Ever since then, I tried to talk myself out of
coming back here. If I need more proof of how different Ellie
and I are, I only need to see the house in front of me. We all live
in the same suburb; our complexes are close to each other. After
all, we orbit around Spring. But while I live in my aunt and uncle's
modest two-storey house, Ellie lives in her sister's three-storey
mansion. My uncle's garage can only fit one car. I often have
to park a half block away since there's no space nearby. When
I brought Ellie home hours earlier, I counted six cars inside. One
of them is an orange Lamborghini, the other a red Ferrari.

I also attempted to change my mind by reminding myself
about Ruby. Stupidly, my skin crawls, but my determination to visit
her strengthens. My common sense, one of the things I like about
myself, tells me that Ellie is not Ruby. Also, Ellie might need my
help. As a friend and recently recruited team member, it's my duty
to check on her. While my logic checks all the right boxes, it fails to
explain why I can't stop thinking about her, about the soft noises

she made when I massaged her head, the feel of her skin under my hands, or why I told her about my dad—a closely guarded secret I've never shared with anyone outside my family.

This is a bad idea.

Bad, bad idea.

I fidget as I stand outside Ibu Lyla's house, a white plastic bag full of heating pads dangles from my fingers. I'm rehearsing the things I'd say to her in my head.

Hi. How're your cramps? I know I can just ask you through a text, but you'll tell me you're fine and I won't believe it. Also, I really wanted to see you. Needed to see you.

'Dion?'

There she is, standing just inside the garage door frame in her shorts and house shirt. Her hair is in a messy bun like she just rolled out of bed. I don't like how pale she looks.

'How are you feeling?' After so many deliberate touches this afternoon, I purposely maintain a respectable distance between us.

'It helps that there's no glaring light, dust, wind, rain, and loud noises around me.' She's using her dry tone that normally makes me smile, but her delivery is weak. My hand twitches because damn me if I don't long to touch her forehead. But I won't, so I jam it into my pocket.

'I'm fine. Just a little tired, that's all,' she adds with a small apologetic smile.

She's a terrible liar.

'I should've called first.' I hand her the plastic bag. 'I, uh, thought you might need some. I'm sure you already have them, but I thought maybe, you know, you need some more. Because you never know? In case. As spares.'

Jesus. What happened to my ability to form coherent, grammatically correct sentences?

She peeks into the bag, looks up, and raises her eyebrows. 'Ten?'

I mumble unintelligibly.

For a second, she seems like she has no clue what to do with the bag before finally putting it on the floor next to her feet. She avoids eye contact with me and chooses to play with her hair. She's nervous too. The thought makes me feel better. I discreetly roll my shoulders.

'Thanks,' she says. 'You didn't need to do this.'

'It's what a teammate does,' I say, trying and failing to sound cute.

She meets my gaze. 'It's . . . weird, you know, talking about'— she gestures towards her stomach—'this.'

'It's not weird at all. As I said, periods are—'

'Natural. Yeah. You mentioned it before. Every part of our body has its purpose.'

'Exactly. It's natural.' For someone who keeps saying natural, I should act more naturally. And yet there's nothing natural about my body language. I don't know what to do with my hands. They're hanging by my sides, purposeless. I can't control my eyes; they always drop to her mouth. I've been obsessed with the tiny dip on her upper lip ever since our close interaction this afternoon. This tiny thing I want so much to taste.

I swallow my groan.

She's right. This is weird.

Bad, bad idea.

'Distract me with your doctor talk,' she says.

'What? Why?'

'Why not?' She smiles. 'So, I won't think about how weird this is.'

Seven years of medical school and I can't come up with a single word.

'What's the purpose of armpit hair?' she starts. 'If your theory is right, people who shave their armpit hair are probably an inch away from death and we know nothing about it.'

I'm stunned silent at her random but hilarious question. Hiding my amusement, I launch into the topic, making sure to throw in some medical terms like pheromones, skin rash, sweat and something about getting a mate.

When I finish the lecture, she peeks at her underarm. 'Maybe I'll grow mine. What do you think?'

I sputter a few encouraging noises. 'I grew mine and they're amazing.'

She stares at me poker-faced. 'Getting a mate, huh? No wonder I never caught any. My armpits are as bald as a baby's bottom.'

I explode into laughter. 'Glad to see your sense of humour is back, petal,' I say. It doesn't escape my notice that she doesn't laugh. She bites her bottom lip to hide a grimace as she rubs her abdomen. My hunch tells me she might be suffering from endometriosis. I'm desperate to tell her that information on the subject is widely available. I wonder why she's holding back when the disease is treatable. Discomfort during examinations? Her monthly discomfort must outweigh the discomfort she'd feel on a doctor's table.

'Will I still be pretty though, if I grow my armpit hair?' she teases.

'Why won't you be?'

'Girls with underarm hair, not an acceptable beauty standard,' she explains.

'Whose standard?'

'I believe it's men's.'

'You'd still be beautiful even if you only ate cheese donuts for the rest of your life.'

I love her smile. Love, love, love it. It's like I've been staring at the night sky my whole life and have only recently noticed the moon. She places a hand on her lower stomach again and I sober up quickly. I take a few steps closer. The shorter the gap between our bodies, the thicker the air.

'Ellie,' I begin, my voice low, 'there are treatments available.'

She cuts me off. 'Nope.'

I suck in my cheeks. 'Why are you being so stubborn?'

'Being stubborn is good. Sometimes it's a sign of resilience.'

'Sometimes it's absurd.'

'Sometimes it's none of your business.'

I close my eyes and tip my face upward. When I look back at her, she's watching me. I can't argue more because she's right. It is none of my business. The best I can do is bring her meds and drive her home. I shouldn't have massaged her head.

Bad, bad idea.

My eyes scan the landscape of Ibu Lyla's immaculate garden before landing on my car. The sky has gone completely dark at 7 p.m. I need to go to the hospital soon.

'If you don't feel good tomorrow, you don't need to attend the meeting. I'll chair the PTA on your behalf,' I say.

Her expression changes. 'The PTA meeting is tomorrow?'

'Yes. We'll finalize the musical budget. Quite boring, actually. We might also compile the issues raised by the members, if we have extra time.'

'How would I know you wouldn't go behind my back and fire me?' she asks, her expression tight. 'Bernadet would love to take Lyla's seat.'

Her blind loyalty to her sister is endearing. I'm jealous because I have never had a sibling who would fight off my enemies for me.

'If I wanted to do that, I would've done it when you were sick and helpless.' I knew that was out of line before I even closed my mouth. 'Ellie . . . shit. I'm sorry. I didn't mean it.'

'It's fine,' she replies, suddenly looking bone-tired. Her hand reaches out and brushes mine. 'Dion. I need to tell you something. I won't change Lyla's proposal. It will stay as it is.'

'What proposal?'

'The one Lyla has drafted. I'm gonna stick with it.'

I narrow my eyes. Though I appreciate her honesty, I'd be lying if I said I wasn't disappointed. 'Look, Ellie. We don't need to decide anything right away. But we owe the rest of the members our time and open mind. Some of the issues they brought up are legit.'

She gingerly holds my right hand. 'I promised Lyla.'

She's warming the seat for her sister. I knew this, and yet, I'm sadder. I had hoped we'd be the change. I'm being naïve. I can't expect her to become someone else just because I happened to spend a short, intimate moment with her.

'Petal,' I sigh, my old frustration rising to the surface. 'Stop hiding behind your sister for a moment. Stay with . . .' I bite my tongue just in time before I say *me*.

She leans the side of her head against the frame and closes her eyes. 'Can we talk about this some other time?'

'Of course.' I can't forgive myself for burdening her with work stuff when she's clearly unwell. We're so close, I can feel her body heat despite the cool evening breeze.

'You know what, petal,' I say lightly. 'The Spring parents will accomplish so many great things if they work together and not tear each other apart. Look at Ibu Sylvia. Everyone rallies behind her. The musical is strong because we work together instead of shoving each other aside.'

She gives me a face that says I'm an idiot. 'Is this a trick statement?'

I chuckle. There are blotches of feisty pink on her otherwise pale cheeks. The soft wind ruffles her hair, and some strands get stuck on the corner of her mouth. As I release them, my fingertips brush her earlobe. Her eyes widen, but she doesn't tell me to go to hell. I turn my hand around, so my knuckles gently slide down her cheek and jaw. I'm entirely enamoured by the pinkish trail the contact leaves on her skin. There's a glint in her eyes, like some kind of dare. Before I re-evaluate my intention, I dip my face and press my lips on her forehead. I hear her sharp intake of breath, but again, she doesn't push me away. She leans into me, smelling sweet and soft, just like a vase of blooming roses. Our bodies move as if they're connected by some invisible string. Her fingers accidentally brush the front of my pants, and my breath breaks in my chest. I hear myself moan as my body clenches. If I ground my teeth any harder, I'd have a headache. With some ironclad effort, I push myself two steps backwards.

'Thanks,' she whispers.

'For what?'

She points at the plastic bag on the floor. 'When the pain is gone and I'm normal again, I'm pretty sure I'll be horrified. I must've made you uncomfortable.'

She *is* making me uncomfortable, but for a whole different reason. My gaze lingers on her mouth. 'You're no more horrifying than usual.'

We both laugh, our voices husky. When our laugher fades, we don't break eye contact, and the air between us feels tight and pulsing. She swallows. My eyes chase the movement like a man who's been denied water for days. I replay our moment in the gym, how her breath blew into my face, how her whimpers stirred something foreign in my stomach. Fuck respectable distance. Tomorrow, we'll go back to being co-leaders. Tomorrow there'll be nothing between us but professionalism. But just for tonight, I won't hide behind my self-made wall. I lean my face close to her and she tilts hers up to meet me halfway. I kiss her right cheek, just above the corner of her mouth. This is the farthest I'll go.

'Never apologize,' I murmur. 'I'm not uncomfortable.'

Her hand slips around my waist and she pulls me into her. Wrapping my arms around her shoulders, I bury my nose in her hair. The plastic bag grazes my left leg as we stand there unmoving. She breaks away first but stays within the circle of my arms. We look shyly at each other, not sure what to do next. My thumb outlines her bottom lip, then my hand cups the left side of her face. I'm relieved to learn that her fever has indeed gone down.

'Good night, petal.' I decide to step back before I mess up and kiss her for real. My legs are a little unsteady. I tell myself not to look back. But like any hero from a romantic movie, I do. She's touching the spot on her cheek I just kissed.

This entire visit is a trainwreck I can't seem to walk away from. A trainwreck that, strangely, makes me very giddy. I haven't felt this way for ages.

No, scratch that. I haven't felt like this *ever*.

My grin splits my face. I'm happy because . . .

Never mind.

I'm happy. That should be enough.

April

Chapter 12

Ellie

Today is the Mondayest Tuesday and it's not even my fault. I check Google Maps for the millionth time, only to find that nothing has changed. Some sleepy driver drove their truck into a board sign on the main street and knocked it off into the middle of the road, thus creating a deadlock congestion. There was no fatality, only the street is swamped by the broken sign and whatever things the truck carried. The long traffic, kilometres away, is way worse than Spring's own. The girls and I weren't badly affected this morning, but going back from Spring to Lyla's house is another story. Because of this, our scheduled PTA for April was cancelled. Most of the members were either stuck or decided to stay home. I can't say I'm sorry about the cancellation.

Since I can't go back to Lyla's place yet, I immerse myself in the stationery and art supplies store in this barely opened mall. Aside from being the closest one to Spring, it's also the newest addition to the numerous malls in the area. The store won't open until ten, but the staff took pity on me and let me in. Forty-five minutes later, my arms are full of new, freshly minted art books, pencils, super glue, and paper rolls.

As I walk out of the shop, I weigh my options: I can wait in the café opposite the store, or I can go back to my apartment. My place is located in the opposite direction of the jam, about a thirty-minute drive from Lyla's house. My parents bought the studio when I was about to start uni. I only used it on the weekends during my college years. I haven't been inside my apartment since I moved into Lyla's house. I bet it's dusty, but if I go back, I can nap on my own bed and snack in my own kitchen. I need to make sure the contents of my fridge are still edible. I can also work at my own desk. The ship prototype needs urgent fine-tuning.

It's decided then. To my apartment I go.

I'm walking past the coffee shop when a familiar figure slumped on one of the tables catches my eye. Half of the face is hidden by the black cap, but I would recognize those shoulders anywhere. My heartbeat trips over itself.

'Dion?'

He squints as he adjusts the brim of his cap.

'Ellie.' My name slips out of his mouth like the taste of morning coffee, deliciously rich and sweet. I curse at how happy I'm to see him.

Bonus point: he, too, looks happy to see me and doesn't hide it from his face.

I quickly take inventory of his appearance. He looks like his typical morning-self, crumpled and beat. His eyes are rimmed red like someone who hasn't slept for ages. What I don't usually see are his blue scrubs. He's thrown a grey jacket over it. The jacket looks soft and comfortable, I resist the urge to run my hands over the fabric.

'Are you avoiding the traffic?' I drop myself on the seat opposite him without being invited.

He rubs his eyes. 'Yeah.' His gaze drops to the materials on my arms. 'You can always ask Jonas to buy them for you. They have a budget for this thing.'

'I love shopping for stationery.'

'What's the difference between those?' He jerks his chin in the direction of my notebooks.

I spread the three of them side by side on the table: red, blue, green. 'They're the same.'

'Hmm. And you *have to* have all of them,' he replies in his deadpan tone.

'That's not true. I didn't get the black one.'

'Because black is not your colour?'

'Because I already have two of them at home.'

He shoots me a mock-grimace, followed by a smile that sends every cell in my body vibrating. We stare at each other, frozen in the moment; my entire face lighting up and him gazing at me with his smouldering eyes. Are his eyes smouldering? Or is it only my imagination? God, I'm getting thirstier the longer I stare at him. I blame him for striking the first flame through his feather-light touches and too-brief-to-analyse kisses during my embarrassing moment of the month. I have no idea how to transport us back to *that moment*. For now, we exist in this undefinable and awkward bubble that's friendlier than colleagues but leaving questionable space for . . . dare I say, something more. I guess I could always ask him to talk, but here we are, playing a game of pretend and handling things like two mature, responsible adults, which is ignoring the tension until it blows up in our faces.

Can't wait.

As though he can hear my internal swooning, he tilts his head and raises one of his eyebrows. I assume his eyebrow is raised. I can only see the movement of the lower side of his face, his eyebrows are completely hidden from my view. The butterflies in my chest flap more aggressively, making my face hot.

'How's Prince Eric's ship coming along?' His jaw flexes as he's killing a yawn.

'We'll build it for real this week.' Just speaking about my assignment brings back the warmth into my veins. Creativity is a poison. It kills and drugs me, and I'm its willing slave. Lately my excitement is overshadowed by my impostor syndrome. Ibu Sylvia wants a wider and taller ship, and I'm grappling with anxiety on whether or not my creation could hold the weight of two adults standing on its plywood steps. Sometimes the doubt is so severe, I'm tempted to quit. Dion's taunt was clear as a bell in my mind. *Quitting is free.*

'Have you fixed the wheels?' he asks, his voice muffled as he swallows another yawn. I feel sorry for him. I bet if someone handed him a pillow, he'd snore straight to dreamland.

I completely forgot about the wheels. I make a mental note to double-check them as soon as I arrive at the art room this afternoon. I give him a thumbs-up. 'Jonas took care of it.'

His eyes narrow a fraction before he drops his chin lower to his chest. He licks his lips and grimaces as if he tastes something bad. 'You and Jonas are Spring's power couple, petal.'

Ah, there it is, Dion's infamous jab. It's good that I no longer react to his sarcasm with bullets and knives. 'Can I ask you something?'

'Shoot.'

'Why do you call me petal? I've always been curious.'

He chuckles. 'You're small and—'

'Fragile?'

'Beautiful.' He studies me closely, like he's unsure of how I would respond to his words.

Well, I *love* to be called beautiful.

'Really?' I ask, not quite believing my ears.

'*Really.* Beautiful. Funny. But yeah, mostly tiny.'

He said beautiful twice.

'Flowers can't be funny. But yay, I'm beautiful.'

'You are.' His voice is low and intimate, making my skin sizzle.

But what does he actually mean? I'm beautiful, so what? What's next? I try my best to ignore the lingering feeling of his fingers on my neck. I try to ignore his scent and the memory of his body heat when he was near me. I don't regret any of what has happened between us, direct or subtle or whatever. But I'm afraid that whatever this is might ruin our fragile . . . relationship?

Pfft Ellie, what relationship?

'Are you on the way to work?'

'From work. ER,' he says, this time not bothering to cover his yawn. 'Now is actually my bed time.'

So, he works the graveyard shift. That explains his crumpled face every time he attends Spring morning meetings. Aside from the hard hours, his work is no doubt challenging. It's the hospital. Then there's the rehearsals he does with the students in the afternoon. Then he goes straight to work. What is he made of? Steel and steroids? Thinking about his schedule makes me sigh. He started off as an irritating, arrogant know-it-all guy, but ever since our weird moment in Lyla's front yard and him opening up about his dad, I also know he's the most gentle and caring man. He's smart and he takes his responsibilities seriously. I can't believe I'm thinking this, but I enjoy being in his company. Whenever I'm at Spring ground, I'm thinking about him. Whenever I'm at home, I'm thinking about him. Everywhere I am, I'm thinking about him. I want to peel his layers off one by one. For now, the *only* layer I can peel off him is his exhausted look.

An idea strikes. It's fucking brilliant.

'Hey, wanna go to my place?'

His eyes widen and I realize how my words sounded. I swear I just wanted to help him, like paying it back for his kindness to me last time. However, now that I uttered the invite, the images follow. A glimpse of him in my space awakens something wild in the pit of my stomach. I can't edit my words, so I carry on what I started.

'I can't go back to Lyla's house anyway, so I'm gonna wait at my place. My apartment is that way.' I point to the direction that's away from the road accident. 'You can nap on my couch while I work. You look like you could use some rest.'

He's visibly stunned. For a long time, he stares at me with his signature frown. He must be truly tired if it takes him this long to formulate a response. The Dion I know, the charismatic and smart one, would have either (1) diplomatically turned down my invite, or (2) sarcastically turned down my invite.

It surprises me when he asks, 'You sure?' There's a doubtful lilt in his voice, but he doesn't outright reject my idea. He must be truly exhausted.

'Yes, I'm sure.' I look down at the half empty cup on the table. Condensation has pooled under it.

'I can't possibly crash on your couch while you work,' he says in a strange voice, like he's arguing against my idea and hoping he'd lose.

'Would you rather have me clean up my room?' I ask.

'Even worse. I can't possibly sleep while you clean. I will have to offer my help.'

'I can't possibly ask you to help me make my bed.'

He crosses his arms in front of his chest. 'How big is your bed?'

'Hobbit-size. You can't criticize it since it's *my* bed and it fits me perfectly.'

His lips quirk up. 'I can't possibly criticize—'

I hold up a hand. 'We can do this all day, or we can start moving.'

A server appears at our table. 'Your chocolate chip gelato, sir.' She puts the cup in front of Dion and leaves.

I stare at the cup with my jaw hanging open. Then I steal a look over my shoulder at the inside of the café. 'They serve gelato at nine?'

'Do we need a schedule to eat ice cream?'

'You're right.' I make a mental note to bring the girls here on the weekend. Without thinking, I pick up the ice cream cup and bring it close to my nose.

'By all means, sniff it,' he comments dryly.

I put the cup back in front of him.

He shakes his head. 'Go ahead. I just had my coffee. I'm bloated.'

'Why did you order it?'

'My mistake. Never order anything when you're hungry. Or sleepy. Take it,' he says when he sees me hesitating. 'You need it more than I do, considering.'

I frown at him. 'Considering?'

He tilts his head up, peering at me from under his hat. 'Do you not crave sugar around this time?'

It takes a moment to realize that he's referring to my cycle. I can't believe he remembers. If the prickling heat to my face is any indication, I'm sure I look like a boiled shrimp. I fuss with my hair, hoping he doesn't notice my embarrassment. I hear a controlled exhale from his mouth. Of course he notices.

'It's natural, petal. No need to be embarrassed about it.'

I grab the ice cream cup and ignore him. 'I crave dessert 365 days a year,' I say. 'It doesn't mean anything.'

'How many of them are cheese donuts?'

'365.'

Indulging me, he shoots me his charming close-lipped smile. 'My dad loved cheese donuts.'

As soon as the words fly out of his mouth, he visibly clenches. Not only a part of him, but *all of him*. The jaw, the fingers, the shoulders, the neck. Like a fortress closing its massive gates with its metal locks and chains. He looks like he wants to bite back his words and crunch them to dust. I hear the painful sound of his teeth grinding against one another. A cold fist grips my heart as I realize I won't be able to rescue him once he locks himself behind the metal bars. Panicked, I shout: 'Bacon. I love bacon!'

He's startled, eyes narrow, mouth slightly ajar. The clanking noise of imaginary metal locks meeting metal gates in my head halts. I notice the exact moment he remembers where we are, and what we were talking about before. Relief sweeps across his features as he exhales; it sweeps across mine too. I'm still breathing hard like I just sprinted up a mountain, but my muscles loosen.

'Of course you love bacon, petal.' His lopsided smirk returns. 'I hate everything with cheese.'

Every part of me wants to ask him about his father, but I know better. I just got him out of the abyss. I will do anything to keep him in the light.

'Are you lactose intolerant?' I ask.

'No. I just don't appreciate my desserts . . . not sweet.'

'You're missing out on a lot.'

One corner of his voluptuous mouth quirks up. 'Name one great savoury dessert.'

'Salted caramel.'

'Sweet.'

'Butter Croissant.'

'If you like eating papier-mâché.'

I give up. Arguing a lost cause while my ice cream melts is not a sacrifice I'm willing to make. 'So, you and mochaccino, huh?'

'It seems the most practical. I need sugar and caffeine in the early morning, or should I say, at the crack of dawn if you follow my body clock. Mochaccino has both in one bite.'

I find him looking at me with amusement and wonder, his gaze is all soft, his smile softer . . . I'm gonna lose my mind. 'Why are you looking at me like that?'

'You don't like it?' he asks.

'What?' I look down. The ice cream is gone. It's nothing but a chocolate pond now.

'If you don't want it, I can always finish it,' he says.

'All of that sugar does nothing to your waist?'

'It does,' he says, 'My waist thanks me.'

I can attest that it's true. His waist thanks him by remaining fat-free.

I hear him sigh. 'Men and women have a different metabolic system, petal. Don't compare it.'

'I didn't say anything.'

'Your face did.'

'Dating doctors must suck,' I mumble into my gelato.

'I'm not sure about that. We know everything about bodies, their function, every nerve ending and their precise location.'

I don't mind the blush that washes over me, but must my face hiss like a piece of steak on a hot grill the moment he mentioned *nerve ending*? Now I can't stop wondering if he was trying to awaken a certain nerve ending when he ran his fingers down my cheek a few weeks ago. Not only does my face get hotter, my stomach feels like someone just set up a campfire there. He only smirks when I glare at him with my very red face. I pluck the napkin from the holder and wipe my mouth. 'Ready?'

'*Or* we can stay here and work on our PTA proposal.' His words sound weak because I assume he doesn't want to put weight behind them. 'Ellie, hear me out. You don't have to do anything other than listen. That's all I ask.'

I can't dodge him forever, but I can dodge him this time.

'I'd rather work on the ship if you don't mind. It's time sensitive.' I'm not entirely lying. It will take more time for me to complete, and their deadline is more severe.

He still doesn't move from his seat, but he picks up his almost empty coffee cup and takes a sip. The ice cubes rattle against the glass. 'Fine.'

I duck a little lower to catch his eyes. 'You go with me, then I'll drive you back here.'

'Why?'

'Because,' I say as I point a firm finger at him, 'You're almost passing out from exhaustion. I won't let you drive.'

'All right.' He pushes his chair and stands. He's about to turn when he notices I'm still sitting. 'What?'

'This is the first time you agreed with me. Oh, wait. Is it the second? I think it's the third.'

'You expect me not to?'

'With you? *Always.*'

He rubs his dead-with-sleep eyes, but his smile is affectionate when he half-heartedly argues, 'Not *always*, petal.'

* * *

My apartment is small, but it has the necessary stuff I need to live comfortably. It's a safe neighbourhood that houses mostly elderly expats, and it's close to Lyla's. It's not much, but I like it. It's my home away from home.

The said home is currently covered with three months worth of dust and smells like a place that has trapped stagnant air inside. I drop my stuff to my desk and open the windows. A handful of dust flies towards my face when I yank the curtain open.

My current guest is surveying my apartment with naked interest. People might think I'm adopting the minimalist trend with my decor. Truth is, I only need a bed, a work desk, a two-seater couch, a coffee table, bathroom necessities, a fridge, and a microwave. And, of course, Wi-Fi and two sets of ACs.

Dion spends a moment studying the scattered old papers on my desk. I tend to doodle when I'm bored. Since I'm drawn towards shapes, my sketches consist of a lot of landscapes, buildings, and furniture.

He tips his head at me. 'Nice,' he says.

For some reason, his one-word compliment makes me want to dance around my studio.

Next, Dion half-crouches to inspect the rows of frames on my table. He would soon see that I got my looks from my mom. He'd see how close I am with my sister and her family because nearly all the pictures on my desk are of Lyla and the girls.

He says the exact same thing. 'You're very close with your sister.'

I shrug despite the pinch in my chest. I miss Lyla and her meddling. 'She's the only sister I've got.'

'What is it, seven, eight years difference?' he glances at me from the photograph of the young me and Lyla in our parents' house.

'Eleven,' I say. 'My mom said the condom broke.'

He's choking and coughing, his face turning red. I have a great time watching him pound on his chest. 'It's natural, Dion,' I say. 'Sex needs to happen before babies. You said so yourself in the sex-ed workshop you conducted for Spring mothers.'

He's coughing harder. When he finally gets his breathing under control, he rolls his eyes at me. 'A broken condom is not natural. It's an accident.' He shakes his head, something like longing shines from his eyes. 'Do you and your family talk about everything?'

'Pretty much,' I say. 'Lyla and my mom would ask me to stop lazing around and to be more ambitious and organized, and I'd reply with *yada yada yada.*'

His eyes flick down to my midsection and linger there for a beat. 'Does the *yada yada* include the talk about your menstrual pain?'

I stay silent because the truth is, my *yada yada* hasn't.

'I don't agree with their assessment,' he suddenly says, facing me straight on. 'I can tell a lazy person when I see one. You're not. An unambitious person wouldn't take an unpaid job in designing 3D props like you have.'

My heart floats around in my chest. I've been told I lack drive and ambition ever since I was a kid and I believe them. I'm *too lazy* to argue with those people. It's nice to hear someone else's positive opinion about me.

'Thanks,' I say. 'Truth is, I don't always know what I want to do with my life.'

'You'll figure it out.' He looks around my apartment once more. I realize he's waiting for me to invite him to sit. He's such a proper guest, my mom would worship him. He even took off his shoes before he entered my house. Double points from my mom, no doubt.

'Make yourself comfortable.' I point at the couch. It's a little dusty, just like the rest of my studio, but I get the feeling he won't mind.

After taking his jacket off, he drops his gigantic body on my two-seater, and immediately, the space is gone, like he single-handedly shrunk my whole living room. He's the giant inside my hobbit house.

'Want something to drink?'

'Martini, please,' he deadpans. He has taken his cap off, revealing a mop of dishevelled hair that strangely looks even better on him.

I give him a bottle of water, then sit next to him. I prop my elbow on the back of the sofa and watch him. From this close, his scent is more pronounced: a sterilized smell, some hint of soap, and a bit of coffee from the café. Now his alcohol-like scent makes more sense. He's carrying the hospital with him. The space between us is so narrow, I feel our bodies transfer heat to one another. If I don't hold myself back, I'll rest my head on his shoulder. I'm starting to feel a bit territorial about that shoulder of his. It was my resting paradise when I was in pain. It still looks comfortable now, inviting even.

I miss him, I realize. I miss *us*. Not as co-captains, but *us* when we're toeing around something we both refuse to talk about. Something that teases the possibilities of *more than colleagues*.

I clear my throat. 'Why do you do this? You attend Spring's morning meetings after your shift. You work with the students in the afternoon. You sacrifice your nap time for more work. You could have played video games, dated your co-worker or something . . . you know, be free.'

I'm aware that I copied the words he told me from our first meeting.

'If you want to know about the special person I'm seeing, just ask, petal.'

Is he flirting? He's formally invited me to ask about his personal life.

'I know you don't have one because everyone at school is trying to hook you up with someone.'

'I could keep the identity of my special someone a secret.'

The twisting in my belly nags me to ask the ultimate question: *Do you have a special someone?*

He turns his head slowly towards me, blinks, then his mouth opens up into a perfect smile. Like a gulp of cold coconut water after a beach swim. Like the juiciest strawberry on top of a chocolate cake. I must be starving if I keep imagining him as food.

He slides a little lower on my couch. 'Thanks for this, Ellie. I really appreciate it.' His voice is deep, heavy, like he's giving everything he's got to fight his sleep and now is on the brink of letting it all go. He closes his eyes, long fingers linked on his stomach, legs spread like those of men who ride the buses.

I feel weird watching him like this. 'I'm gonna start drawing.'

'Mmmm.'

But I don't move my ass to my desk. Instead, I rest my right cheek on my arm and watch him.

* * *

I wake up with a start. The scent hits me first. Male and foreign and something like antiseptic. Dion is still sprawled and napping the way he was before. I glance at my wall clock and have to blink a few times to make sure. It felt like I had slept for hours—I was that comfortable—but turns out it was only a few minutes. I yawn and shake the remnants of sleep out of me. The dust must have tickled my nose because all of a sudden I sneeze. Dion's eyes snap up and he jerks ramrod straight. Covering my mouth to avoid another sneeze, I gently say, 'Hey.'

He looks at me for a long beat. 'Hey.' His voice is rough. He leans back to the couch and the cushion whooshes under his weight. He puts his hands together on top of his stomach and closes his eyes. 'How long have I been asleep?'

'Twenty minutes,' I say.

'*What?*' He laughs and wipes a hand down his face. 'I felt like I've slept for weeks. Did you clean your apartment?'

'Twice.'

He does a little stretch that causes his top to ride up and exposes a strip of tanned skin and a line of body hair above his scrub pants. I nearly groan when he drops his arms, and the scrubs fall back into place.

His eyes remain closed when he asks, 'Have you scrubbed the bathroom floor?'

'The walls and ceiling too.'

'Laundry?'

'Folded and stored. I even ironed your jacket.'

He laughs, then groans. 'It's a crime to be this tired.'

'Studies have shown that this type of fatigue is common in old people,' I reply.

'Thanks. I'm twenty-five.'

'In that case, yes, it's a crime to feel this tired.' After a moment, I add quietly, 'If you're tired, you can always quit Spring.'

He doesn't say anything for the longest time. When he moves his head to look at me, his expression is guarded. 'I like to help. It's the right thing to do.'

'Not at the expense of your health,' I mutter. 'And the right thing to do for *whom?*'

'I'm fine, petal.'

I know when to butt out of a conversation. 'You want something to eat?' I untuck my leg from underneath me.

He catches my wrist and pulls me back next to him. 'Stay.'

My cells explode into tiny fireworks, loud and hot. The skin where his fingers touch pulses alongside my quickened heartbeat. I flop back into my previous position and watch him rest his head against the back of my sofa. Since he has closed his eyes, I unabashedly inspect him. His facial skin is a typical guy's, clean with some roughness. Spots from old acne and soft facial hair. I itch to feel that uneven stubble with my fingertips, my left hand hovers inches from his chin. He must have sensed my movement because he opens his eyes. He's slightly disoriented but alert enough to notice my hand.

'May I?'

He nods, but it's clear that he's confused. I touch the chin first, then slide my palm against his jaw. The skin is softer than I imagined. The friction from the stubble sends goosebumps up my entire arm.

'You lack facial hair,' I say. 'But the texture has character.'

The tips of his mouth curve up slightly. 'I can't grow a beard to save my life. I don't know why.'

'You must know why,' I say casually despite my dry throat. With some reluctance, I pull my hand back. 'You're a doctor. Everything has its purpose. What's the purpose of facial hair? Why are you not able to grow it?'

'Ah, *that*,' he says with his expressionless face. How he manages to switch from laughing to deadpan is beyond me. 'You see, everyone—'

The rest of his words are mumbled as I clamp a hand over his mouth. Snickering, I tell him, 'I'm not interested.'

He continues mumbling against my palm, sending mini jolts into my body, jolts that get stronger with each second where his breath fans my skin. My whole body is vibrating. Hell, my whole couch is vibrating. He captures my wrist and moves my hand a centimetre away from his mouth. 'Have you grown your underarm hair yet?'

I slap my hand back onto his mouth as we're both reduced to chortling madness. He still circles my wrist and does a poor job of getting it away from his face. When our eyes meet, the intensity of it punches me in my chest. I stop laughing. I stop breathing. *That* moment from Lyla's front yard is back—stronger and more urgent. It doesn't cuddle me like the last time; it's now slamming against me, slapping me, pushing me to do something about it, to initiate, to respond, to coax. *Anything.*

Slowly, he guides my hand back to his jaw, rubbing the back of it against the roughness of his skin. Then, inch by fucking inch, he brings my hand up to his mouth. I swallow the thickness in my throat the moment he presses his lips on the tender skin where my pulse beats. He must notice how erratic it is. My gasp is loud in my ears. He makes a low noise in response, a similar sound to when he unexpectedly kissed my cheek last month. Both times, he was so gentle with me, always pausing for a second to give me a chance to pull away.

I don't want to pull away. I want to do the exact opposite.

The urgency travels to my centre. I feel heavy as I sink deeper into the sofa.

He looks at me from beneath his long eyelashes with a little shyness and a lot of desire. He has those sleepy eyes that are too intoxicating to look at. His chest moves up and down, his Adam's apple bobs hard. I yank my right hand from his grasp. He lets go, eyes searching my face for an answer. I answer by straddling him. It's almost impossible for me to draw breath, like my lungs are on fire, the air hazy and smoky. My chest is tight with want. I want to breathe. I need air. I need him against me. I slam my mouth down on his and kiss him raw. The instant he kisses me back—with a hunger that exceeds mine—he lifts my entire being.

I'm bouncing into the clouds, I'm feathery, the butterflies in my stomach keep me afloat. He feels this too, whatever unnamed thing this is.

'Petal.' My nickname comes out tortured. His fingers dig into my ass as he hauls me closer to him. I'm dazed. In a trance I can't break.

We're kissing like we're each other's air. The sounds of our laboured breathing, soft moans, and wet lips smashing against each other are like an orchestra to my ears. One of his hands runs up my spine, wrecks my hair, and clasps my nape. My own hands roam his silky hair, marvelling at how thick and wavy the texture feels against my touch. His mouth, oh god, his Julia Roberts look-alike mouth. It's exquisite, juicy, soft, and pretty damn bossy. He certainly knows how to use it for things other than pouting and frowning. He kisses like he's the leading man on the dance floor. The pressure, the rhythm, the jazz of our tongues; he's taking me on a ride and I'm breathlessly trying to catch up. I cup his face in my hands. 'Better than apple juice,' I murmur as I thumb his bottom lip.

He huskily laughs. 'What?'

His arms are now linked across my back, locking me tightly to him. I feel the warmth of his body and the firmness of his muscles through our clothes. Something hard is pressed between my legs. By instinct, I circle my hips. Maybe I'm being inappropriate, yet I don't feel self-conscious at all. I usually am as I was raised by conservative parents and religious schools. I have no experience with sex. I don't know what I'm doing or if I'm doing it right, but this moment with him doesn't feel wrong.

He groans into my mouth as he thrusts his hips against me, creating a dangerous friction we're both so desperately seeking. I grasp his shoulders in a deathly grip. He frames the sides of my face, tilts it a little so he can deepen his claim on my mouth. My apartment walls are closing in on me. I break away from his kiss only a fraction of a second to yank my shirt off my head. His eyes are half-lidded and fogged with lust.

'Fuck,' he whispers as I pant in front of him in my far-from-sexy black cotton bra.

He runs a finger along the strap, and I nearly die. He cups both my breasts through the fabric. My stature might be petite, but my breasts are not. They fit well into his hands.

'Ellie,' he grunts. My name sounds like a prayer. His hips jerk into mine and I throw my head back, enjoying the feel of his hands on my feverish skin. Our hips move frantically on their own, grinding against each other through his scrub pants and my jeans, faster, harder, faster . . .

I trust him. I trust he won't hurt me.

I suck on the side of his neck.

As abruptly as someone has switched off the light, he stops. Not only that, he throws me aside. I find myself discarded on the couch, shirtless and gasping for air. My lips and nipples are swollen, my skin burning.

He's standing with his back to me. One of his hands is running through his hair, the other clutches his jacket.

'Fuck. Fuck.' His voice is hard, fierce, and hotly mad. '*Fuuuck.*'

His shoulder blades rise with the deep breath he takes, then they fall. He drops his hand from his hair.

'Ellie. We can't.' He's still not facing me. His wipes his face and shakes his head, like he's weeping. 'This is . . . *wrong*. You . . . a mistake. I'm so sorry.' Then he runs out of my apartment like his ass is on fire. He slams the front door closed, leaving me confused, horny, and embarrassed in my own apartment.

I register my discarded shirt, and I feel like I've been slapped for a second time. Nobody can see me here, but I cover my chest with my arms in panic. I'm so ashamed, I can't bring myself to move from where I am. I can't even make myself put my shirt back on.

What the fuck just happened?

He stopped and ran out of my apartment. He refused to look at me. He didn't even bother to turn around as a courtesy because I assume the sight of me must have disgusted him. I have never felt so humiliated in my whole life, and this by a guy I tried so hard to befriend since the beginning.

A mistake.

How, *how* did I become a mistake when he wanted me too? His kisses were hot, his touches were kind. He brought me heating pads. He cared about me, I know he did. *He did.*

Slowly, I curl up on the couch. The cushion is still warm from our bodies, my mouth still tingles from his kiss, my skin is still raw from his fingers.

I cover my eyes and cry.

Chapter 13

Dion

I punch the elevator buttons like they're my enemies, then run across the apartment lobby and into the street, clutching my jacket strategically in front of my crotch. I can't believe I almost came by dry-humping Ellie on her couch. I completely forgot about my vow to maintain a safe, friendly distance, like my uncle always advised. She only needed to touch me once and all power to my brain short-circuited. I'm weak.

My feet take me to a filthy, vandalized bus stop. I drop my ass on one of the dirty seats, then stoop low with my elbows on my knees and my face in my hands.

A long time ago, I promised myself I wouldn't be caught in this situation again. And yet, here I am, kissing the sister of the most influential parent at Spring. Here I am, making a fool of myself in front of a girl whose family's social and economic step on the ladder is way above mine.

Haven't I learned my lesson?

Apparently fucking not.

My uncle would be ashamed of me. I'm ashamed of myself.

I push away from my knees and slump in my seat. My eyes drink in the chaotic street, but my mind hasn't moved from her couch. She felt so good. She looked damn good too.

Fuck.

My dick hardens, remembering the feel of her in my arms all too well. I clench my fists and thump the back of my head against the shelter's wall. My god! She was reckless and unapologetic. She wanted me and didn't hide it. It was fucking hot. I loved it. *I loved it.* My frustrated grunts turn to a bitter laughter. I angrily run a hand over my mouth in an attempt to erase the memory of her lips on mine. I'm not sixteen anymore. I'm a twenty-five-year-old grown man. I'm a competent doctor. I will *not* almost come in my pants twice in the same morning.

A black Mercedes Benz S-class slides to a stop a few meters from the red light. My reflection blinks back at me from its tinted dark window. I'm looking at my young high school-self in Spring uniform.

Ruby rode this type of Mercedes to school. The car was personalized with an *R11BY* plate number. But unlike her posh car, Ruby didn't belong in the cool kids club. She was a nerd like me. That was probably why she and I were friends.

I was always aware of my status when I was a student riding on a full scholarship in Spring. It was hard not to when all my friends came from the crème de la crème, top of the top families. They had the best gadgets, rode the most luxurious cars, wore designer shoes and accessories, had nannies, maids, drivers, and assistants to their name. But whenever I was with Ruby, I felt like we were the same. We were just two kids talking about pop culture and homework. I don't remember when our platonic friendship turned into more. But I remember *she* started it.

It was innocent at first. She'd ask me to accompany her to the library, just the two of us, whispering like two naughty kids in the corner. She'd ask me to sit with her during recess. She'd ask me to hang out with her after school in the parking lot. She initiated the touches. A hand on my arm, on my elbow, on my back. Then she got bolder. She would trail her fingers on the inside of my thigh. She'd shoot me lingering looks, biting her lips, and batting her eyelashes. I was shy but I wasn't an idiot. When she proposed a casual date, I eagerly said yes. I didn't have any close friends. I was never unwelcome in any groups, but they always found subtle ways to let me know I wasn't one of them. To be included in Ruby's circle, however small it was, felt like a welcoming party. I finally belonged.

Ruby's family was known for their prestigious status in politics; her father worked in one of the minister's offices. They were the kind of parents who were paranoid about who got close to their daughter. They were the type of people who assumed everyone would take advantage of their wealth. I was sixteen, and in love. I *thought* I was in love. The complex fabric of society hadn't truly sunk in beyond the simple *they're rich* and *I'm not*. When Ruby's mother secretly followed us and found out she went on a movie date with me, her family freaked the shit out.

I will never forget my uncle's alarmed expression when Ruby's parents demanded that the board expel me because *we can't have a kid like him mingle with ours*. Their words. As if I carried a virus and that poorness could be transmitted by touch. The board rejected their demand outright, but Ruby's father's insult stayed with me.

To make matters worse, Ruby threw me under the bus and watched me die without an ounce of guilt. In a rehearsed, choked voice, she told her parents and my uncle that I kept bothering her even when she repeatedly told me she only wanted to be friends. The whole time we spent together, I failed to notice how intimidated she was by her family.

Her betrayal stunned me into silence.

My uncle could not do much in that meeting other than listen and apologize. He did a lot of apologizing.

'Ruby has a bright future ahead of her,' Ruby's father said. 'She can't get involved with someone who can't keep up with her.'

It took years before I understood the depth of that insult. The anger pounded less, but the humiliation trickled in, drop by drop, filling in the hole until my chest was full of it. Ruby's father insulted me and my family simply because we were not crazy-rich like them. He was right. I couldn't keep up with them. I couldn't keep up with the generational wealth Ruby's family had. I was an orphaned kid who went to the most exclusive school in the country because the board felt sorry for me for losing my father. I was a charity case.

I got the message loud and clear.

'I know it's unfair, Dion,' my uncle said when we were alone. 'I know you were telling the truth. I believe you. You did nothing wrong. But I think it's best if you maintain your distance from Ruby. Focus on your studies. Don't let these people define your value.'

I promised myself I wouldn't let anyone define my value. If I couldn't match these arrogant asshats financially, I could *outmatch* them in fields where results are absolute. Academic records. Sports performance. Debate club. When I was an A student at Spring, I was an A student everywhere in the world. I would never be one of them, but I would earn their respect. I worked alongside them, I existed among them, but I wouldn't get involved with them.

Until today. Not only did I break my promise, I let myself go. My stomach tightens, a weird feeling between disgust and pleasure.

Pleasure. God knows how long it's been. I've lived my adult life like a monk. What Ellie and I did was juvenile, but the pleasure was real. It managed to liquify my bones. And expand my hope. She's on my team.

The Mercedes purrs and glides away from my view, taking my high school refection in its window with it.

What if it's different this time? A voice emerges from the deepest corner of my mind. *I could go back to her. We could sit down like grown-ups and talk. Yes, yes.* It's humiliating how high my heart soars at the thought of me and Ellie together. The possibilities tease me with happily ever afters. Yes, we'll make this work. We're both adults; we make our own decisions.

But does she though? How can I be sure it's not her sister who makes decisions for her? She admitted that the two of them are close. They share *yada yada yada* between them.

Damn it. I'm making the Ruby mistake all over again. I can't get involved. I won't put my uncle in the position where he has to defend me against Spring parents. I'm big enough to defend myself now, but it doesn't mean I want my family to experience this shit again.

But I can't stop thinking about her. I want to hear about her ship and drawing design. I want to support her supporting her nieces. I think about her when I see donuts. I want to call her petal and watch her narrow her eyes at me. I want to take away her chronic pain. I want to massage her head and neck. I want to accompany her to see a doctor. I want to share ice cream with her. When it comes to Ellie, all my thoughts can be narrowed down to a single dot: I want her. I want her so much, I ache. But I shouldn't.

I'm too wound up to think straight. Time to order a Grab Car.

May

Chapter 14

Ellie

It's been more than a week since that humiliating experience in my apartment. I avoid Spring gym like it's my religion, devotedly. I also ignore his onslaught of messages, missed calls, and work emails.

> Ellie. I can explain

Pfft, please. Like he can explain himself. Mistakes are mistakes. It's not a word that requires a lengthy description. As if my luck has been tinted since that cursed day, I feel miserable all the time. Today, it looks like it's gonna rain shit. Just as I think I can nap during my second day of period cramps, I get a call from the school, informing me that Aureli is ill. The news throws me into a cold ice tub.

Aureli meets me outside the gates, teary-eyed. 'My head hurts,' she says.

'Let's get you home, okay,' I say, gently running my fingers through her hair.

As we're walking back to my car, I silently grumble about the fact that Lyla's driver has to take a day off *today*. It's not his fault, but it frustrates me. My car is parked a little farther from the junior building. I hope, by some miracle, I have enough time to take Aureli home and then get back to pick up Ashley. On paper that's possible. On Spring ground, it's fucked. But like the fool I am, I still hope I can make the round-trip in time.

I put Aureli's stuff in the trunk, then settle her in the back seat. After turning on the car and blasting the AC, I hop back out and survey my situation. The sight nearly makes me tear my hair off. My parked car is boxed in from every side. The only way to get it out is to fly it. Desperate drivers and parents have parallel-parked in any space available, including the pathway and side road. They do not care if their cars block other cars. It's a giant car prison, that's what it is.

I take in a deep breath and climb back in. *Think, Ellie, think.* I will have to use superpowers to get us out of this confinement.

I turn around to check on Aureli. The weight in my chest worsens as I look at her, pale and gloomy and so unlike her usual cheerful self. I press my palm against her forehead and neck. She's not feverish, but her skin is cold and damp with sweat.

'From one to ten, how bad is your headache?' I wish on everything that Lyla was here.

She gives a soft whimper. 'I want Mommy.'

'I know, sweetie, I know. We'll call her as soon as we're home, okay?'

After about fifteen minutes of pushing two other cars inch by freaking inch, then manoeuvring my own out of the spot, my shirt clings to my back as if I've just run a marathon. My palms are red from all the work and black from dust, my lower stomach screams every time I exert extra power to push, my period flows like a waterfall. My Toyota is out of the hellhole only to be stuck bumper-to-bumper on the way to the exit. A distance that can be reached in less than five minutes will stretch to an hour if there's a deadlock somewhere inside this compound. The expert parents know what to do and what to avoid, but I'm new, and evidently, I have chosen the wrong spot. Why can't someone from the school fix this fucking mess?

'Auntie Ellie,' Aureli whines. 'I wanna poo.'

No! How?

'Umm, Aur. Can you hold it?'

She's openly crying in the back seat. 'My tummy hurts.'

We're fucked.

I can't leave my car in the middle of queuing, even when the line hasn't moved much. Everywhere I see is cars, cars, cars. Security guards are standing nearby helplessly. I don't trust Aureli to walk by herself to find the toilet in her condition. I don't even know the nearest toilet from where we are. I'm a bad, bad aunt.

Aureli whimpers again.

I grab my phone.

He picks it up on the first ring. 'Ellie?'

The hopefulness in his voice pierces my chest like a hot arrow. 'Are you here?'

He must have noticed the panic in my voice because his words sharpen. 'Is everything alright?'

No, not really. Why did you leave me like that?

I take in a lungful of air. 'I need your help.'

* * *

Dion

I happened to be holding my phone when her call came through. Had I left it inside my backpack, I wouldn't have heard it ringing.

With some effort, I find her a few minutes later. My black shirt sticks to my body from jogging all the way from the gym to the other side of the campus. Her choice of parking is unusual. It's probably because she's driving . . . Wait, why is she driving? Where's their usual driver?

I don't get the chance to ask any questions. I see her face from the front window and notice how relieved she is to see me. Without saying anything, she gets out of the car and hurriedly opens the back door. She pulls Aureli into her arms.

'Where's the nearest toilet?' she asks me.

I point to my left. 'Second floor.'

Aureli wraps her arms around Ellie's neck and hides her face on her aunt's shoulder. Can't stop being a doctor, so I check Aureli's temperature. No fever. That's good, at least.

The car behind me honks. I throw my deadliest glare at the driver because (1) no honking inside the school, (2) can't he see the line hasn't moved? (3) can't he see we have a situation involving a sick kid?

I get into the driver's seat and bump my forehead against the door frame and hurt my ribs against the steering wheel. Despite the less than ideal circumstances, I smile as I adjust the seat to accommodate my long legs.

The traffic doesn't move much when Ellie is back with Aureli a few minutes later. As Ellie settles Aureli in the backseat, our eyes meet through the mirror. She quickly looks away. Sweetness floods my tongue. It feels like ages ago that we kissed. I screwed everything up by reacting like a jerk. No matter how valid my reasons are, my execution was pathetic. There's also the problem with my body. My blood sings every time I'm near her.

Aureli wipes her eyes. 'I'm hungry.'

'Let's get your lunch box,' Ellie says. She sounds tired.

'It's finished,' Aureli says, then curls into a foetal position in the back seat.

Ellie mutters a curse under her breath. I guess she doesn't pack snacks or extra water bottles in her car. Her expression melts my heart. I'm close to telling her that it happens to everyone. She's not a bad aunt; just an inexperienced one. Spring traffic can bring the nastiest surprise on even the most experienced parent.

'There's a small canteen behind the gym. The one next to the pool,' I say. 'I can get her some food.'

She looks at me like she just remembered I was there. 'I'll go,' she says after a moment. 'Can you stay with her for a few more minutes?'

'Of course. But you sure? It's far.' I adjust the mirror to see her eyes. Her complexion is deathly white.

She nods, then leans down to smooth Aureli's hair and murmurs, 'I'll be back, sweetie.'

Her posture hunches when she stands next to the car, her hand cradles her lower stomach. I'm familiar with her telltale signs; it's her chronic monthly pain. No wonder she looks beaten. Not only do we have a sick kid in the car, but her aunt is unwell too. I cover my mouth to hide my frustrated sigh.

Aureli makes a hiccupping noise from the backseat.

I turn my head slightly to look at her. 'Hey there, little Nemo. What time did you go to bed?'

'Twelve.'

'Twelve, *midnight?*' I ask in disbelief. I loosen the seatbelt strap to further twist my body.

She opens one eye, stares at me like I'm dumb. 'Twelve like ten, eleven, twelve.'

How neat. I just got schooled by a second grader. 'What were you doing up so late, Aur?'

She yawns and rubs her eyes intensely. I'm about to pull her tiny hands away from her face when she says, 'Netflix.'

A huff of laughter escapes me. 'Way past your bedtime, isn't it?'

'Auntie Ellie said okay,' she responds, suddenly sounding fierce.

I make a disapproving face. 'On a school night?'

'Nothing's wrong with it.' Her tiny hands are balled in fists.

Apparently sticking to one another no matter what is strong in this family. From behind me, Aureli says in a tired voice, 'But don't tell her I told you, okay? It's a secret.'

I mime zipping my mouth and throwing away the key. After a moment of silence, there's a tap on my back. I'm so alarmed, I nearly put the car in reverse. I look over my shoulder and find Aureli kneeling on the seat, her pinky is extended towards me.

'Promise?' she asks.

For such a tiny person, Aureli has the most ferocious eye-contact I've ever seen. Then I remember who her mother is. I put forward my most solemn face and link my pinky with hers. Aureli doesn't immediately let go. She's searching my face, like daring me to whimper or something. I clench my teeth, so I won't explode with laughter in her face. When she's satisfied with what she sees, she flops back against the seat and lets out a big-ass yawn.

'I'm hungry,' she proclaims. 'My head hurts.'

'Your aunt will be here soon.' She's been gone for quite some time, but the canteen is far, I reason. Also, she probably has to walk slower than usual.

'Hey, Aur.' I try to distract myself from worrying about Ellie. 'What do you usually watch with your sister and aunt at home? What's your favourite show?'

It takes a while before the respond comes. 'Netflix or Disney?'

I eye her from the mirror and smile. 'What's new in Disney?'

'I don't know.' She turns petulant. 'We haven't watched anything for a while other than last night. Auntie Ellie was not feeling well so she stays in her room a lot.'

My stomach drops. 'Not feeling well how, Aur?'

I hear another yawn. I turn my torso around. She lies on her side, one hand rubbing her eyes. I reach out and hold her wrist.

Déjà vu. A month ago, I held her aunt's wrist before she could bruise her temple.

'Don't rub too hard,' I tell Aureli.

I turn back around and move the car a little. Just as I broodingly stare at the buildings on my right side and chant *come on, come on* for Ellie to show up, a sleepy voice floats from behind. 'She's quiet.'

I catch Aureli's eyes through the mirror. 'Who?'

'Auntie Ellie,' she says. 'Ashley thinks Auntie Ellie is sad. Maybe she misses our mother like we do.'

If I gnash my teeth any harder, they'll break. I'm pretty certain I'm the reason Ellie is sad. I swear I'll make things right as soon as she and I find the right time. I'm also struck by how much I know what Aureli is talking about. I know everything about missing a mother, how deep that feeling is that we grapple with words to express ourselves. I press park and undo my seatbelt. The car alarm begins beeping, so I grumpily put it back on.

'You know, Aur, I miss my mom too.'

'Why?'

'I live with my aunt and uncle. My mom lives in Kalimantan. You know where it is?'

'Is it the one next to the island that looks like K?'

I chuckle. She knows her geography. 'Yes, that's the one.'

'Why you're here and she's there?' she asks.

'Because we have better schools here than in any other city, Aur. It helped me get into a good university.' From the mirror I see her nod.

Her next question punches me in the gut. 'What do you do when you miss your mom?'

I can't answer her with complete honesty because *I blame myself* is not the direction I'm aiming for with her. Or with anyone.

'I call her,' I say. 'Your mother will be back soon, right?'

She visibly brightens. 'Yeah. Mom will be home before the musical. She's gonna watch us play.'

'That's awesome, Aur.'

'What about you, Kak Dion? Will your mother come and watch you in the musical too?'

'Err, no.'

'Why not?'

I hope my simple answer is enough to satisfy her curiosity. 'Because she's working, and she can't take days off.'

There's a pause. Then her face fills my rear-view mirror. We hold eye contact for a few beats. Aureli's expression is a picture of genuine sympathy. 'Your mother must miss you so much, Kak Dion. Just like my mom misses me and Ashley.'

I never imagine that a little girl's words could gut-punch me so painfully, and so accurately, twice in the span of mere minutes. I rack my brain trying to find the right words to say back to her.

I get none.

* * *

Ellie

I have a cup of steaming instant noodles in one hand and a plastic bag full of protein bars and bottles of drink in the other. Just to be on the safe side, I bought everything I saw on the counter: water, tea, milk, and electrolyte drinks. I drop the bag on my feet once I'm in the car. I pass Aureli her cup of instant ramen. 'Be careful, it's hot.' I give her the plastic fork next. Immediately, the whole car smells like soto mie. Aureli gingerly puts the cup on her lap. I sit with my back against the back of the passenger seat and my head in the gap between two front seats. If I lean a few inches to my left, I can rest my head on Dion's shoulder. Wouldn't that be nice?

Now that I'm aware of him, my entire body tightens at our nearness. Dion's eyes on me are like a feathery caress against my hot skin. I meet his gaze in the rear-view mirror, holding his dark stare longer than necessary. I hope he can see my whole face from that rectangular piece because, my embarrassment and hurt aside, I mean what I say. 'Thank you.'

His eyes soften. 'Anytime, Ellie.'

I notice how ramrod straight Dion sits in the driver's seat. 'Why are you sitting like that?'

'I'm sweaty,' he answers.

I reach through the gap and gently press his left shoulder until his back meets the seat. He makes a surprised sound but doesn't resist me. He has adjusted the driver's seat to accommodate his long limbs, so right now our faces are practically next to each other. He's facing forward; I'm facing . . . him.

I pluck one of the cold drinks and hand the bottled tea to him. He looks at it, surprised again, before taking it. Our eyes meet. One beat. Two. Three. I see raw joy in them. My heart hurts. Despite everything that happened between us in the last seven, ten days, he's a decent guy. A guy whom I can depend on when I need help. Lyla was right. He's a good kid—a good guy.

He unscrews the cap and takes a hearty gulp.

'Is she okay?' he asks me quietly.

'Gosh, I hope so,' I say.

'And are you?' His voice has gone deeper.

I lean my head against the side of the passenger seat and briefly close my eyes. I startle when his fingers lightly touch my cheek. The air between us is so magnetic and bristling, I won't be surprised if the car fills up with smoke next.

'How bad is the cramp?'

Since he mentions it, I'm feeling it everywhere at once.

'Better than yesterday,' I say, glad that it's the truth. Yesterday was like death to me. Coupled with emotional distress I've experienced since the horrible day in my apartment, my body feels like it's been run over by a tank. I'm not going to tell him that.

He's quiet for a while. When I peek at him, his face is super close to mine. His right hand goes up and in the next breath, he's awkwardly massaging the left side of my head. It's so good, I nearly burst into tears.

'Finish!' Aureli's timing shocks us both into reality. I flinch; the muscles in Dion's jaw jump. His hands grip the wheel like he wants to tear it apart, his knuckles white.

I take the cup from Aureli and drop it into the trash bin. I roll my canvas bag for her to use it as a pillow. She wiggles a little until she finds the most comfortable position. Then she looks up and smiles. My heart blooms in my chest. *This* is the Aureli I know. Her cheeks are pink from the hot meal, her eyes are a little sleepy, but there's a glow. Hopefully her headache is from sleep deprivation and hunger and not from some nasty virus or something.

I tap the tip of her nose. 'You scared me there, Aur.'

'Can we watch *Percy Jackson* when we get home?'

'What? No.' Schooling my face to resemble a proper responsible adult, I repeat, 'No TV on school days.'

'But we have only two episodes left, Auntie Ellie,' she says in a tone that suggests she's being betrayed. 'We haven't watched anything since last week.'

Last week was hell. When I live by myself, nobody pays attention to the state of my mood. But now I have these girls. They noticed the change in me despite my best effort to hide it. Just last night, Ashley asked why I didn't touch the mie tek tek that the chef cooked for dinner. This particular dish from my East Java hometown is my favourite, especially if it's sweet and spicy, made with yellow ramen-like egg noodles—with shredded chicken, tomatoes, fried shallots, and crunchy cabbage as toppings.

'We'll save it for the weekend,' I tell Aureli. I silently beg her with my eyes to not make a scene.

'*Weekend?*' she screeches. 'But Auntie Ellie, it's *Tuesday* now. Saturday is . . . is . . . so far.'

Of course she makes a scene. On the other hand, I'm glad that she does. She must be feeling better already.

'Bed by 8.30 tonight,' I say.

Aureli gasps, pushing her tiny frame up by her elbows. 'You'll watch it without me!'

Dion snorts and quickly covers his mouth with the back of his hand.

'Aur,' I begin, then punch Dion's shoulder. 'Stop it.' He shakes his head, his body trembling with silent laughter. Aureli seems oblivious to the entertainment she provides for our guest.

'Aur,' I sigh her name again. 'You're feeling bad today because you went to bed at ten last night.'

'Twelve,' Dion coughs.

How the hell does he know?

'No more TV on weekdays. No more junk food either,' I tell Aureli with the stoniest expression I can pull off. Surprisingly, it's not that hard with all the pain rummaging inside my own body.

She cries. 'You sound like Mom!'

'Geez. Do I?' I rub my temple.

'Yes, you do,' Dion answers. He catches Aureli's eyes from the mirror, then he winks at her. 'See, Aur. It's like you're talking to *your mom*, right?'

I have no idea what he means, but Aureli's face beams.

The car moves a little.

'Aur, if you're feeling better, we need to let Kak Dion go back to his rehearsal.'

'They can survive a few minutes without me,' he repeats the exact same words he told me when it was me who was writhing with stomach pain.

The sparks of electricity are back, pulling me taut with want. I take my earlier position between the front seats. His shoulder is an inch away from my nose. His scent blends with my car's and Aureli's ramen—it's the best smell. I close my eyes again. Aureli is not the only one who is sleep deprived. The three of us went to bed at 12.30 a.m. I wince mentally. I'm a bad, bad aunt.

'Hey,' his deep voice shakes me from my thought.

Something warm and unfamiliar coils at the bottom of my stomach. He's still holding the tea bottle I gave him earlier, the contents almost finished.

'Why are you driving today?' he asks.

'The driver took a day off.'

'Who will pick up Ashley?'

I shake my head because the answer is obvious. It's *not* gonna be me. I'm not yet out of this predicament. Aureli might be okay now, but I still have another niece to take care of.

'This is so messed up.' The need to share my story with him is overwhelming. 'I couldn't get the car out of my parking spot. I was blocked from all sides, Dion. *All sides.*' I am so angry, I cry. His thumb wipes the tears off my cheek, and I let him.

'Nobody was around to help. I had to push the other cars just to get out. It's like they don't care anymore where they park as long as they park.'

The car slides forward a little. Dion shifts closer to me. 'You should've called me earlier. You should be at home, resting, not driving, and pushing cars.' The frown is back, pulling the corners of his mouth down.

'I—'

Why am I a mistake?

'You might be busy.'

He shakes his head, his voice low and unyielding. 'With me, you can always call. *Always*, Ellie.'

His words are an echo of my own. While mine were delivered as a joke, his make me cry harder.

'You won't make it back for Ashley.' There's a shake in his voice, making me wonder if he missed me as badly as I miss him.

'No shit.'

'You said shit, Auntie Ellie,' Aureli comments. Then, she bolts up straight. 'Auntie Ellie, you're crying!'

'No, no.' I hastily wipe the tears off my cheeks, but she's seen them and knowing Aureli, she won't let it go until she believes I'm not. 'I'm angry,' I say.

Her jaw drops and she points at her nose. 'At me?'

'Ah no, no, no, sweetie, no.' I hug her, crushing her face against my chest and mine against her hair. 'I would never, ever, ever be mad at you.' I must've craved human contact so badly ever since my disastrous moment with Dion, I pour my warmth and affection into my little niece. I drop kisses at the top of her head until she squirms and giggles. I smile with my eyes closed. When I open them, Dion is smiling at us. It's a smile I haven't seen before, soft on the corners of his lips, but deep in his eyes. My stomach flip-flops as I stare at his mouth. Now that Aureli believes I'm not crying, she wiggles out of my arms and lies back down on the seat, ignoring the adults.

'I'll take care of Ashley,' Dion offers. 'You need some rest.'

I'm too drained to pretend I'm not in discomfort. I study the side of his face, helpless and grateful at the same time. 'You don't mind?'

'*Petal*,' he says in his gruff voice.

I haven't heard that nickname for days. I swallow the hot ball in my throat. Our faces are practically touching in that middle gap. I can kiss him. I can run the tip of my nose against the roughness of his jaw.

I shift my attention to Aureli. 'If you need another toilet run, we'll do it now while Kak Dion is here.' I won't get caught in the same hell like before.

My niece shakes her head.

I kiss her forehead and open my door. Dion opens his at the same time. He waits as I climb in. The whiff of his scent, the heat of his body, his breath on my hair; they're too much for me and my migraine. In a lousy attempt to ignore him, I hop into the driver's seat and slip. Oh God, how far back did he push the seat? My hands can't even reach the steering wheel.

'Ellie,' he says.

I take a quick glance at him, then regret it immediately. I dislike him a lot, I won't deny it, but seeing his tortured face doesn't give me satisfaction either. I turn my head away. The radio panel is more interesting to look at.

'Ellie,' he repeats my name, this time it's a whisper. 'I need to talk to you about . . .' He swallows. 'Can I call you later?'

I'm tempted to say no. If he asked this question yesterday, I would've spat the word in his face. I'm still raw from his fresh rejection, but now I also feel grateful for him. I don't know what I would have done if he wasn't around this afternoon.

'It's okay, Dion. We're good,' I say without looking at him. Even if we're not, I'll have to pretend that we are. We still have jobs to do. We have one or two more PTA meetings where we need to present the proposal. The musical is important for everyone. I can't jeopardize it just because someone rejected me and made me feel bad about myself. I'm doing this for my nieces and my sister. I want the three of them to be proud of me. I want to show Lyla that she can depend on me. I want to show my mom I'm not lazy. Most of all, I'm doing this for me. Working with the Spring art team has reminded me why I love architecture. I love designing; I love building stuff. I love working with my hands. I'm pretty good at what I do. For these reasons, I will endure Dion for just a little bit more. I will pretend I didn't kiss him, seduce him, or grind my hips against his. I will pretend he hasn't broken my heart.

Yes. We're good. There's no hesitation about it now.

From the corner of my eye, I see he straightens. After quietly closing my door, he moves to the back and taps Aureli's window. I watch them high five each other through the glass. Without a backward glance, he walks away, his strides as wide and fast as always, but his shoulders are a little hunched, his head a little low. The almost empty tea bottle dangles in his hand. There's suddenly a big lump in my throat.

He can call us mistakes, but *he* clearly is not. I'm starting to see why all the mothers in this school adore him. He doesn't spread his charm like a player. He's genuinely charming because he cares. He cares about this school. Probably just as much as these mothers do. Just as much as Lyla.

I cling to the warmth he left on my seat, letting the memory of his heat travel into my own skin.

Chapter 15

Dion

'Someone is in a good mood.' Sherly, the head nurse, pokes my shoulder blade with her pen.

'I'm always in the good mood,' I reply.

'Liar, liar, pants on fire,' Ayu, another ER nurse, comments from her station without taking her eyes off the monitor in front of her.

Sherly agrees. 'He looks like someone who's in love.'

'Who's in love?' Budi, my friend from medical school, asks from the other side of the counter while passing out patient's charts to Sherly.

I look up from my own monitor and grin. 'Shut up.'

Ayu twirls her chair. 'Is it the new ophthalmologist? I heard she used to be a model when she was in high school.'

'Which one?' I ask, not because I'm interested but because I'd rather they talk about someone else than me.

Ever since Ellie's call two days ago, I've been living in fluffy clouds. She said we were good. I haven't seen her since then, but I believe her. I plan to text her tonight. No, not tonight. It's almost midnight. Tomorrow then. I'll casually drop some texts.

I'll ask about how she is. I could offer to get her more heating pads, or painkillers. I don't realize I glow like a star the entire time I imagine my future interaction with Ellie. Three faces stare at me with various degrees of gleeful expressions.

'Maybe I'm happy because I did a good job lately,' I say, quite lamely, to my co-workers.

Budi snorts. He gestures widely towards the empty hall behind him. We rarely have emergencies. The most we ever handled was some incidents at home, fever, or stomach ache. The non-life-threatening ones.

'The patient in curtain three called him a pretty nurse,' Ayu says, 'and Dion didn't correct her.'

'She had him at *pretty*,' Budi says, feigning annoyance. 'This is what happens when you forget your doctor's coat.'

'All right. I'm leaving,' I say, holding up my hands.

The dispatcher on Sherly's desk crackles. The noise is like a crack of thunder in our quiet ER wing. We pause whatever we're doing and listen. There was an accident on the highway involving a forty-feet container and three family cars. Everyone sucks in a breath. The air in the room drops a few degrees.

'Shit,' Sherly mutters.

My ribcage collapses into my chest.

Multiple casualties are headed our way.

* * *

While the surgeons and specialized doctors rush to the operating rooms, the rest of us deal with the other victims who suffer from less severe injuries and don't require major surgeries. The thirteen-year-old boy I've been tending to for the past hour barely speaks a word. He has those vacant glassy eyes, the look of someone who's still in deep shock. His body trembles despite being buried in the multiple blankets I wrapped him up in. Considering the fatality of the accidents, he's lucky to only have suffered a few cuts on the face and chest, and a gash on his right forearm. He will need to go through more tests to make sure we haven't missed any internal injuries, but for now, his wounds have been cleaned and stitched. I'm trying to engage him in conversation, if it's still called a conversation when I'm the only one who talks. I calmly describe what I'm doing and tell him he's going to be okay.

'Where's Mama?' He turns his eyes to me, and something underneath my skin turns to ice. The truth is, I don't know the other victims' situation. 'I'll go find her. You stay put, okay Anton?'

He gives me a weak nod. I step outside and draw the curtain back. The view around me is of carnage. In the two years of my residency in this hospital, this is the worst night I've ever seen. What can three small family cars do against a forty-feet container? The image of long traffic comes to mind. I shake it off in the next second, feeling incredibly ashamed of myself. There are families who are injured, probably even in critical condition, and what I can conjure up in my mind is traffic?

Ayu passes me. There's blood on her scrubs. 'Dion. Sutures.'

'Right.'

We all freeze when we hear a piercing scream from the opposite direction of where Ayu leads me. The curtain behind me is thrown open and Anton, bandaged, shocked and tangled in blankets, shouts, 'Mama!'

I immediately hold Anton back. 'Hey, hey. Easy.'

He flicks my hand off, and with a power I didn't know he has, surges forward to where his mother is. Ayu and I run after him. We round a corner and stop just in front of an operating room. Mother and son slump on the floor in each other's arms. A senior doctor crouches next to them. The ER nurses try to help the mother sit, or act as a wall for her to lean on. The woman screeches in a voice that's not human, a cry so broken it pricks my eyes with fresh tears.

Ayu shakes her head, then whispers to me, 'We lost the father and the other son.'

My stomach sinks to the floor. 'No.'

I see my own mother, young and beautiful, slumped on the floor, holding a boy in her arms and screaming my father's name. I close my eyes; the image follows me into the darkness. 'We lost your father, Dion.' She framed my face with cold, trembling hands. 'We lost him. Oh my God.' She fainted not long after, and other people's arms came around me, taking me away from my mother and into the waiting room. My uncle and aunt stayed with me that night. They have stayed with me all the way to now, fifteen years later.

I walk out of the ER and into the outdoor garden. The cold, damp air shocks my body, but I barely register the shiver. Lights from the ambulance flash red and blue. Security and hospital workers walk past me. It's a busy night. It's a night we will remember after the blood has dried and the dust has settled. I walk until I'm far enough from the crowd. I lean against a cold, white hospital wall and rip off my medical mask. I'm going wild. I want to run but my feet can't move.

Breathe, I tell myself. *It's not you. It's not you.*

But it's Anton, a boy I barely know, and yet I want to carry him in my arms and take him as far as possible from the wreckage that's this ER hall. He lost his father and brother in one night.

It's not me, but it's someone like me. Someone whose world has been rocked upside down.

I pull my phone out of my scrubs. My fingers shake, my gloves feel icky, so I rip those off too. I tap on a name and wait. Subconsciously, I know that she likely wouldn't be awake at this late hour. After what feels like forever, a sleepy voice answers me.

There's a block of hot coal in my throat; I can barely get a word out. Wiping the tears from my eyes, I finally say, 'Mami.'

'Dion.' Her voice sharpens. 'Are you okay? Where are you?'

'I'm fine. I'm fine. I'm at work.' I let out a shaky laugh that sounds more like a person drowning, but the weight in my chest has lessened and the burning in my throat is manageable. 'Nothing happened. I just wanted to hear your voice.'

And then I break down.

* * *

It's nine in the morning when I arrive home, three hours later than my usual shift. My aunt rushes to meet me at the door.

'Busy night,' I say.

'I figured,' she says. 'Your mother called.' My aunt is a tall woman, nearly as tall as me. The gene runs well in her and my mother. 'I cooked you bubur manado. Let's . . . oh.'

I pull her into a hug and refuse to let her go. I slump against her, the burning behind my eyes and nose returns. Once again, I lose the ability to speak.

'*Oh honey.*' My aunt whispers, her own arms going around me. She rubs my back, just like that night many moons ago, a movement that soothed me, a reminder that she'll always be there to help me stand tall.

After a few minutes of silence, I finally let her go. I'm embarrassed by my outburst. My aunt clasps my arm and leads me to the dining room like the schoolboy I was. 'Something warm in our belly will make everything better.'

I smile. 'It definitely will.'

'You want spicy or plain? I separate the non-spicy one for your uncle, but you can have it if you want.' She rolls her eyes. 'That old man, I tell you, he's always complaining about my cooking.'

The mundaneness of bubur manado conversation anchors me in the present time and not what happened a few hours ago in the hospital.

'How spicy is your spicy? Like, level two, three-ish?'

She mischievously side-eyes me. 'Maybe close to five, seven-ish.'

I snort. 'All right. I'll take the level five bowl, please.'

'That's my boy,' she says. 'By the way, Agatha called. You missed a meeting, she said?'

My brain is so sluggish, it takes me a minute to remember what meeting it was. Anyway, I can't be bothered with Spring right now. I just want to sit with my aunt and hear her talk, just like I did with my mother earlier. I want to surround myself with the voices of people I love. A reminder of how fragile life is. A reminder of how fortunate I am to have these people.

'I'll text Ibu Agatha later,' I say.

She scoops me a bowl and hands me a spoon. 'The lightbulb in the kitchen broke again. Asked your uncle to change it last night, but . . .' She throws her hands out.

'I'll do it.'

'Let your uncle do it.'

'I can do it faster.'

'I know,' she says, lovingly watching me spoon a full chunk of porridge into my mouth. 'Not too salty?'

I shake my head.

For the next few minutes, the only sound in this kitchen is the soft clank between my spoon and the bowl.

'You work too hard.'

'Mm-hmm.'

'You don't have to do everything the Spring people ask, including your uncle. You know that, right? Tell me you know that.'

'I know that,' I say. 'Don't worry. I can manage. It's almost over anyway.' I make a silly face, trying to erase the worry lines that frame her eyes and mouth. 'One last time for Spring, Auntie. I will make you both proud.'

'We already are, son.'

My eyes water again at the word *son*. I fidget with my spoon.

'When this gala is over, you should focus on your career, you hear me? Leave Spring alone. It's your past, not your future,' my aunt says.

I'm surprised that the first image that pops up at the word *future* is Ellie's face, followed by me in a white doctor's coat, and not my old and inaccurate image of my father's face smiling down at me. I like the new image better. A lot better.

I smile up at my aunt. 'I promise.'

Chapter 16

Ellie

When the invitation to attend the principal's meeting finally landed in my inbox, it had been two days since Dion sat with me in my car. He took Ashley home later that evening. I should've sent him a thank you text right away. The longer I waited, the harder it was to do so. I'm thrilled at the prospect of seeing him today, but also terrified. I don't know what else to say to him after that belated thank you. I don't know how to act normal with him in the same room. Every time I think of him, I feel a tightness in my stomach, followed by a heat in my neck, and finally, tingles in my lips. The inside of my chest seems to fold into smaller pieces until I can't breathe.

The meeting is being held in the management building where top Spring executives reside, including Mr Goh. Unlike other pristine, minimalist offices, the Spring executive offices buzz with noises. The desks are cluttered with books and papers. Student's art pieces are hung on the wall. The colours of the beige wall and the green/maroon carpet kind of clash but it adds to the eccentricity of the place.

Since I'm early, I wander around until I find Ibu Agatha. Her corner cubicle is more spacious and private than that of the other staff. She sits next to a window that overlooks the small fishpond.

I knock on her cubicle wall. 'Good morning.'

She looks up from her desktop and her smile splits her face. 'Ellie. Come on in.'

I step into her office and take a seat, glad that she doesn't bow waist deep anymore.

'I'm early,' I say.

'Always good to be early,' she replies. 'How have you been? Ready for the last PTA meeting?'

A simple question with no simple answer. 'Yes, yes. Everything's good,' I say through my smile. Dion and I haven't gotten the chance to discuss the new items submitted by our colleagues, but I'll wing it. I've been winging these meetings for four months. Surely this last one is no exception. Even if I'm wrong, I can always call Lyla later. She will solve whatever problems that might arise today.

Lyla's original PTA plan includes things like canteen management, additional roles for the school counsellor, and improving the standard for teachers hiring. I spotted a few charity initiatives and international competitions in the list, but didn't see anything about homework, extracurricular activities, school fees, or traffic. I'm a bit disappointed not to see the congestion problem in her proposal because if there were one person who could solve anything, that'd be my sister.

Anyway, my job today is *only* to get Lyla's proposal signed and approved by the school for next academic year so my big sister can drive them when she's back.

It gives me a feeling of insurmountable relief—and bigger disappointment—when Ibu Agatha says, 'I'm afraid you're a lone warrior today, Ellie. Dion can't make it.'

'Oh. What happened?'

She shrugs. 'Work, I guess.'

Why does my heart feel like it's shattered into a billion pieces? What is this contraction I feel in the middle of my stomach? I know it's not my menstrual cramp. It's something else. Stronger, hotter, and tighter. My hand goes there to gently massage it.

'I heard the ship is coming together quite nicely.' Ibu Agatha speaks the way an aunt is speaking when our parents are not around, in a proud whisper that promises sweet treats.

I blush. 'It's a team effort.'

'But it was your idea. You designed it. Ibu Sylvia showed me a picture yesterday. My goodness, it's twice her height.' She laughs.

I fuss with the hem of my shirt. I need to learn how to chill and accept compliments. 'It still requires a lot of fine-tuning,' I say. Maybe because I feel safe with her, I blurt out the words without much thinking. 'Dion seems to think I have too much on my plate. He asked me to quit PTA a few times.'

'Nonsense,' she says but her expression turns tender at my mention of Dion. 'He's teasing you, Ellie. That boy likes you, you know. Never seen him this animated before.'

Her words almost make me tell her everything: the kiss, the moment with Aureli, me missing him so much, me hating him so much. I open my mouth. The words are almost out.

'If anyone is taking on too much, it's *him*.' Ibu Agatha shakes her head.

I bite my own words just in time.

'He doesn't know where his limits are.' She talks like my mother. Her exasperated sigh is a cover-up, a mask for the unconditional pride and love underneath.

'He said the school asked him for help,' I say.

'The school formally invites every alumnus for this fundraising project, on a voluntary basis. No pressure whatsoever. But you know Dion.'

No, I don't.

'He can't say no. And we can't say no to him either. He's family.'

I bob my head. 'Because he's Mr Goh's nephew.'

'That's not what makes him family.' She eyes me differently, like she's debating with herself. In the end, she gives in. 'He didn't tell you about his father?'

'Only that he died when Dion was young.'

Her face breaks. 'Sad, sad thing indeed. Heart attacks are so cruel.'

His voice from the rehearsal afternoon echoes in my head: *heartbreak is a serious business.*

'His father taught Chemistry here. He was one of the student's favourites.'

My chemistry is better than yours.

No! I hope he didn't interpret my lame-ass joke as rude, like my *chemistry* is better than his because I have a father and he doesn't. Knowing Dion, he wouldn't take it like that. I'm overthinking this, but fuck, still.

'Dion looks so much like his old man. When the board approved his scholarship and he moved here, it was like we got his father back,' Ibu Agatha says. Her eyes are distant for a moment. 'I remember it was supposed to be on a trial basis, but Dion impressed us all with his academic and non-academic excellence.' Ibu Agatha beams with nostalgic pride. I smile at her, because who wouldn't? I'm looking at the purest kind of love. He didn't lie when he told me everyone here loved him. They do.

'He was on the basketball team, swimming team, science team, and debate team. You name it. He was the president of the student council for three years. You should have seen him then, Ellie. You two could be best friends.' Ibu Agatha pats the desk in front of me. 'Enough about that boy. What about you? You just graduated last year, I hear? What are your plans?'

Older people are so fascinated with plans. I have none at the moment. I'd better not throw her a bone. I know her type. She'll grab the edge of the bone and won't let go until I relent and open up all my deepest fear and darkest secrets.

Just as I mull over how to best answer her, a head pops in. 'Agatha, where's . . .' He stops when he sees me. 'Oh, my apologies. I didn't know Agatha has a guest.'

Agatha excitedly waves the man in. 'Mr Goh, I'd like you to meet Ellie.'

I quickly stand and shake Dion's uncle's hand. He looks nothing like Dion, so I assume Dion is related to his wife. He's a man of medium height, a little round in the middle, hair all grey, half-moon glasses on his nose. He's wearing a Spring uniform minus the tie.

His grip is firm. 'Pleased to meet you at last, Ellie. I've heard so much about you.'

I like his smile. He looks more like someone's grandfather than the principal of one of the most intimidating schools in the country.

'If you heard it from Ibu Sylvia or Pak Jonas, my answer is *team effort*.'

He chuckles. 'I don't know what that means, but no. I heard about you mostly from her—' he points at Ibu Agatha '—and Dion.'

My smile trembles a little.

'You and Dion manage the PTA well.' He winks at me. 'I hope we don't scare you too much.'

'Speaking of PTA,' Ibu Agatha says, 'it's now, Mr Goh.'

'What is?' he asks.

'The PTA meeting,' Ibu Agatha answers, tilting her head slightly towards me.

'Oh.' He checks his watch. He looks up and smiles apologetically at me. 'I wouldn't get anything done without her. I'll join you in a bit. Ellie, it's been a pleasure.'

I love that he treats me like one of his students and not Ibu Lyla's little sister. He doesn't bow to me; he's not being formally stiff around me either. I wonder if that's what he does with Dion at home, be an easy and loving uncle to the nephew who lost a father.

I gotta stop thinking about Dion.

After he leaves, Ibu Agatha leads me to the meeting room.

'Do they prepare a buffet for this meeting like in the other big meetings?' I say as we march together towards the other side of the hall. 'I haven't gotten any breakfast yet.'

Ibu Agatha laughs. 'We shall find out.'

* * *

There must be something wrong with me and Spring meetings. Every single one of them is cursed. My eyes nearly leap out of my sockets when I see Bernadet and Netty in the meeting room. Judging by the friendliness Ibu Agatha extends to them, these two must be formally invited. I wonder why they're joining a meeting that's supposed to be between the school and the PTA chairperson only.

My throat closes up but thankfully I manage to say, 'Good morning.'

As I take a seat opposite them, my mind clicks like a jigsaw puzzle slipping into slots. They must be here because Dion asked them to. Dion couldn't make it, so as a counterbalance, he sent in Lyla's strongest opponents. My palms begin to sweat. I have no clue how far reaching the formality of this PTA proposal is. Is my signature and Lyla's name enough?

* * *

'Ellie, do you want to start?' Mr Goh says to me in a grandfatherly manner. He places himself at the head of the table. Though I appreciate his kind gesture, it doesn't help my case. It makes me look like a kid, especially with Ibu Agatha sitting on my side and occasionally patting my forearm.

I pull the file out of my bag and go through the proposal quickly. When I'm done, there's a few seconds of stillness. Then Bernadet clears her throat.

'Forgive me,' she begins in a tone that clearly says she is not asking for anyone's forgiveness, 'I can't help but notice that there's not much change in the proposal from last year's. It doesn't represent every one of us.'

My heartbeat turns erratic. I want my sister. She would know how to deal with this. I'm not her. I'm a kid at this table. I'm glad Mr Goh is there. It calms me that there's someone older and wiser leading this meeting. I can be a kid for the duration of . . . however long this is.

'Ibu Bernadet, this is coming from the current PTA management, the same PTA that's democratically chosen by all Spring parents. I believe whatever is proposed there has been thought through thoroughly,' Mr Goh says.

'In that case,' Bernadet continues calmly as if she expected this answer, 'some of the parents would like to suggest that there be a time limit for the PTA management position. To make sure that there's balance and objectivity.'

Ibu Agatha scribbles furiously on her notebook. I look helplessly at the principal. Mr Goh nods his head several times as he swivels his chair. He reminds me of his nephew, who also swivelled his chair when he was in deep thought.

Stop thinking about him.

'Totally understandable. If you remember back then when we sat together to draft the rules and roles for our PTA, we put democracy at the top of everything else.' Mr Goh then turns to me, smiling, like a parent about to depart wisdom to his young daughter. 'Just to bring you up to speed, Ellie. Every year, the Spring community will submit names of other parents who they think are suitable to lead the PTA in the coming year. Once all the names are submitted, the school will run a poll digitally through our portal. Every parent will anonymously vote for their choice. The one with the largest number of votes becomes the PTA chairperson. This person can then choose their team based on the names already in the poll, or submit names of their own members to the school for our approval.' He turns his head towards Bernadet and Netty. 'We're very open with the voting process. In the past two years we saw that Ibu Lyla led the voting by more than 75 per cent. We're honouring democracy so, to answer your suggestion, no, the school won't interfere with the current system, Ibu Bernadet.'

My stomach, which has been clenching from the moment I entered the room, is starting to unclench. Perhaps this meeting is salvable. And wow, Lyla. More than 75 per cent? I knew it. My sister could rule the world if she put her mind to it.

Bernadet sits forward and rests her forearms on the table. 'If we run a motion of distrust, can we still fight for inclusion in the proposal?'

My stomach clenches again. What is this? And why does it sound like a political coup?

Mr Goh shrugs in a friendly manner. 'We support democracy thoroughly. Motion of distrust should be backed by 51 per cent of PTA members to be in action. I gather you've gotten 51 per cent?'

Bernadet nods. 'Sixty.'

'If I may ask,' Ibu Agatha says, 'what are the items you need to add to the current proposal?'

Bernadet's eyes flick to me. 'We've been submitting our suggested items to Dion. And yet as we can see here, none of our suggestions made the list. Either it was a mistake, or it's intentional, but it's disrespectful all the same. I personally think it's not in their best interest to work for a school they're not a part of.' She swings her laser eyes to Mr Goh. 'We've included a petition to remove the current chairpersons.' She pauses after stressing the plural form.

'And I suggest we appoint a new leader. *Preferably* someone who's currently available here and not somewhere overseas.'

My jaw drops. *A motion of distrust.* What the fuck? What the actual fuck? Is this a school or a government office?

I'm so livid, I'm shaking. I put my hands on my lap and will them to stop trembling. So, this is how Dion and his cronies sabotage Lyla. He didn't bother discussing the new items with me because he would rather send these two into the meeting and let them fire Lyla.

A small voice in my head says, *but they fired him too.*

But—a louder voice in my head argues—*he never wanted the role since the beginning.* He was here to babysit me. He was the school's safest choice. He didn't want to, but he had no choice. Bringing these two mothers in while he hides behind some hospital work is a cowardly move.

But it doesn't sound like the Dion I knew. On the other hand, it sounds exactly like the Dion who called me a mistake.

It's like someone has snapped their fingers in front of my eyes. That's it. *A mistake.*

I'm a mistake; I was one from the very start. Everyone saw that, even the school. Everyone felt that Lyla had erred in her judgment about me. I'm so caught up in my own turbulent thoughts that I completely miss the conversation, until Ibu Agatha gently nudges my arm. I jolt back into the room. The participants are currently staring at me.

Mr Goh smiles. 'What do you think, Ellie?'

'Umm . . . about what?'

He gestures casually around the room. While I'm sure I look stricken, he treats this meeting like we're discussing lunch. I'm outclassed in every way.

'Do you mind if Ibu Bernadet joins you as co-chairwoman so that we can have a more comprehensive program for the next year?'

'But I thought I'm . . . fired?'

Mr Goh chuckles. 'Nobody is firing anybody. I prefer we put our energy on improvement rather than destruction. We're nearing the end of our school year. There's a big gala coming up. Everyone is excited about it. I suggest we all work together to make our school year memorable. What do you say?'

When he puts it like that, I can't refuse. I also know I can't bail and use Lyla's name as a shield.

Oh, Lyla. I have failed her. She asked me to guard one thing, *this one thing only*, and I failed.

'Sure,' I say, unable to meet everyone's eyes.

'Perfect,' Mr Goh exclaims. 'Shall we extend the submission deadline by a week?'

Mr Goh alternates his attention between me and Bernadet. I'm frozen in my seat, trying to decide if my anger is louder than my fear. In the end, my fear and my aversion to conflict are stronger. I mutter a yes under my breath.

Bernadet turns to Mr Goh. In her firm and strong voice, she overrides me and cements her new position as the stronger ruler. 'You'll have it in *less* than a week, Mr Goh.'

And just like that we have three chairpersons on the PTA management on behalf of Lyla. One is more than enough, but three! I can't with this school.

This last PTA meeting sucks balls.

Chapter 17

Ellie

My anger takes me to the gym. I arrive a few minutes before the rehearsal starts. The longer I wait, the more furious I become, rumbling gigantic volcanoes erupting every few seconds under my skin.

When he sees me, he does a double take. Then he smiles and his steps quicken. By the time he reaches me, his smile has already taken over his entire face. Dion smiling is the stuff of legends, even when he looks dead tired all the time. This afternoon, he looks more crumpled than ever. Lines on his face have deepened, and the hollow that surrounds his eyes seems darker. His hair is wild as if it hasn't met a comb. No matter how pissed I am, my traitorous heart races at the sight of him; it also breaks at seeing how exhausted he is. Despite all that, my rage is fresher than everything else today.

At the look of my face, his smile wavers. 'What's wrong? Are the girls okay?'

Stabbing a finger on his chest, I hiss, 'If you want to kick me out, you tell it to my face. You don't go behind my back and stab my sister, you coward.'

His mouth drops and his eyes flash with hurt. 'What are you talking about?'

'I need to remind you, *all of you*, that Lyla has done nothing wrong. She hasn't violated the mandate given to her by the parents of Spring, nor has she failed in her job. PTA is still hers. We owe it to Lyla to respect and trust her leadership.'

'I agree,' he interjects.

'No, you don't!' I whisper-scream, then pull my hair out because I don't know how to make him *see*.

'Only cowards will try to take over her role when she's away. Just because you've been here all your life, it doesn't mean you can do whatever you want to other people. There are ethics, you . . . you entitled, selfish brat.' I shout the last sentence forcefully, my spits rain on his shirt.

His eyes turn dangerous, like a predator about to shred their prey. Taking a step towards me, his body is pulsing. Good. *Good*. Now we fight like equals.

But he doesn't shout. He doesn't even move his mouth. He brings his thunderous face close to me and hisses in a voice I don't recognize. '*I'm the entitled, spoiled brat? Me?*' He chuckles with so much bitterness, it sends a chill down my spine. I take a step back, my instinct detecting danger even when my brain refuses to acknowledge it.

'That's rich. Coming from someone who's exactly *that*,' he snaps. 'The likes of you are always the same.'

My breath hitches. *The likes of me?*

'Everything is about you, isn't it? *Every. Fucking. Thing!* It's you and your sister and your sister's proposal and back to you again. You called when you needed something. Then you threw me away when you were done. How very *generous* of you. Well, guess what, *petal*. Everything is *not* about you. Sometimes it has fucking nothing to do with you!'

My blood is roaring in my ears, and I want nothing else but to slap him. The security guards who stand by the gym doors turn their heads towards us. I take a deep breath and force my shoulders to roll away from my ears. Dion must have realized we have an audience because he takes an insane amount of air into his lungs and blows it out slowly through his mouth, his fists clenching and unclenching by his sides.

One of the guards salutes us. 'Afternoon, Kak Dion.'

Brother. He's always been their brother. Always will be.

Dion plasters a tight smile and nods.

'Is everything okay, Kak?' the guard asks, his eyes zeroing in on me.

'Yes, yes, we're fine,' Dion says. 'Problem with props,' he lies smoothly.

The guard smiles. 'Of course.' Then he sits back down and ignores us.

As soon as they leave us alone, Dion's dark eyes spare me no mercy. I'm pissed at him, but I'm also on the brink of tears. I hate our fights. I hate where I am now. I'm the world's greatest failure. This is why I shouldn't have taken the extra work. I can't handle pressure. I can't handle confrontation. I can't even handle my own life. I can't push myself to finish writing my resume. I shouldn't have been involved in Spring affairs at all.

As if he could hear the exact words in my head, his mouth curls menacingly and he says, 'I don't give a fuck about PTA and their politics. I told you before and I'm telling you again: you would have been better working together as a team rather than picking each other apart.' He rubs his eyes; they're red like he hasn't slept for ages. 'I just want to contribute to my alma mater the best I can. I owe it to them for taking me in and giving me a lifetime of an opportunity. I owe it to my parents and my uncle. I don't have that kind of entitlement to make every single fucking thing about me, *Ellie*. I just want to pay it forward. That's it. I just want to be there for these kids and my uncle.' His voice catches at 'uncle'.

Tears flow heavily down my face, and I don't even know what causes them. Funny how fast my boiling anger melts into crushing sadness. I don't want to fight. I don't want to see him broken. I've always wanted to be his friend, ever since we first met. I wipe my nose with the sleeve of my shirt. He must have mistaken my tears for something else. Maybe I do look like a spoiled brat who cries when they're being scolded.

His face hardens. 'When was the last time you took a risk, *Ellie*? When was the last time you fought for anything? That's right. You don't. You live your life so comfortably because you can afford it. Somebody will come and fix things for you. Your sister will swoop in and save your day. Not everyone has half the safety net you have, so spare me that privileged bullshit. Fix your own mess. I'm done. I quit your little PTA.'

No, no, no. He can't quit. How am I supposed to handle the other mothers, especially Bernadet and her gang? I need him to manage the PTA members. I need him to help me save Lyla's position.

'You can't quit,' I say a little breathlessly. 'Please . . .'

Help me.

Oh God. He's right. He's absolutely right. I'm a little girl who hides behind other people. I wait for them to clean up my messes.

I can't utter the rest of the words. I'm ashamed and desperate.

His posture stoops low, like he can't bear the invisible weight he carries around with him. He looks older, more tired, and vulnerable. He wipes his eyes, purposely not looking at me. The rise and fall of his chest has slowed; he's quiet when he says, 'Ellie. These mothers are not your enemies. You're equal to Ibu Bernadet or whoever you think challenges you. Stand up for yourself. You and the other mothers can sit together and be a team. We're here for the kids, yes? That's what PTA stands for: for the benefit of the school and the students, and not for an individual power flex. Am I wrong?'

I shake my head and hastily wipe my face.

He takes a closer look at me, and his expression turns tender. His fingers flex, his right hand is halfway raised, like he's about to touch me. Then he drops it. 'God, Ellie. How could you? Is that how you see me?' he whispers, and I cry harder.

For the longest time, none of us speaks. The dismissal bells ring through the quiet complex like a crying banshee. In the next few minutes, this place will be swamped by kids, parents, nannies, security guards, and school staff. Everyone will be eager to rehearse and work for the musical. Dion is too. And he looks so burnt out.

Dion is staring ahead at the parking lot. I feel what he feels. I want to run away too. I want to tell him that he can. He doesn't have to be here. He doesn't owe them anything. My blood is boiling again, but this time I'm angry *for* him.

High school students approach the gym in groups, their loud and merry banters reach my ears like a thousand thorns prickling at my skin. They wave at Dion when they see him. 'Hey, Kak Dion.'

Big brother. I smile despite myself. These kids adore him; he cares about them perhaps more than they know. What I see in Dion's face crushes my heart. From looking so distraught, he forces a smile out of his mouth, all the way to his eyes. I watch each of his facial muscles work, stretching in sync to create a perfectly, unconditionally happy face. I can't imagine the kind of mental manipulation it takes for him to do that. I can't even lower down the roar of blood in my ears, or stop the burning in my eyes. The urge to close this widening spasm between us and grab his hands is overwhelming, I bite down my teeth until I hear them crack.

Dion hoists his backpack higher and follows the students into the gym. Both times he left me like this—on the couch half naked and now by the gym doors crying a shitstorm—I want nothing more than to run to him and wrap my arms around his waist and ask him to stay.

Chapter 18

Ellie

'Why didn't we have a homework policy in your proposal?' I ask Lyla during our video call in the late evening. After I said goodnight to the girls, I went into my room and prepared myself for this conversation with Lyla. I have notes scattered in my bed.

'Homework policy?' She thinks about it for a moment. 'It's complicated, Ellie. I know what the concerns are. Always not enough; always too much. There's no single policy to fit them all. There are many studies on it and I'm sure Spring adheres to the international standard. I'm not an academic; it's very possible that the root of the things we need to change goes far deeper than this.'

That's Lyla the thinker.

'Even when I know a review is needed, I won't touch it. It's not where my expertise lies. I'd rather drive programmes that I know can provide results. Anything related to curriculum, the school would lead, as it should be. We're not driving the bus, you know what I mean?'

That's Lyla, the result-driven individual. A part of me agrees with my sister.

'Why do you ask?' Lyla says.

I shrug, trying to appear casual despite my anxiety and the heaviness of my heart. The issue with my feelings for Dion is personal, so I decide I won't share that with my sister, even when I very much want to. We share *yada yada yada* together, all the time, about almost everything.

'I noticed that the kids are swamped with homework after school,' I say. 'They have to stay up so late every day, even on weekends. Seems stupid to me.'

'It *is* stupid,' Lyla agrees. 'One thing that contributes to this situation is the dual curriculums we're running. Unfortunately, nobody gets more than twenty-four hours a day. It's a classic problem.'

I blanch. One curriculum is already tough. Imagine doing two. I'm glad I graduated high school years ago.

'Traffic is killing everyone,' I tell Lyla.

She groans in solidarity. 'I admit I don't miss it. Must be crazy with the musical approaching its big day.'

'Yes, it's worse,' I say. I'm glad she can't see me squeezing my fingers together. Lyla might be biased about Spring, but she's the only one I trust the most. I'm dying to pick apart her brain about this. 'Some parents have asked me to suggest staggered dismissal to the school management.'

'It won't work.' Her reply is fast and firm and sure.

My hope and confidence shatter. I always see Lyla as a problem-solver, a dictionary or a Google search, who always, *always* has a solution ready for every single problem. The fact that she was so certain nothing could help Spring's traffic situation is heartbreaking, not to mention demoralizing.

'How far are we going to *stagger* it?'

For a moment, I don't realize it's rhetorical.

Lyla says, 'The big kids would go home later, yeah? Teachers would go home later than the big kids, correct? That means the workers and staff would go home a lot later than the students and the teachers. There'll be costs to consider, Ellie. I don't mean Spring can't pay them. I just want you to understand that it's never *that* simple.'

'I didn't think of that,' I confess. I didn't think. Period.

I sink lower in my bed. 'So, there's nothing we can do? We have to live like this forever?'

'Oh, there's always something we can do,' Lyla says with a smile. It's silly how relieved I am to see it on her face. Lyla can't lose hope. Throughout my entire life, Lyla has meant hope. 'The gain, however, might not be worth the effort, Ellie. It won't bring much relief to the chronic problem we face. Remember, we have time and resource constraints. Gotta choose our battle wisely.'

I won't be discouraged by Lyla the logic. 'I have time, Lyla. I want to try something about the flow inside the school. Do you mind if I play around?'

'*Do I mind?*' Lyla laughs. 'Are you seriously asking me this?'

Umm . . .

'Ask for general affairs. They will show you the layout of the school. Play around. Ask for their input.'

I jot down the information in my phone.

'Talk with Dion too,' Lyla instructs. 'He's been with Spring longer than any of us. He's smart. He can fill you in about the issues he sees from the student's point of view.'

'I will.' It's scary how easily I lie to Lyla. Dion's exhausted and anguished face has been haunting me since yesterday. His words hurt; his dismissal hurts more. I'm the selfish, privileged kid who has a wide safety net under my feet. The more I think about it, the more convinced I am that he's right.

'Anyway.' Lyla brightens. 'How is the progress with my proposal?'

'I submitted it yesterday.' I don't exactly lie. I submitted it, but it was being bombed, thus we need a new one. Lyla doesn't need to know this . . . *yet.*

'Everyone okay with it?' she asks.

Kill me already.

* * *

The following week, I chair our last PTA meeting with Bernadet as my co-chairwoman. Since every meeting room in the school is occupied, naturally the mothers move the venue to the fancy café in a nearby mall. Ironically, it's the same café where I rescued Dion from the morning traffic. It was only last month, but it feels like it was ages ago. I haven't heard from him since our blow-up last week, not that I reached out to him. I'm scared to even try. There's nothing we can do to come back from the hurt we've caused each other.

Everyone dressed as immaculately as ever at 8.30 a.m. on a Tuesday morning. We exchange greetings and order ourselves cute little cups of coffee. Though the menu consists of only two pages, these women take forever to complete their orders. They get themselves almost everything, in double portions, all under the *we'll share* pretense.

Since I'm a bundle of nerves this morning, I avoid caffeine. I get myself a cup of ginger tea and a plate of peanut butter kaya toast. Tara insists I must try their half-boiled eggs. I politely decline but of course she orders it for me anyway.

'You and I can share,' she assures me.

Bernadet and I sit opposite each other in the middle of the long table. Everyone seems to acknowledge the tension and the *it's-no-joke* vibes from us, so the other mothers are on their best behaviour this morning. Even Tara looks sober on this bright day.

Putting on my big girl pants, I dive straight into the matter. 'I've been thinking about each of the issues you brought up, with special focus on homework policy and traffic situation, as per your request, Ibu Bernadet. I agree with you. These two are urgent.'

Bernadet looks at me with calculating eyes for a minute. Then she nods and says, 'Call me Bernadet, Ellie.'

I'm taken aback by the lack of venom in her voice, but I welcome every positivity thrown my way. This time, I came in prepared. I worked with the mindset that there was no safety net under my feet. I researched like my life depended on it. I talked to Lyla in great length about PTA roles last weekend. I asked for a copy of PTA's vision and mission from Ibu Agatha.

'Lyla has a point of not trying to spend our time on things that we can't control. On the other hand, I trust that the vision of PTA is to be the balancing voice that will notify the school if something is not right.'

It's for the kids, Dion's voice whispers inside my head.

'Complicated issues require complicated solutions.' I look at the faces around me, faces I have become familiar with in the past few months. They bicker, they laugh, they bitch, they complain, but they are also the first to lend a hand whenever the school, the kids, the PTA organization need help. I learned my lesson the hard way for labelling these mothers as one thing. They are many things. They're far from perfect, but they're the best comrades Spring has ever had. They're in the right place, in the right shape, with deep enough pockets to make a difference. I won't say their methods are always right, though.

'Homework policy.' I clear my throat. 'Without trying to create too many earthquakes, let's say we choose a certain grade level and try the new approach with them for a year. I see many of you have kids in primary. What if we begin our homework trial with them? Before we continue our discussion, I'd like to remind everyone that the school will have a final say on this.'

'If the school will have the final say on this'—Bernadet tilts her head—'what is our role here?'

'Our role is to provide data to the school, not the sporadic complaints we throw at the teachers. It's *homework*. Work to be done at *home*. Who knows it better than parents?' I put in my own experience as a student when I cooked up this solution. I know a thing or two about homework.

There's a shift in the weight Bernadet assesses me. I think it's called respect, but I won't let my ego fly with it. I sip my lukewarm tea. It tastes horrible, but maybe it's just my nerves.

'What does Lyla say about this?' one of the mothers asks.

'I'd love to know what you think first,' I answer, incorporating Dion's diplomatic gesture when dealing with these mothers. The powerful, smart, helicopter, ambitious type of mothers.

They're harmless, Dion's voice is like my uninvited conscience. *They just need people to listen to them and take them seriously.*

The truth is, I haven't told Lyla about these additions yet. My best defence is, if I only add small suggestions on top of Lyla's original plan, I think I can convince my sister to go along with me.

Bernadet sips her coffee. 'How about the traffic?'

I like that she wastes no time in coming to me with another strike. The scene from my first morning flashes behind my eyes, and then my panic attack when I had a sick Aureli in the backseat. I don't stutter when I reply to Bernadet. 'We could start by proposing some small changes around the campus. As a matter of fact, I'm drawing them into the proposal.'

I reach into my canvas bag and pull out a piece of folded paper. The mothers who sit close to me help clear the table. It's trace paper I usually use for my architecture class. I've copied the Spring original blueprint, then added the new adjustments as per my discussion with the general affairs manager. I spent a few sleepless nights finishing this and I'm proud of it.

I tap a few points on the paper. The mothers circle me, our heads bent over my drawing. 'We'll try to introduce a different flow in the afternoon dismissal, here and here. We'll also be setting up ground rules in our parking spaces. Over here, here, and here. Some entrances to the parking area will be closed.'

I answer a few questions from these mothers. After a few minutes, everyone sits back at their seat. I put the paper back inside my bag. If they agree, I'll redraw it with the proper scale and attach it to our revised proposal to Mr Goh. It means another sleepless night, but with Lyla's chef at my disposal—she literally can make anything I request, including the strongest coffee and the meanest chocolate cookies as a midnight snack—sleepless nights have nothing on me.

I sip my drink while I nervously, and excitedly, wait. It's like presenting my project to my clients. My mother is right (of course she is). It feels different when it's my own effort. It's sweeter.

To my absolute astonishment, Bernadet smiles at me. 'Impressive, Ellie. Your 3.8 GPA really shows.'

I let out my breath slowly. 'Thank you.'

'I'd say go for it,' one mother on my right says.

'Yes, let's do this,' the other echoes.

'I agree. A fresh perspective from an outsider always helps put things into focus,' Bernadet compliments me, and the intense air around us relaxes immediately. She holds her cup in front of her mouth. 'So, when is Lyla back? The school is not the same without her. No offence, Ellie. You're a sweet kid, but your sister is a riot.'

My table whoops with buzzes and giggles and the now all too familiar motherly chit-chat. I sit back and watch them. My heart is full *and* in pieces at the same time. I wish Dion could see this. I want to gloat to his face, 'I'm not a quitter, doll-face,' and eagerly hear his sarcastic comeback.

'Lyla misses home,' I tell the mothers. 'Hopefully she can come back to catch the musical.'

'Oh, she must,' Tara exclaims.

'It'd be weird to be a part of the school's momentous milestone without Lyla,' Netty adds.

'I'm glad that you were there for the meeting with Mr Goh,' I tell Bernadet quietly.

'Me too,' she says, not unkindly. 'I bumped into him at the Chinese restaurant upstairs. Have you tried it, Ellie? Their dim sum is legendary.' She turns around to address the other moms who are eager to listen to any bit of gossip about their principal, 'He and his wife had just finished dinner when my family arrived. It's been a while since the last time we had a casual chat. He invited me to the meeting, so I went.'

My blood turns cold. I lashed out at Dion and accused him of worse things when in fact, he was innocent. Shit, *shit.*

The chit-chat merrily goes on. I hear snippets of excitement here and there.

'Do we know if the president will attend?'

'The minister of education will. I heard his office has sent back the RSVP.'

A fierce feeling that gives me goosebumps spreads through me, followed by a slight tremor of pride. I'm so proud of Spring's musical and their cast and crew. My two nieces are in it. They're part of their school's history. My creation is in it too. The ship is the biggest, most complicated piece of work in the whole prop set, and I'm—*me, Ellie*—the design lead of that team.

The talk pivots, and my ears pick up a familiar name.

'Poor Dion. I can't imagine what that's like.'

'I remember somebody texted me about the accident. Was it you, Rosa?' Bernadet shakes her head in dismay. She takes one glance at me, then explains, 'He missed our principal's meeting because of it.'

My throat burns. 'Because of what?'

'The highway accident. You didn't read the news? It happened the night before our meeting,' Bernadet says, clearly failing to notice how fast the blood has drained from my face. 'Multiple casualties.'

Tara makes a low, sympathetic noise. 'Only one boy survived.'

'The mother and their youngest son survived,' someone corrects Tara. 'Dion had to stay with the kid through the night,

I heard. I cannot imagine. Ibu Agatha often tells me she suspects Dion is still traumatized from losing his own father at such a young age.'

My ribcage collapses onto itself. I can't breathe.

Everything is not always about you.

The mother next to Bernadet gasps, a hand to her chest. 'We should throw him a proper farewell party.'

'Wh-what party?' I'm so lost here.

'Dion's party,' she replies, grinning at everyone.

'Why a farewell party?'

Tara gives me a *duh* look. 'He's due for his internship.'

'But it wouldn't happen until . . . later?' I need some air. I'm about to faint. There are dark splotches in my vision.

Tara shrugs. 'It doesn't matter. We'll throw him a party anyway.'

It matters to me, I want to scream at Tara. It matters a lot to me. 'Tara.'

She turns to me with her bright smile.

'When will his internship start?' I'm so afraid to hear the answer, I grip the edge of my chair like I'm going to shred it apart.

She must've sensed the urgency in my voice because she doesn't ask any more questions. 'I heard him say at least one or two years from now.'

Like a puppet doll that has been released from its string, I collapse against my seat. Relief floods into my body like cool waterfall and I savour every moment of it. 'Thank god,' I tell Tara, laughing rather hysterically now. 'I thought you guys meant soon after the gala or something.'

Chapter 19

Dion

'I have something to tell you,' I say as I sit at the dining table with my uncle and aunt. The news I'm about to share is huge, and I only have less than an hour to do it before I have to leave for work. I purposely took a day off from rehearsal this afternoon so I can catch my uncle at home before my shift. 'I'll start my mandatory internship soon.'

My uncle looks up from his plate. There's no surprise on his face. We all know this was bound to happen sooner than later. In a way, they've been encouraging me to complete it as soon as possible so I can continue my study in the cardiovascular field after I come back from it.

'How soon?' my aunt asks.

I made my mother promise not to tell my aunt and uncle because I wanted to be the one to deliver the news to them. They deserve to hear this from me.

'2nd June.'

My uncle's jaw drops. 'Right after the gala?'

I avoid his stare. Truth is, my original start date was 20th September. But that night, after Ellie accused me of sabotaging her sister's PTA, I was so mad, so sad, and so eager to move on, I was twitching to do something. *Anything*. In those lonely hours, I drifted back to the past. Why did I study medicine? Why did I choose cardiovascular? The answer: because I was drowning in sorrow almost two decades ago. I felt my mother's arms around me, trying to pull me to her, but I couldn't move a muscle. And then my face morphed into Anton's, and I was the one who tried to keep him afloat. More than once, I fought the urge to get the boy's medical record and steal his contact number. I needed to know how he was doing. I desperately needed to know if he was okay.

The internship would put me in remote place outside the main island of Java. The purpose is to help the underprivileged get better medical treatment, while at the same time test our skills and knowledge. Every med student has to do it for a year. In my hazy fog of passion and anger, I volunteered myself to fill any immediate spot the government might have. I put down my parent's hometown as preference, knowing well I wouldn't be lucky enough to get it. But surprisingly, I did. In the next few days, I'm going back *home* to where my mom is. It feels right that the next phase of my life will bring me back to my birthplace. The date though, is a little bit shocking because it cuts so close to my other big responsibility. I wouldn't have signed up had I not fought with Ellie. I might have stayed back and tried to get to know her. I might have wanted to be her friend, and if she let me, be more than her friend. But now, I'll never know. Things have broken between us before they could take shape. I also hate myself for making one of the biggest decisions of my career based on what happened with her. I let someone else dictate my actions. Too late to cancel now. The paperwork for this kind of cancellation is said to be longer than my medical textbook.

'I'm stationed in the suburb of Samarinda. I told Mami already.'

My aunt covers her mouth with her hand. 'That's great news.'

'Thank you,' I say. I turn to my uncle. 'I'm sorry about your holiday plan.'

My uncle waves me off. 'We can always have our holiday after you're back. I'm just surprised. This is sudden. You only have a few days left.'

'Do you need to prepare anything? Something to buy?' my aunt asks.

'It's not like I'm gonna live in the jungle. There's no need to prepare anything.' I throw my aunt a mischievous wink. 'I'd like to remind you that this is my national duty. I can't go there looking glamorous.'

They laugh.

'You know what,' my aunt says with a flourish, 'I'll take you.'

'To the airport?' I ask.

'To Samarinda, silly. I wanna see the place where you'll work and visit your mother.' She claps. 'Oh, this is going to be wild!'

I stare at her, bewildered. 'Didn't you hear what I just said? I'm going there for work. This is not a school fieldtrip.'

'Oh, school fieldtrips.' My aunt throws her head back and snorts. She nudges my uncle. 'Do you remember that one time when he forgot to pack underwear and had to spend a week on the trip going commando?'

My mouth drops. 'I did not!'

My uncle joins his wife in laughing at me. 'I don't remember that, but I do recall his goth phase when he only wore black. We had to scour every mall to find him all-black underwear.'

They dissolve into chuckles. I sit there defiantly denying all false accusations while my heart quietly melts until there's nothing inside me but a pool of happiness.

'He used to be this tall.' My aunt indicates my height by comparing it to our dining table. She leans back. 'Look at him now. We have a smart-ass doctor in the house.'

My uncle holds his wife's hand, his eyes fondly regard me. 'I think we did alright.'

'In raising a wise-ass? You bet.'

For a moment, they both just sit there looking at me but not quite looking at me. They're looking at me through time and memories. Bittersweet memories. My eyes are suddenly hot as hell.

'So, your internship takes one year,' my uncle says, 'then your specialty study is . . .'

'Five to six years.'

My aunt whistles. 'That's a lot of years.'

'Dion. Listen.' My uncle leans forward, so I do too. 'We know your mother has prepared some savings for your study . . .'

I tense up immediately.

'Your aunt and I have saved some for you too.'

Oh no, no, no. 'No need, Uncle. I can look for a scholarship, or a job—'

He holds up a hand. 'You don't have to apply for anything. The money is there and it's yours. You can use it for your study now and keep your mom's money for future use, or vice versa. Totally up to you. The point is, it's there.'

No matter how hard I inhale, I can't seem to get any air in. I choke out, 'I can't.'

'Of course you can,' my uncle says, gently. 'We want you to take it. Your mother too. We planned this together.'

Next to him, my aunt nods, her eyes misty.

I shake my head. 'I can't pay you back, Uncle. I don't even know how I'm supposed to pay for all the years I lived here.'

My uncle's and aunt's excited expressions change into shock.

'Pay me back?' my uncle says, his voice has gone low. He's using his principal tone, the one he uses when he's displeased with something. Without ceremony, he pushes to his feet and leaves me and my aunt alone in the dining room.

But he must understand, right? He must know that I can't possibly take more generosity from him. I've already died from carrying the burden of his past kindness, I can't possibly add more. I glance helplessly at my aunt. When she speaks, I hear only disappointment in her voice. 'If you were fifteen, I would've defended you. I get where you're coming from because your mother is the same. But you're *twenty-five*, Dion. You *choose* to self-sabotage your life. You choose to hurt him.'

I look down at the table, surprised to see my own tears dripping onto it.

'Well, what are you waiting for?' my aunt demands.

I look up at my aunt, wishing nothing more than her to hold my hands and tell me what to do like she did when I was still a child. 'What should I say?'

She makes a sharp *tch-ing* sound. 'You already know what to say. Just say it. The world won't stop turning just because you utter them.'

* * *

I find my uncle standing before his bookshelf in his study. He has his back to me when I enter. Whenever I'm in this room, my uncle seems bigger than he actually is. I look up to him. This is the man I respect. The man I'm trying so hard not to disappoint.

I know he heard me come in but he chooses to ignore me. I don't take more steps from the threshold. A few seconds go by. Then he exhales. 'Have you told the kids that you're leaving soon?' He means my *Wrecking Sea* teammates.

'After the show. They're already nervous enough, no need to add more pressure,' I say.

He finally turns and faces me. I deserve longer silent treatment from him, but just like that, I'm forgiven. I don't deserve it. I don't deserve him, a father figure who took me in and raised me. Fifteen years, and I still can't believe my luck. I'm often gripped by terror that one day he'll be taken away from me too and I'll lose two fathers. The fear I groom inside my head is so enormous, I'm aware how often it overshadows my logic. I'm experiencing the sudden thickness in my throat. I still haven't said the words I need to say. From my spot near the door, I watch him pace in front of the bookshelf.

'Is there anything else you need me to tie up before I go?' I ask.

'Don't worry about Spring. By the way, PTA has submitted their newest proposal. It's quite different from the ones I usually get.'

Nobody knows I quit PTA but Ellie. I wonder if she told anyone about it.

My uncle pulls out his phone and taps the screen a few times. He shows it to me. 'Impressive work.'

I take the phone from him. Using my thumb and index finger, I enlarge the pdf file and begin to read. They have put, among other things, traffic and homework initiatives, the two major ones that have always been ignored by previous management. There's an attachment of the suggested traffic flow at the bottom of the file, in perfect scale, in some sort of architectural 3D drawing. There's no mistaking whose drawing this is. Looks like she managed to handle the other mothers by herself. If I could name what I feel right now in one word, it'd be pride.

I hand the phone back to my uncle. 'It's all Ellie.' Though I appear calm in front of him, my emotions are loud.

'Oh?' my uncle says.

So, he doesn't know that Ellie and I are no longer speaking to each other.

My uncle shakes his head in amusement. 'It won't make any difference during peak hours, but it might avoid unnecessary blockages in certain areas. Who knows, this might work.'

Her crying face when she told me she had to push some cars just to get out with Aureli sick in the backseat comes back. 'It's better than what we're dealing with now.'

'Oh boy, I agree,' my uncle says, sighing a little. Congestion has been a headache ever since the school was built. It'll be a forever-headache for Spring. If I were the principal, I'd welcome any suggestions on how to make our life more bearable. Improvement is a long shot, but comfort can be fought for and won in nooks and corners.

'Can I have a copy of that?' I ask. This is probably the closest to Ellie I can be for now. I convince myself it's for the better. I'm leaving anyway. She will too, once her sister is back from London. We were always meant to move in a separate direction.

'I'm sending it to you.' My uncle comes over to me and taps on his phone.

He's so close, our arms are almost touching. I break the walls around me and hug him, so tight I knock the breath out of his lungs.

'*Thank you.*' The two words that've been teasing my tongue for as long as I can remember but have no courage to leave my mouth. My aunt is right. The world doesn't plunge into total darkness after I say them.

My uncle freezes, but then his arms go around my shoulders and he squeezes me back. We break apart just as suddenly and turn slightly away from each other to discreetly wipe our eyes. We're not used to showing physical affection to one another. This is a lot for both of us.

My aunt finds us exactly like that, standing close but avoiding each other's eyes. She takes a quick look at us and folds her arms across her chest. 'Are you gonna be here forever, or will you come back and finish dinner?'

As we walk back to the dining room, I loop an arm around my aunt. She side-eyes me affectionately before wrapping her arm around my waist.

'I'll do the dishes,' I offer.

She scoffs. 'Of course you will. Who did you expect would do them? Me?'

I laugh. My chest hurts when I realize I'm going to miss them like hell, the way I miss my mother. I will forever carry a part of guilt for not being able to be everywhere for everyone all at once. I will always worry that something bad might happen to one of them while I'm not there. I know this is the price of choosing. But if this is the price I have to pay for having three parents who love me unconditionally instead of one, I'll take it.

I'll take it. I'll take it. I'll take it.

Chapter 20

Ellie

When I arrive at the multi-purpose hall in the afternoon, the gym is incredibly packed. Every cast and crew member is here for the dress rehearsal, including the support system like the staff, PTA members, and third-party contractors and vendors.

Since I'm on the stage, I have a bird's eye view of the gym. I find Dion easily because apparently my internal body is a compass and he's my North. As though we're tied by some invisible rope, we're acutely aware of each other despite the distance between us. One of us will immediately look away, feeling embarrassed for being busted for staring. But after a few games of cat and mouse, we decide to drop our pretences and hold each other's gaze and dare the other to look away first. His eyes on me are as sharp as the pinch of a needle on my arm. Other times, it's gentle, teasing me with softness, like the feeling of sipping a cup of warm tea. Sometimes it's dark like a mystery I dare not solve.

'How's our ship?' I ask my teammates. These students look tired, but they move like they're fully charged. The blessing of youth and many, many cups of coffee.

The ship will be fully used in all the scenes that require it today. The performers will control the ship movements manually with various combinations of ropes. Our Prince Eric will christen the deck with his presence later, for the first time after five months of rehearsal. He'll be standing and singing from inside the ship, on narrow steps made out of board and plywood.

My deepest worry is its height. The two additional steps that Ibu Sylvia requested make the ship a little too heavy on the top. I'm so nervous, I had a nightmare that the ship sank into the bottom of the gym. I can't imagine what it's like to be the cast. The day after tomorrow is the *grand day*. In front of a VIP audience. A thousand seats, fully booked since a few months ago. Ashley whines of having cramps every time before rehearsal. Aureli still giggles like a happy child but even that carefree kid has started going to bed early every night without being asked twice.

I press my palm against the hull. *Please behave.* My creation answers my prayer by standing firm in all its glory in front of me. I still can't believe my eyes. I designed and built the biggest 3D prop in this musical. This will go on my resume for damn sure.

'Should we call Roy now?' One of my teammates asks, referring to the student who is cast as Prince Eric.

'Can we test it first without passengers?' I stall.

'Everything will be perfect,' the other teammate says beside me. 'Just chill.'

I want to put my hand on her mouth because what she said sounds jinx-y.

'It's show time, team,' Jonas says, warming up his hands. 'Ellie, wanna do the honours?' He tosses the rope to me.

I seriously do not, but I guess I have to. It's my big baby after all. I flex my fingers as my team cheers me on.

Ibu Sylvia saunters towards us. 'While waiting for Roy, can I have a go first?'

I close my eyes. *No.*

'I'll do it,' comes a familiar, deep voice. Dion and his team materialize on the stage. 'Might as well,' he tells Ibu Sylvia. 'It's us who will push and pull the ship anyway.'

Jonas and Ibu Sylvia look at me expectantly. The weight of Dion's eyes is like a hot brand against my skin—poking, twisting, burning. I can't keep finding excuses not to start the testing just because I have impostor syndrome. I avoid Dion's eyes at all costs when I answer the unspoken question with a small nod. I join my crew on the side while Jonas, Ibu Sylvia, and the members of *The Wrecking Sea* form a circle. A lot of hand gestures happen before they step away from the huddle. Ibu Sylvia stands at the edge of the stage by herself, her posture rigid, expression tight with controlled excitement. Jonas and Dion crouch down to place the ropes. Then Jonas joins Ibu Sylvia as Dion climbs into the ship and stands in the front, holding onto the plywood banister I've assembled myself. Despite the distance between us, our eyes meet. My mouth moves. 'Careful.' I doubt he can read it from where he stands.

'Hold tight, Kak Dion,' the boys from *The Wrecking Sea* shout from below, three of them holding the ropes in their hands. He gives them a thumbs-up. I ball my fists so tight, the nails dig into my palms.

'On my mark,' one of the students yells, 'three, two, pull.'

They give the ropes a tug. The ship jerks forward at the first pull. It looks like it's gliding on the waves. My chest explodes with relief. Thank god, it works.

My teammates cheer. Ibu Sylvia shouts something to the dancers. Jonas links his hands behind his head and stares up at the ship.

Dion signals his team to stop pulling. The ship gradually sails to a stop, then it sways towards the stage wall. It goes so very slowly, thanks to the weight of the ship, but there's no mistaking what is about to happen next. Everyone around me shouts and jumps into action but I'm paralyzed. My eyes widen with terror and I can't tear my gaze off Dion. As the ship tilts, so does he. And he's a few meters high above the ground.

'No,' I whisper. 'No, no, no.'

Dion tries his best to balance himself with nothing much but his own body. *The Wrecking Sea* crew, technicians, Jonas, and Ibu Sylvia try to push the ship to the left. For a moment, their attempt halts the ship's descent, but the damage is already done. The top of the mast pierces the props on the wall. It finally crashes. I see Dion get thrown against the wall. He hangs on the banister for a moment before he slides down the wall and onto the floor. It happens fast, but in my mind, it goes blow-by-blow like a slow-motion movie scene. I know exactly when his right shoulder makes contact with the wall. I know exactly when he grunts, when he uses the wall to push himself upright. He's pale, all the way to his lips.

My hand flies to my mouth.

People crowd the spot where he fell. I can't see him. From the gym floor, young kids run to the stage amidst the shouts from their teachers to stay clear. Commotion is everywhere, just like that first day when students and nannies and mothers were running towards the maroon gates to beat the bell. The whole gym transforms into one gigantic wave, and it sweeps me off my feet. I'm without ground.

* * *

Dion

I've lost count of how many times I sat here on this small single bed. Sport injuries were common since I played almost all the sports, but the occasional nosebleed, case of cold, or food poisoning also brought me here. The school nurse, Ibu Ninik, was alarmed when my crew and Ibu Sylvia rushed me in.

After a glance at my right arm, she quickly dismisses everyone. When they stubbornly remain by my side, filling the already small room to a point where we can all smell each other's sweat, Ibu Ninik raises her voice and orders everyone out. One by one my friends exit the clinic. Ibu Sylvia stays.

'Let's take a look,' Ibu Ninik says to me. Her face has age spots and lines; she's also gained weight, but her eyes and smile are as motherly as I remember them. I pull up my sleeve. The two women bend their heads to inspect my wound.

'Lucky boy,' Ibu Ninik says, adjusting her glasses. 'Only scratches.'

I know my wound is only skin deep, but for the sake of the musical I agree to let them fuss over me.

Ibu Sylvia leaves me with a gentle rub on my head. 'You're in good hands.'

When it's just us, Ibu Ninik sighs my name with a head shake. 'You have to injure yourself two days before the big day.'

'I didn't ask for it,' I reply. 'I think I hurt my back too. My right shoulder blade.' I take off my shirt.

She moves behind me and clucks her tongue. 'What did you collide with? It looks like your skin has been shredded by tiny bears.'

'Must be the sharp panels.' The wall is decorated with some rocks and seashells. I try to take a look at my back, but I can't see much without a mirror. I inspect my shirt instead. From the tears and the holes on the fabric, I can imagine how my back looks like. It's not pretty.

'It's already swollen.' She gingerly presses the skin around the wound. It stings. 'Good news is, I don't think you need stiches, but the wound is wide. Can you still dance?'

I roll my right shoulder and stretch my right arm in front of me. Don't feel any cracks or twists other than the localized burns. 'If I can't, Martin is more than ready to take over.'

'Let's clean it and we'll see.' She hums as she prepares Betadine and rolls of bandages. Her movements are slow, and sometimes she has to adjust her glasses to see her hands. I don't remember ever thinking of her as anything but a strong and capable nurse. But that was a decade ago.

'I can do it.' I try to take the scissors from her.

She slaps my hand away. 'I'm the nurse.'

'I'm the doctor.'

'Can the doctor dress a wound on his back?'

I grin sheepishly. These people always manage to make me feel like I'm seventeen again. 'No, ma'am.'

'That's right, Mr smarty-pants. Now hold still. This will sting.'

I clench my teeth and brace myself.

Thirty minutes later, my wounds are all cleaned and dressed. I took some painkillers. For old time's sake, Ibu Ninik offers me candy, which I decline, and a bottle of water, which I accept.

There's a knock on the door. We both turn and find Ellie standing at the threshold. I can't describe the feelings I'm having at seeing her this close and not from across the gym. It's like my stomach has bottomed out and my heart is shooting up to the sky at the same time and I'm left stranded in the middle, not sure which way I want to go.

But gosh. How much I missed her.

'Can I help you?' Ibu Ninik asks.

Ellie's eyes flick to me. 'Is he okay?'

'Oh, he's . . .' Ibu Ninik smiles at me. 'He can answer that for himself. Come on in.' She drags a plastic chair that's been in this clinic for years closer to my bed and gestures for Ellie to sit. Ellie awkwardly holds the back of the chair like it's a shield between us. She remains standing, biting her lip and fidgeting with her fingers.

Okay, she's nervous. So am I. My heart is back in my body and it's now racing like nobody's business. I find myself unable to tear my eyes off her. She looks a little pale but nonetheless, sweet and adorable. The splotches of red on her cheeks remind me of rose petals. There is dirt and grease on her arms and shirt. Last time we met, we were shouting hurtful things at each other. Nothing much has happened between us since then, but there are big leaps that have happened to us since then too. I feel like I'm found, but I'm still lost.

'Do you want some tea?' Ibu Ninik asks Ellie.

'Oh, no thank you. I won't be long,' Ellie answers.

I clutch the bed sheet a little too hard, one of the fitted edges pops out.

'I'll get you tea,' Ibu Ninik says like a boss, then to my horror, winks at me before she leaves.

The moment we're alone, Ellie shoves the chair aside. I jump to my feet because for a fleeting second I think she's going to kill me. She charges forward like a military tank, her face thunderous. She rounds the bed and sees my back. 'Fuck!'

I quickly hide my wound from her view. We're circling the bed like two kids playing a game of tag. The clinic is such a small space, there's really not a lot of room for us to run around. Eventually my back will meet something hard, most likely wall. I halt her by raising my hands in front of me.

'Turn around,' she demands.

'No.'

'For god's sake, Dion.'

'I'm fine.'

She screams, 'Your back doesn't look fine.' She points at my injured arm and shouts, 'That doesn't look fine.'

Shocked by her outburst, I mutely watch her put her knuckle into her mouth. The moment she releases her hand from her teeth, a rush of words tumbles out of her. 'I don't want you to think that I purposely sabotaged the play. I was afraid this might happen with the additional height, but I didn't deliberately plan for this disaster. I didn't expect it to crash.' She touches her forehead and briefly closes her eyes. 'I knew we should've tested a few more times. I knew it, I knew it. Now you're hurt and it's my fault. I'm making a fucking mess. Fuck, fuck, fuck this!'

It takes me a while to realize that she's talking about her threat a long time ago. I'm engulfed by a wave of nausea and sadness. Am I that horrible that she thought I would think of her like that? I must be, because other than this, she also labelled me as a spoiled brat. I know my personality is not always sunshine and rainbows, but I'm certain I don't suck that bad in making an impression.

Without thinking, I pull her into me. It's like holding a statue, her arms stay at her sides, her fists are balled tight. The only indication that she's a human being is the warm air she breathes through her mouth and the wetness of her tears on my chest.

'It was an accident, that's all.' I'm afraid to let her go, afraid that if I do, she'll break into pieces. 'I'm okay. No harm done.'

We remain standing like this for a long moment. Our own breathing is the only thing I hear. I close my eyes and smell her hair. I've imagined holding her again so many times after our fight.

'You ran out of my apartment.'

The words are soft, almost like a caress against my skin. My eyes snap open. I knew I'd screwed up, but it's not until I hear the accusation that I realize how much, and how deeply, I've hurt her. I tighten my arms and lower my face until my mouth is next to her ear. 'I shouldn't have done that. I'm sorry, petal. I'm so, so sorry.'

Her hands move along my sides before resting on my waist above my pants.

'I trusted someone once,' I continue, 'and she hurt me. I vowed I would never put myself in that position again. You reminded me of her. I was scared.'

'I'm not her,' she says softly with her mouth pressed against my beating heart.

'You're not,' I murmur. Quite the opposite, in fact. I smile as I feel her body melt into me. 'You make me happy, Ellie.'

There's a choking sound, then she fiercely hugs me. A small oof escapes my mouth. I snuggle my nose against the crook of her neck. She responds by pulling me closer, if that's even possible. Her hands are now splayed on my lower back, holding me in place. I'm so happy, I might cry.

'I don't know what to do, Dion,' she says after a while. She angles her face up. 'What if I can't fix the ship in time?'

I look at her smiling eyes that are now wet with tears. 'Don't you dare quit, okay? I won't let you.'

She pushes me off, and for a split second my heart drops. She must be mad at me, but then she sob-laughs into her hand, and mutters, 'You pompous ass.'

Butterfly wings flutter in my ribcage. I run my fingers down her cheek. I love seeing the blush that trails after my touch. There are so many things I want to say to her, and I don't know where, or how, to begin. But she's here now, I tell myself. If I got struck by lightning inside this damn clinic, I'd have no regrets.

She touches my forearm, then looks at me. Something in her expression shifts the air between us.

'I heard about the accident,' she says. 'I'm sorry about your patients.'

It's like I'm being punched in the gut. I stagger backwards, my arm swings down from her face. I don't know how far she's aware of what that accident and what happened to Anton meant to me, what they reminded me of. My whole body suddenly feels as heavy as lead, so I sit back down at the edge of the bed. My deep-rooted anger and all the bad memories are slowly eating me alive.

Someone grabs my face. Before I can blink, she's there, standing between my legs and kissing me. She kisses me so urgently; the force nearly topples me off the bed. I think I hear her chant *stay with me, stay with me* into my mouth. I'm not sure how, but her presence pushes my anger to the side. I kiss her back like she's my freedom. My other senses rush to the surface.

'Ellie.' My voice is rugged and I'm breathing hard. 'I didn't mean what I said about you and your sister. I was furious and I took it out on you.'

Her expression mellows. 'You did mean it. And you are right.'

'No, no, I was wrong. I swear I had nothing to do with Ibu Bernadet coming to the meeting—'

'Shhh. I know. I know.'

I'm frantic, panicked, momentarily caught in a world where confusion and relief clash. I register how my hands shake as they stumble to touch her. I kiss her again. It's the only thing I can think of that will anchor me to the present. She tastes so good, sweet and salty, like the best combination of all desserts.

Salty.

I seem to be the reason for most of her crying. I wipe her cheeks the best I can. 'Petal, please don't cry.'

She smiles. 'You first.'

Puzzled, I wipe my own face with the back of my hand. I'm surprised to see it wet.

There's a strong emotion on her face I can't quite describe.

'*I won't hurt you*, Dion,' she whispers, 'I promise.'

There's a savage burning in my throat. '*I know.*'

With me sitting and her standing, we're basically at the same height. She gently dries my face with her thumbs. 'I missed you.'

I'm melting. Gooey, wobbly, and incredibly silly. I'm blind with happiness. Her scent is everywhere around me. My body explodes in a confetti of sensations. I pull at her waist and flush our mouths together. There's a raging fire in the pit of my stomach. I remember our first kiss in her apartment, how it burned us both, how we almost lost control. I can't do that to her here of all places. Despite the urgency in my gut, I force myself to breathe and just be. It's like pressing the brake when the car is heading towards a collision with the wall. I won't survive the impact. But if it means she will, then so be it.

Our foreheads rest against one another.

'Are you really okay?' She runs her fingertips gently over the bandage on my arm.

'Yes.'

'Can I inspect your back?'

'Can I kiss you?'

'You just did.'

'One more time?' I'm one giant ball of repressed angst and desire, I don't care if I sound desperate.

'Here, now?'

I make a big show of looking over my shoulder. 'You'd prefer we kiss in the corner?'

Her smile comes in pieces, small and uncertain at first. Then it spreads wider, showing her teeth and tongue and making the corners of her eyes crinkle. To be the sole recipient of it makes me feel like I'm god.

'You and your stupid comments,' she says.

That's all the permission I need. The kiss is like coming home after a long shift at the ER to a bowl of hot porridge and a glass of warm tea. Her laughter echoes in my mouth and I groan into hers, my fingers tangled in her hair, and hers in mine.

'People can see,' she says in between our mingling breaths. 'There'll be gossip.'

'I hope it's hot,' I grunt.

'So hot, it'll be included in the PTA agenda.'

I break the kiss because I'm shaking like mad. I love that I'm able to do this with her, trade insults and see who can suppress our laughter the longest.

'So hot, they'll fire us,' I say.

'They already did.'

I raise my eyebrows.

'Lyla is flying home as we speak. We're officially fired,' Ellie says.

I bark out a victorious laugh. 'That's the best news ever.'

There are footsteps and noises outside the clinic. I drop my hand as she steps away from my personal space. 'You should put your shirt back on.'

I subtly—I hope it's subtle—flex my chest and biceps. 'What, *now*?'

Her eyes travel down, and instinct tells me to cross my legs but I don't. She swallows, and I feel that in my groin.

'What time do you have to leave for the hospital?'

I blink. I don't have a hospital I need to go to anymore since last night was my last day. The residency stops when the internship is ready to begin. The pain that stabs my stomach when I realize I have to break the news to her is excruciating. How am I supposed to tell her when we're *this* happy?

'Can you stay a while? I might be here long. Have a ship to fix and all that, and someone annoying just told me I can't quit.' She rolls her eyes.

I speak against the tightness of my throat. 'Sure, I'll stay.' There's still time to tell her, I convince myself. I *will* tell her. Just not now.

Ibu Ninik barrels in without any sound and startles us both. I suspect she's been spying on us outside the door for quite some time. These Spring elders might look ancient, but their minds are sneaky like that. I quickly throw my torn shirt over my lap.

'Here's your tea,' Ibu Ninik says to Ellie.

Ellie accepts the Styrofoam cup and thanks her.

'You want some?' she offers me.

'He can get his own tea,' Ibu Ninik says in the sweet old woman's way that tells me she will make me pay for all the stolen kisses that defiled the room in her absence.

Putting a hand over my heart, I feign hurt. 'Ouch. I'm the patient here.'

'Who is capable of making his own tea,' Ibu Ninik says.

Ellie looks amused. 'I'll see you back there.' Then she leans over and—under the watchful eyes of a Spring senior nurse— kisses me squarely on my mouth. It's a ballsy move, not to mention territorial. I'm too stunned, and too drunk on ecstasy, to respond.

The moment Ellie leaves the room, Ibu Ninik harrumphs from across my bed. 'Are you in trouble, Dion?'

I push my head into my shirt, glad to hide my wide-ass grin from her eyes, and say, 'Yes.'

Chapter 21

Ellie

'Surprise!' Lyla shouts the moment I step into the dining room.

'Oh my God!' I slap my cheeks as I stare at her. Then I run to the table to bear-hug her. We're screaming nonstop for a few minutes before we finally let go of each other. Lyla takes my face in her hands, and we're back to screaming,' Ahhhhh!' at the top of our lungs.

'You said your plane wouldn't land until tomorrow morning,' I say between my laughter.

'We took an earlier flight. I was so bored in London.'

'Nobody's gonna believe that.' I pull a chair next to her and flop into it. 'Do the girls know you're back?'

'They didn't want to leave my side.' Lyla snorts. 'I had to threaten them with no Wi-Fi if they refused to go to bed.'

I hear someone approaching and I whirl around. Ferdinan walks with his nose buried in his phone, he nearly collides with the dining table.

'Ferdinan!' I shout, my face hurts from smiling so big. I missed these two so much, I'm about to pee myself.

Ferdinan looks up, blinks through his specs as if for a second he can't remember where he is. 'Ellie!' He comes over and hugs me. 'Where have you been this late? Do you have night classes?'

'It's only nine-thirty, Ferdinan. And I graduated, remember?'

He blinks. 'You did? When?'

Lyla makes a hand gesture that tells me to ignore her husband.

'I missed you two.' My chest expands a few inches with love, and relief. Finally, there are real adults in this house. Yes, I'm an adult, but I'm the *baby adult* among these people. I wonder if there will come a day when I feel like I don't need their protection anymore. I can't imagine that.

Lyla's face melts. 'I missed you too, darling.' She reaches out a hand and I grasp it tightly. 'Can't wait to see you girls in the musical. One more day!'

Ferdinan glances up from his phone. Despite looking like he could use a month of sleep, his posture is alert. He reminds me a lot of Dion. 'What's one more day?' he asks his wife.

'The Spring musical,' Lyla answers.

'What musical?' he asks, sounding more baffled than before.

I choke on laughter as Lyla rolls her eyes. I get up and hug my sister again. 'Welcome home, Lyla.'

She crinkles her nose. 'You smell weird.'

'It's glue,' I say.

She clicks her tongue. 'Shower with warm water now.'

I know better than to argue with the PTA chairwoman.

June

Chapter 22

Ellie

Though I spent the past two weeks in this multi-purpose hall and have seen all the preparations from scratch, the actual sight still manages to make me gasp. Arriving together with Lyla and Ferdinan, our car inched slowly from the street all the way to the front gate. Lyla chose to get off near the marketing building—the one where I chaired my first disastrous PTA—and took a leisurely walk towards Nusantara hall. The walk was often interrupted by people who were ecstatic to see Lyla. Shrieks and laughter filled my ears, and I couldn't help smiling. This place has become so familiar to me without me realizing it.

The school has been prettied-up from the ground up. They hung colourful lights, lanterns, and ribbons on the ceilings. Posters and student's art pieces decorate the walls. Hundreds of medium-sized plants line up the halls in pretty cream-coloured pots.

All school personnel have cleaned up quite nicely too. The helpers, security guards, and technicians wear maroon, pinkish batik shirts or dresses. The administration personnel and teachers wear their formal evening attire with pins of Spring and our national flag adorned to their chest. The guests who consist of parents, alumni, businesspeople, and government officials follow the black-tie dress code.

I wear an old, black strapless dress I bought a few years ago. My hair is up in a soft, messy bun. I balance my simple dress with bold accessories, a pair of dangling gold earrings and layered necklaces. I borrowed Lyla's nine-centimetre, black, pointed Jimmy Choo's. I'm a world taller this evening.

After our frequently interrupted walk that felt like it took forever, we finally arrive at the gym. As we queue for registration, more and more familiar faces come up to us. My sister and her friends spend a few rounds hugging and talking. As expected, photo-taking ensues, involving many devoted Instagram husbands. Ferdinan does his job well, patiently answering calls to be a photographer or a videographer for the ladies' Reels and TikToks. He even bends his knee and swings his hips here and there to get the perfect shots.

I scan the hall for Dion even though I know I won't see him. All performers have been on the ground since morning, including Ashley and Aureli. They woke up with so much energy today, the whole house thrummed. I think of Jonas and my art team. They are probably hunkered backstage too.

Ibu Agatha is engaged in an animated conversation with my sister before she turns to me and envelopes me in a motherly hug. 'You look gorgeous, Ellie,' she says.

'You too, Ibu,' I say with a big smile. She wears a long sleeved black dress. She has sprinkled some glitter on her hair, her makeup glamorous enough that for a moment I can't see the stern Ibu Agatha I saw every day on the school grounds.

'Ibu Lyla. Welcome back.' Mr Goh has joined our circle, looking sharp and dazzling in his classic tuxedo. Ferdinan takes a short break from being an Instagram husband and comes over to shake the principal's hand. Like kids who know when to make themselves invisible whenever the adults are talking, the other parents quietly leave my sister alone.

I step into their circle and shake Mr Goh's hand. 'Everything looks splendid tonight, sir,' I say.

'You had a hand in making this happen, Ellie.'

My face heats and I hunch my shoulders, fighting the pressure to tell him that I only designed the ship. It's nothing compared to what the performers or the people who are responsible for transforming the gym into a castle are doing.

'She's a godsend,' Mr Goh tells Lyla, then grins at me.

'She is,' Lyla agrees.

I wish I could be as certain and as unapologetic as Lyla when people pay me a compliment.

Our circle gets merrier when some gentlemen from the board join us. While the adults continue speaking, I spend my time being a passive listener and keep my eyes on Lyla. I hear some big words in their discussion, words like expansions, teacher-training, non-profit organizations, and tuition money. Surrounded by all male acquaintances, Lyla commands the air with her presence. She knows when to listen and when to assert her opinions. Some people are born with leadership qualities and know how to wield them.

A moment later, Ibu Agatha ushers us to our seats. It's not surprising that they reserve VIP seats for the PTA members. But Ibu Agatha leads us past the VIP and straight to the VVIP front row along with Mr Goh, the board members, and our government officials. I feel dozens of eyes on my back . . . no, not on me. *On Lyla's back.* My sister has dressed simple, in her black pantsuit and a pair of red stilettos. Her hair is down in lazy waves. Unlike me, she adorns herself minimally with jewellery. I always thought everyone looked at Lyla with fear. I was mistaken. They look at her with respect. Perhaps with envy too, because how could one not feel jealous when they see another person so put together?

I wish my nieces would one day see what I see. Their mother is a badass and they're gonna be proud as heck of her. Just like I am.

My eyes move to Ferdinan, who's beaming with excitement but clearly not in his element. This is not a hospital, obviously. Tonight, Ferdinan is like the rest of us, a spectator who's looking at his wife like she's his entire world and he can't believe she's with him.

Suddenly the bows, the adoration, the kissing-ass attempts, and the motion-of-distrust coup make perfect sense. Power inspires. It calls out to kindred spirits, fire to more fire, wind to more wind. It also invites fear, vulnerability, and a sense of inadequacy. It's even more amazing that Lyla doesn't come from a privileged background. This is a girl who dropped out of college because she had no choice. She built her passion from home. From now on, whenever I hear cynical comments about housewives and their lack of ambition, I'll present my sister, along with Bernadet and the bunch of Spring PTA mothers. They're loud. They're a lot. They're funny. Their demands are ridiculous, but they're also willing to work for the things they believe in. *They care.*

My comrades are currently sitting in the front section of the hall, their colourful dresses and sparkling jewellery looking like balloons and ribbons at a kid's birthday party. On my first day of school, they were divided into two warring rows. It doesn't matter now. We're all on the same side. We fight for the same school and care for the same students.

'Lyla.' I touch her elbow and she turns. 'I'm gonna sit over there.'

Lyla's eyes follow the direction of my finger. Her face lights up when she sees *who* occupies the row. 'Sure, Ellie.'

I pivot back and approach the VIP section. Bernadet clasps my hand as I pass her seat. Somehow, they manage to magically spare one empty seat in the middle of the row. I squeeze between

Tara and Poppy, a mother who once complained about the tuition fee in one of our PTA meetings many moons ago.

'Any room for two more?' Lyla is standing at the edge of our row with Ferdinan smiling widely by her side.

My row erupts in giggles, whoops, and shit—me included—so deafening that other people in the audience mistake it for the start of the musical. After another round of scooting, one vacant seat magically appears next to me. Ferdinan fetches an extra chair from the row behind, and—after some more scooting—I have Lyla on my left and Ferdinan on my right.

'You're not sitting with the *Very, Very Intimidating People?*' I whisper into Lyla's ear.

'Nah. This is where I belong,' Lyla says.

I briefly put my head on her shoulder. Six months ago, I didn't know who Lyla was as a friend. Now I do, and I love what I see.

Chapter 23

Dion

Through the small gap in the side curtain, I peek into the hall. The auditorium is packed. The VVIPs are on their way. The adrenaline is swirling in the air around us. We will open in less than thirty minutes.

I gather my *Wrecking Sea* team backstage.

'Guys,' I begin. 'In case I don't find you after the show, I wanna say that I'm very proud of you. Congratulations to the seniors for graduating.'

They clap. Half of the crew are grade twelve students. Tonight, as the gala closes, they'll leave Spring as graduates. I'm feeling all sort of things from within me: pride, sadness, excitement, all surfacing with equal power. 'I also wanna tell you that I'm leaving for my internship tomorrow. I hope we can still keep in—' My voice gets swallowed by their noises. I'm being grabbed and hugged from every side. My eyes begin to feel hot in between *Good luck, Kak Dion* and *We're gonna miss you, Kak Dion*.

I clear my throat. 'All right, listen up. We will do our first number as practised.' The first number involves the backflip only

I can do. My eyes find Martin, my understudy. 'Then Martin will carry the rest.'

'But Kak Dion!' Martin protests.

'No buts. You're ready.' As one of the graduating students, tonight will be Martin's last chance to bid the school goodbye. He deserves it more than I do.

After a moment, Martin grins. 'Are you going to watch our performance from the audience, Kak?' he asks me.

'Of course. Won't miss it,' I say. 'But first, I need to find my girl.'

The whooping I receive from them is ridiculous. I forgot this is what happens when you talk about girlfriends and boyfriends with high school kids. Who-dates-who is a very big deal to them.

'You got a girl, Kak?'

'I do.'

'WHO?' They hoot at the same time, causing several heads to turn our way.

I laugh. 'None of your business.'

* * *

Ellie

I've been holding my breath the entire time the ship was out on the stage. Dion is magnificent to watch. There was no sign of his minor injuries from his energetic performance as an angry sea. I can't see his face from where I sit, but I feel his movements in my heart.

I excuse myself to the restroom the moment Dion's and Ashley's scenes end. I linger at the doorway nearest to the pool instead of rushing back to my seat. On this very corner not so long ago, I was writhing with a stomach cramp so severe, my vision was covered in black dots. Across from these doors were other doors. A few weeks ago, I stood outside those doors and hurt the boy I care about.

My eyes slowly take in the unrecognizable gym, trying to recount the many hours I spent inside, outside, and backstage. The multi-purpose Nusantara hall is majestic tonight, showcasing the very best of everyone's efforts and talents. The view brings out the melodramatic in me. This was my life for six months. This school is far from perfect, but it's a home to these kids, to the staff, to the workers, to the parents, to the entire Spring community. I met someone amazing here despite the stress over congestion, the demanding mothers, and the PTA drama. Meeting Dion is worth all of that and more.

I'm gonna miss this place very much. I'm gonna miss the shouts, the shrieks, the giggles, the chaos in the meetings. Now that Lyla is back, I doubt she'll allow much shrieking or giggling in her meeting room.

'You know you're standing near the toilet, right?' a male voice cuts through my thoughts like a hot knife through a pack of butter.

I whirl around and my jaw hits the floor.

My Prince Charming. The doctor, the heartthrob, the wrecker of the sea, in his black suit and black tie and . . . black-rimmed glasses? His hair is combed smoothly to the back and not falling down on his forehead. I stare at him, totally mute.

Dion in scrubs is drool-worthy.

Dion in his doctor's coat? Heaven-sent.

Dion in his sweaty sweatpants and tank? Sweet baby Jesus.

Dion in a suit? A killer. Chef's kiss, the soft cream on the top of cupcakes. The ultimate apple juice.

But Dion in a suit and nerdy glasses? He's not playing fair. This man knows what he's doing.

'Wow,' he whispers, thus breaking my internal drooling. He looks starstruck, eyes heated like molten lava. 'Wow, Ellie.'

My name is delivered in a fervent murmur, a silent sigh, like it's painful for him to say it. I forgot that I, too, cleaned up quite well.

'Wow yourself. You wear glasses?' I lick my dry lips.

He touches the side of the specs. 'I had to find you in this huge room full of people. I need my eyesight to be perfect.'

'It isn't already?' I always imagine him as the most perfect specimen.

'I don't need glasses for day-to-day life, only for work.' He pauses as he looks at me. Thanks to my heels, he doesn't have to lower his face too much. He reaches for my hands and holds them between us. 'This is so much better than I've imagined.'

'You imagined me in a dress?'

'I've imagined you a lot in my head. Dresses, or . . .' He abruptly clears his throat, the tips of his ears burn red.

He was about to say *dresses or no dresses.* My stomach gives an unexpected flip, delicious and hot. I bite my lower lip to stop a whimper. I want to smash our mouths together, with him wearing his ridiculously sexy eyewear. I wonder if he's thinking the same thing.

Dion says, 'Have you seen the pool? It's beautiful.'

He leads me out of the hall and into the open air. It's warmer outside. As we stand by the pool, Dion drapes his jacket over my shoulders. He's standing close to me, one of his hands grabs the railing next to my elbow, half of his body is behind me. I rest my forearms on the waist-level gate separating the pool and the canteen. For a moment, none of us speaks. When I smile up at him, his eyes drop to my mouth, and I swear I hear the sizzling of heat in the air between us. He slides to my right side, his arm bent on the railing.

'You're very quiet,' he says. 'I've been waiting for the snarky comments about the crooked lights they looped on the tree there. The one that looks like a strangled snowman. Or that the stars are actually poorly formed rectangles. No criticism about the decorations at all?'

Now that he mentions it, I notice the lopsided yellow lights on the tree opposite us. I laugh, he chuckles. The sound sinks into my chest like a cupid arrow.

'Have you seen the garden?' he asks.

'The front garden, yes. Wait. They decorated the *whole* garden?'

He smiles. 'We went all out, petal. Nothing is left behind.'

'I'm gonna miss this place,' I tell him softly. It's ironic that the minute I realized I loved Spring is the last night I'll spend inside it.

'You can always come back. They'll love to see you.' He touches my hand loosely; his thumb is playing with the tip of my fingers.

I turn around and rest one elbow on the railing. We're eye to eye now with him leaning. I see the reflection of the lights on his glasses. I can't help reaching out and smoothing his already perfect tie. I like the feel of my hand on his chest, so I keep it there.

'Petal.' His voice is a hum. 'There is something—'

'There you are!' a voice booms from behind Dion.

I drop my hand; Dion mutters something unintelligible.

'Hey, Jonas,' I say as he struts towards us. He looks sharp and eccentric in his skinny black pants that are a few inches above his ankles. His jacket fits his frame like a second skin. He's clearly redefining the term 'hot nerdy Art teacher'.

'Jonas,' Dion greets him, begrudging as always.

I suck in my cheeks trying not to laugh. His attitude towards Jonas used to annoy me, but I'd also be grumpy if someone interrupted our moment. But it's Jonas. He's harmless.

'What a show, right?' Jonas beams at us. 'What. A. Show.'

I beam back; Dion doesn't.

'You're not performing in the second act?' Jonas asks Dion.

'Martin will.'

Jonas aims his grin at me. 'The ship is magnificent. The whole room gasped when it came out.'

My cheeks flush with pleasure. We've worked our asses off in the past two days to fix the wheels and redistribute the balance of the ship to make it stable.

Dion is looking at me with fierce softness that melts my heart. He says in a low voice, 'Very proud of you, Ellie.'

Jonas keeps smiling, clearly oblivious to the dripping tension between me and Dion. 'You guys coming in or what?'

'Later,' I say. 'I want to spend time with *him*.'

Dion's face draws blank. He's surprised. And pleased, I hope.

There's a moment when everyone is silent. Jonas's mouth forms an O, his eyes dart from me to Dion. 'Shit. I'm being a third wheel. Sorry, sorry.' He backtracks from us, hands held in front of him; he's grinning from ear to ear. 'Enjoy your evening, lovebirds.'

'See you later, Jonas,' I say.

'Yeah, see you later, Jonas,' Dion echoes. His voice is not exactly warm but at least he doesn't sound like he's chewed on something bitter.

Once we're alone again on the side of the swimming pool, he turns to me. 'Lovebirds, huh?'

I pry open one of his balled fists. 'No need to act like you're about to punch him.'

'He deserves it.'

'He doesn't.'

'He spent so much time with you.'

'And whose fault is that? You put me in his team.'

His smile is part sheepish, part pride.

'I love it when you're jealous,' I say.

He makes a face. 'Of him?'

I raise my eyebrows.

He sighs. 'Maybe a little.'

I lean my back against the railing and hold his left hand in my right. Occasionally when someone opens the back door, the sound from the ballroom hits us like a blast. Dion and I would tilt our heads in that direction, replaying the scenes from rehearsal in our mind. I don't know how long we've been standing and holding hands without speaking until he clears his throat. 'Petal. I have something to tell you.'

He has that softness in his face again when he looks at me. Up close, his eyes seem to be sparkling from the reflection of the lights. He pushes his glasses up and swallows a few times. I have the urge to smooth his Adam's apple.

'I'm leaving for my internship soon.'

My hand is still in his. I'm still smiling. 'When?'

He looks over at me. 'Tomorrow.'

I stare at his mouth. Then at the knot of his tie. I'm still smiling as my stomach slowly disintegrates. *Tomorrow*? Impossible. I must've heard him wrong.

'Did you say tomorrow?'

He drops my hand and looks away, his face a shade whiter. 'Fuck, this is all my fault.' Closing his eyes, he takes a deep breath. 'The day after the accident, I called the office and offered to take whatever urgent spot they had on their list. I just wanted to get away from here as soon as possible. I wanted to do *something*.'

That day of the highway accident was the day we fought. I called him a privileged fraud, not knowing of the horror he had just witnessed the night before. If there was one day I'd like to remove from my life, it's that day.

Dion keeps talking. 'I tried so hard to cancel this, but unless I fake an illness or something, there's nothing much I can do. The bureaucracy is complicated, I don't know . . .' He trails off. 'I'm sorry.'

'Don't be,' I manage to say after haphazardly holding my breaking heart together. 'It's your job. You gotta go when you gotta go.' Is this what it means to be someone else's safety net? You put aside what you want for somebody else's greater purpose? Turns out I'm not only saying goodbye to Spring Academy tonight. I'll be saying goodbye to him too.

I notice a flicker of disappointment in his eyes. Did he expect me to beg him not to go? I won't. This is his future. I want him to live his dream. I want him to stop doing things for others and for once, be selfish and do things for himself. He's done so much for this school because he thought he owed them. He owes no one. He doesn't owe me either.

'Where is it?'

'Samarinda.'

'Isn't that where you are from?' I infuse some lightness into my voice. 'Your mom lives there, right?'

'Yes.' He looks surprised that I remember. 'Won't stay with her though. The hospital I work for will provide the accommodation for me.'

My effort to halt the tears fails. 'What time tomorrow?'

'8 a.m. flight.' He cups my chin and angles my face to his. 'Ellie. I'm sorry. I wanted to tell you before, but you were so worried about the ship, then we were so happy together, I couldn't. I still don't know how to tell you *this. Everything.*' He taps angrily at his chest.

I hold his hand and put my happy face forward because, truly, I'm happy for him. He's been feeling guilty about his time in Spring for his entire life, I won't add my name into his guilt list.

In the background, the intro of *Under the Sea* is playing, its upbeat tune seducing our limbs to a dance. We tilt our heads in the direction of the doors and listen. When we look back at each other, we're both smiling. Whatever emotions we're feeling right now will have to take a backseat because this is Aureli's scene. I'm not gonna miss it even if my world is crumbling around me.

'C'mon,' he says, pulling me off the rail and showing me his charming smile, the one he showed the audience during the sex-ed workshop. He takes back his jacket and drapes it over his arm. 'Our little Nemo is waiting.'

* * *

Dion

I link my fingers with Ellie's as we stand at the back of the ballroom. Everyone is clapping to the blaring beat. The lights from the stage bathe the entire room with bursts of stars and moving jellyfish. The younger primary kids dress as fish and dance on the stage before they spill down, swimming and waggling their fins between rows of audience seats. It's been the highlight of the show. Parents are overwhelmed with joy, especially the ones whose kids are a part of the swimming fishes. In a proper theatre, everyone would remain seated while the show is ongoing. But here, the families and teachers whip out their phones and gleefully snap picture after picture of the dancing kids. People shout and wave and cheer. Some kids get distracted by their loved ones, they forget their dance routes. Everything is a little chaotic, and that's exactly why it feels like home to me. I see pieces of me in every corner of this school, from my younger years to the present. The conversation about me leaving hangs heavy in my heart, but I manage to push it aside. Nobody can be gloomy when there are happy fishes circling around our legs as they dance to the upbeat song.

I crane my neck to find Aureli in the sea of small kids. 'Over there,' I whisper in Ellie's ear.

Aureli is dressed in a Nemo-inspired orange striped costume. She skips and bounces merrily between rows. Ellie throws both arms in the air to get her niece's attention. Several kids notice us and wave back. The moment Aureli sees her aunt, she drops her dance moves and rushes over. She reaches her aunt and wraps her tiny arms around Ellie's waist. She hugs my legs next before joining her friends back on the stage.

I bump Ellie's shoulder, grinning. Then I see her face and my amusement dies. Tears run down her cheeks in an endless stream. Her eye makeup is slightly smudged, making her look even more heartbreaking. She doesn't say anything; she doesn't look away from me. We're suspended in time, the noise around us gradually fades away into muted buzz.

'I'm gonna miss this,' she says fiercely. 'I'm gonna miss *you*.'

All I can manage is a nod.

Under the Sea wraps up. As the young dancers run backstage, the audience rise to their feet. For a minute or two, all we can hear is applause and whistles until the next scene begins. Sebastian walks around the stage in circles.

Ellie and I don't move from where we are.

'I'm gonna miss all of this too,' I say quietly, so quietly it's drowned by the music from the loudspeakers. *I'm gonna miss you too*, I want to tell her that. But just like with moments with my uncle and mother, the most important words always refuse to leave my head. They stay until they denotate inside my body. They leave me nothing but ash and a bittersweet taste on my tongue. I don't want to be a burden to anyone. Years of hiding my vulnerability from people around me, it feels impossible to unlearn it.

'I haven't properly kissed you tonight,' Ellie says out of the blue.

I close my eyes. *'Ellie . . .'* The heaviness sinks both of us back to the lower ground of the gym. It's tempting to tell her I'll breach the contract. But I know she wouldn't want that.

My thoughts must have been plain in my face because she smiles. 'Hey. We still have the rest of the evening.'

I half smile, then gently hold the side of her face and press it against my chest. The room serenades us in a love song ballad between Prince Eric and Ariel. The lights dim. I wrap my arms around Ellie from behind and sway her as the audience waves their glow sticks in the air and Sebastian the crab urges us to *kiss the girl.*

Yes, we still have tonight. And what a triumphant, unforgettable night this is.

Chapter 24

Ellie

It's a whirlwind of laughter, hugs, kisses, and pictures afterwards. In the middle of endless photo sessions, my purse buzzes. Dion has sent a shot of me laughing at something Tara and my sister said. Three dots appear, then his text says:

> The most beautiful thing.

After a moment of searching, I finally locate him. He's standing a few feet away, also surrounded by people and his *Wrecking Sea* teammates. After saying a few words to his friends, he approaches me and solemnly addresses my sister. 'Evening, Ibu Lyla.'

My sister brightens at the sight of him. I watch them formally shake hands.

'You were great up there,' Lyla says. 'That flip was amazing.'

'Thank you,' Dion says. His eyes slide to me for a fraction of a second, then he squares his shoulders. 'Ibu Lyla. Do you mind if I borrow Ellie tonight?'

'No, no,' Lyla says, a little distracted by other conversations around her.

Dion takes my hand. 'Can I bring her back a little late?'

That gets Lyla's attention. She tilts her head at him, then narrows her eyes at our joined hands. A flicker of understanding passes over her face.

'Excuse us for a sec.' Lyla holds my arm and moves us a few steps away from everyone. 'No,' she sternly tells me before she even turns around to face me. If I were someone else, I would've cowered under her unflinching glare. But I am not *anyone*. I'm her sister.

'I'm twenty-three. I don't need your permission.'

She crosses her arms. 'As long as you're my sister, you do.'

I sigh. 'Lyla. He's leaving tomorrow.'

'So?'

I raise my eyebrows. After a moment, she makes her infamous *tsch* sound. 'I see. How long?'

'One year.'

'More reasons to say no. You'll say yes to anything he asks. I won't allow it, Ellie. I need to be the cool-headed one here.'

I stomp my feet and regret it instantly. Not a smart move with heels. 'God, Lyla. I don't have time for this.' I can't believe I have to do this in a public space with Dion standing only a few feet away from us, probably anxiously witnessing our interaction.

Lyla grips my bare shoulders. 'I get it, Ellie. I've been there before. I don't want you to repeat the same mistakes I made.'

'Ashley is not a mistake,' I retort.

Lyla drops her hands and takes a step back, her eyes flash with hurt. 'That's low, Ellie. You know what I mean.'

I know what she meant, and I feel bad. My frustration at her for treating me like a kid deflates. Not entirely but enough to make me mumble an apology. I study my sister's face. 'Do you regret it? Ferdinan?'

The answer is fast and fierce. 'Not a fucking second.' Her eyes scan the space behind me and I know exactly when she spots her husband. It's like watching a snowy mountain melting into a sea of hot spring. Her tender gaze finds me next, and she gives me a rueful smile. 'I only want what's best for you, Ellie.'

I grab her hands and hold them close to my chest. Lyla, my forever safety net, my pillar of the unshakeable wall. 'And I'm grateful for that. To be honest, you do know what's best for me more than I do, Lyla.' My cheeks warm when she returns my smile. 'I may not know much, but *I know* that if I don't go with him tonight, I'll regret it for the rest of my life.'

She's quiet for what it seems like forever. At long last, she takes in a deep breath, a resignation in her eyes. 'I'm gonna talk to him,' she says and firmly stalks back to where Dion is.

'What? Lyla! No.'

But nobody can stop Lyla from anything.

'Ellie said you're leaving for your internship,' she says sweetly to Dion.

'Yes, ma'am.'

It's comical to see a tall man like Dion hunch his shoulders and fiddle with his hands in front of my petite sister. If this was a movie, I'd have laughed.

'Have you met my husband?' Lyla asks as Ferdinan wanders into our group. 'Darling, I'd like you to meet Dion. He's a doctor.'

I've never seen Dion flabbergasted before. He stares at Ferdinan like he's just met Tom Cruise, his jaw dropping, his eyes wild. The two men shake hands. The handshake lasts a long time.

'Sir, wow, sir,' Dion blabbers. 'It's an honour. I love your work very much. I mean *respect* your work, not love. Though I do love your work. Of course I love it. It's . . . wow. *Wow.* I can't believe I'm meeting you.'

'Thank you. It's nice meeting you too.' Ferdinan doesn't seem to register the effect of his presence to this young man, or the fact that his hand is still being shook. 'What field?'

When Dion remains mute and starry-eyed, I supply, 'Cardiology.'

'I have a few cardiologist friends I can introduce you to if you want.' My brother-in-law is smiling genuinely at Dion because that's who Ferdinan is. He's a kind and loving person, who also happens to be a genius neurosurgeon. I move closer to Dion because I get the feeling he might pass out. Lyla puts a hand on Ferdinan's arm, thus ending the ongoing handshake.

'You'll take care of her, won't you?' Lyla asks Dion. My sister wastes no time in getting right to the point. 'You'll treat her right?'

My skin burns from embarrassment. '*Lyla.*'

Dion blushes but he's holding his ground steady. Gotta give him credit for being able to face-off my sister without retreating, or worse, agreeing to everything she demands. Not many of us can.

'You have my word,' he says solemnly. 'I won't do anything inappropriate.'

I've had enough of this circus. I point at Dion. 'Stop talking.' I turn to my sister. 'You too.' Ferdinan gives me a delighted, blank look like he has no clue what we're talking about but he's happy just to be included in our little gang.

Dion is watching Lyla with a lot of caution and respect, like watching a lioness from a short distance. He knows he's going to be eaten, but he can't ignore the beauty and the grace of the hunter. I've been in his shoes my whole life.

After a few intense beats where my blood pumps in my ears and Dion stands mutely under Lyla's x-ray glare, my sister finally says, 'Ellie is a magnificent young woman, Dion. I hope you know that.'

I clench my teeth as a wave of emotion overtakes me. Despite everything, despite her constant criticism on my lack of ambition, she's proud of me. She's defending me. My sister is my world.

I'm very grateful to have her in my corner, even when that corner is currently biting my ass with its sharp teeth.

Dion's eyes stay on me, the dark pupils burn bright, like the lush, rich brown glaze on his mochaccino donuts. 'She is,' he agrees. My stomach flaps because what he said sounds like a promise, I can already taste the sweetness in my mouth.

Lyla must have caught that too because her expression is a mix of satisfaction and love, also resignation and exasperation. 'I'll tell Mom he's a catch.'

I take that as my exit cue. 'Thanks. Bye.'

'Ellie,' Lyla calls.

I peek over my shoulder and see her making the finger gesture between her eyes and us. Dion's steps slow. I bet he wants to assure my sister *again* that there's nothing to be worried about. I drag him away before he can say another word.

* * *

'What was that?' Dion mutters under his breath as we sprint into the relatively quiet parking lot. Only a handful of security personnel and drivers are mingling around between shadows of cars.

'That's Lyla the sister.'

'That's scarier than Ibu Lyla the chairwoman.' He shudders. 'Ellie. She made the fingers thing at me.'

'Don't worry,' I say, 'Ignore her.'

He takes off his jacket and drapes it on me. The hem reaches my knees. 'My car is outside.' He's proud of it. This kind of knowledge is the difference between freedom and forever stuck in Spring's ground. 'A bit far, but we'll go straight into the street. Can you walk in those shoes?'

He offers me his arm and looks down at my feet with a frown. By now, I'm fairly familiar with the meaning behind his facial expression. What I thought was an arrogant frown is genuine concern.

These heels on uneven asphalt will be a bitch. 'I can manage,' I say.

The night air isn't chill, but it feels smoky. Whatever the rain shamans did to move the cloudy sky away from Spring hometown, it worked. Not even the breeze dares to disturb us. I inhale the smell of him on the jacket. Who doesn't like being hugged by a soft, oversized, smooth material that smells like your most favourite person?

'You must be hungry,' he says. 'Let's see . . . What's open at this hour aside from McDonald's?'

'We can go to my place.'

He doesn't say anything, only extends his left arm and begins rolling up the sleeve. He slows his steps to a point where my relatively short legs are ahead of him. I stop and watch him. He works deftly, neatly, block by block. The sluttiest thing a man can do is roll his sleeves with full concentration, in the middle of a dimmed parking lot, under a cloudless night sky. He finishes with the left side and moves to the right. He struggles to unbutton the cuff, so I swoop in and help. He looks down on my hands when he clears his throat. 'Ellie. I don't have anything with me.'

At first, I thought he meant he has nothing to prove yet, like career or status or something along that line. Not that I care about those things anyway. But he sounds almost shy and young, it doesn't add up. 'What do you mean?'

He turns scarlet like someone has dropped a bucket of red paint onto his head.

There are tingles on the back of my neck when understanding dawns on me. '*Oh*.' I keep rolling his sleeve. Now I understand why he's doing it. The methodological but numbing action gives our brain a moment to regroup after being shocked into silence.

'Don't drugstores sell condoms?' I ask.

There's a beat when he freezes, then he roars with laughter. 'Oh, petal,' he says, shaking his head. 'Yes, I suppose they do.'

I grin up at him, feeling my own face mirror his colouring. I've never bought condoms before. 'Do they sell them in individual packets?'

He doubles over, clutching his stomach in one hand. 'We will stand here a lot longer if you keep making me laugh.'

'Sorry.'

He takes both my hands in his, then bring them to his lips. 'Ah, petal,' he murmurs.

A large group of students emerge from the hall, bringing music and noise out into the night. When they close the doors behind them, the sound is muted, but their laughter circles us from every corner of this quiet space.

I watch Dion watching the students and the multipurpose ballroom behind them.

'Eight years as a student, seven years as an alumnus,' he says, his voice sounds far. 'I still don't know what I feel about this place.'

'You're allowed to not know,' I say.

'I feel like I should, you know? This was a safe, beautiful home, with lovely people in it. On the other hand, this was also the place where I felt like I was a species from another planet.' He puts his hands inside his pockets and stares broodingly at the building. 'I should have one answer that sums up my whole life here. *One word.* And yet, I can't find it.'

'Life can never be summarized with one word, Dion.'

He glances at me. 'Since when are you so wise?'

'3.8 GPA,' I deadpan.

'Of course.' He regards me with a half-smile. He looks back at the building before us, eyes burning with passion and memories. 'I don't want to sound like an ungrateful brat because *I'm* grateful to be given the opportunity. The people here have helped me so much. But there were also many occasions when they made me feel like—'he shakes his head—'Never mind.'

'Like what?'

'A fraud.'

'You're real,' I say. 'Your accomplishments are real.'

'So are my doubts.' He turns to me. 'I'm only here because my dad isn't.'

'He would've been proud of you,' I say quietly.

He doesn't reply for the longest time. Then, softly, so softly I almost miss it, he says, 'I know.'

'Isn't it enough?'

He looks down; his chest expands as he breathes. There's a lingering sadness behind his hunched back. 'I don't know.'

He's more than enough, but he won't believe my words even when I shove them down his throat.

'If you ask Lyla, she'll tell you that my favourite phrase is *I don't know*. I don't know what I'm doing. I don't know what I want to do with my life. I don't make plans and jot down bullet points. My mom calls me lazy.'

'You're not lazy,' he stops me. 'So, you need more time to figure things out. Is it a crime? No. Is it lazy? No. A lazy person wouldn't bother to attend her nieces' rehearsals every day. A lazy person would not work her ass off to finish the ship. A lazy person wouldn't research high and low to find answers to our PTA issues. My uncle showed me the proposal, petal. I'm proud of you and you should be too.' He pauses for a second to take in a breath, then he continues, his voice a little tender, 'You're a very passionate person, Ellie. Next time someone calls you lazy, I'll have a word with them. Nobody messes with my teammate.'

I'm glowing. I turn to him, my reflection stares back at me from his lenses. 'It's a good thing that I got *you* on my team, huh?'

It earns me his rare and sweet quarter of a smile. He teases me, 'How do you know it's a good thing and not a bad thing?'

'I don't know. I'm not a psychic.' I laugh, then give his hand a tug. 'What I do know is, right now, you're my greatest thing.'

He doesn't move. Slowly, he closes his eyes. His face softens, then breaks completely. He shifts closer to me and presses a long, hard kiss on my temple. I experience first-hand what it feels like to be loved fiercely but quietly. He's so gentle with me—his touches barely make any contact with my skin—but his whole body is trembling from the intensity he tries to rein in underneath. I nervously watch him, worrying that he might retreat into a corner of his mind where I can't follow. I'm preparing myself to do something drastic, like break into a dance or kiss him stupid, but to my absolute relief, this time he stays with me. Smiling, he entwines our fingers together. 'Thank you.'

For the last time, we turn and face the school in silence. The building stands like a Christmas tree. On top of it, the words *Spring Nusantara* shine with yellow blinking lights. I finally understand what Macaulay Culkin in *Home Alone 2* must feel when he stood under the majestic Central Park Christmas Tree. Spring Academy is a big and loud world. It's so easy sometimes—too easy—to feel small, intimidated, and lost. No matter how I feel about this place and the people in it, it's time to say goodbye. Close the book and begin a new chapter.

I lean into his uninjured arm. 'Ready?' I ask.

He spends a few seconds staring mutely at the light above the gym, then down at me, his eyes bright, his grip on my hand firm. 'Ready.'

We only walk a few steps when he tells me in his regretful tone, 'I promised your sister no inappropriate things.'

I roll my eyes. 'Yes, you did. But thank god *I didn't*. Technically, *I can* do inappropriate things to you.'

He grins with his whole blushing face. 'I can't win with you.'

'Do you want to?'

'No,' he answers quickly, gently, one more time with a heavy emphasis. '*No*.'

'That's right, so don't even try,' I deadpan.

His laughter is the sweetest music I hear tonight, the reward I get when I successfully make him stay with me in the light. It's impossible to maintain a blank facade when he so freely lets himself go, so I break down giggling too. With that, we bid Spring Academy goodnight.

Chapter 25

Ellie

Every step towards my apartment is nerve-wrecking. I worry about a lot of stupid things like, are the lights in my room okay, when was the last time I changed my bedsheet, is my underwear sexy enough, what if my makeup smears on his shirt, what if there's a spider on my pillow.

I'm driving myself insane.

We didn't talk much in the car and we don't talk at all inside the elevator. My bare shoulders and arms are hyper aware of every brush of his clothes against me. The small paper bag which contains a blue box full of condoms dangles from his hand. I avoid staring directly at it, but I slide my hand on top of his, so we sort of carry the bag together. Because that's what we are. *Together.* Whatever happens tonight and afterwards, we'll do it together as a team.

I enter my studio and click the light switch. He quietly closes the door behind him. We're standing with a healthy gap between us, still not talking but there's a new urgency in us, I can feel it. The stilted air around us begins to throw sparks of electricity. His eyes are all dark and laser-focused on my mouth.

'Why haven't you kissed me all night?' I ask.

My question catches him off guard. 'I don't want to umm . . . ruin . . .' He gestures in the general direction of my face.

I pull a few sheets of tissue from my clutch and wipe off my lipstick without much ceremony. 'You won't.' I'm certain I look like a clown, with the remnants of red lipstick on my lips and maybe on my chin, but I don't care, I don't care, I don't care. The need to be touched by him is so painful, it's the only thing I can think of right now.

He steps closer until all I can see, hear, smell is him. His finger slides under my chin and he tilts my face up while his other hand stays on my waist. He lowers his face, stops a second only to inhale me, then his mouth lands on mine, gentle at first, then heavy with pressure and repressed hunger. My body sings, the heat in my lower stomach singes me from within.

'There,' he whispers.

I have no idea how he can still sound amused after that kiss. With my heels, I'm almost reaching his nose. I tuck my head under his chin; he lays his cheek on my hair. Though we're pressed against one another, there's this invisible thick line between us. A line he can't yet cross.

He murmurs from above my head. 'I'll follow whatever you decide to do.'

It fires up the confidence in me, knowing that he trusts me. He'd catch me when I falter; he'd be my safety net. I nod into his chest before I kick off my heels. My height drops significantly but for once I like it down here. My eyes never leave his as I take a few steps backwards. He watches me from the other side of our invisible line, anticipation dancing in his eyes like a pair of candle flames.

'My bed might not fit you,' I blurt. As always, when I'm nervous, my filter takes off on a long holiday.

His chuckle is low and deep and does a weird thing to my stomach. 'Why, is it a kid's bed?'

I don't want to stall anymore.

I touch the side of his face, loving the familiar prick of his stubble against my fingers. 'Hey,' I whisper, the beating in my chest making my voice shake. 'Stay with me, alright? Give me all of you.'

His dilated pupils find me, dark and hungry and dangerous. He blows a controlled breath, then rests his forehead against mine. 'With you? *Always.*'

I offer my hand. He clasps it, then takes a symbolic step forward, formally putting himself on my side of the line. I lead him to my bedroom.

* * *

Dion

We lie spooning, her sweaty back to my sweaty front. One of my arms is extended under our pillows and she currently rests her head on it, careful not to press on the bandages. My wounded back hurts more after our strenuous activity, but I do my best to ignore it. I thought leaving Spring was my before and after. I was mistaken. *This* is my before and after. I won't be the same after tonight.

I leisurely move my left hand along the side of her body, feeling every bit of her curves and softness. 'I changed my mind about my favourite dessert,' I confess.

'Not mochaccino?'

'Not anymore.' I kiss her neck. '*You're* my favourite dessert.'

She laughs. 'Are you saying I'm salty?'

'Hot,' I say.

My hand continues trailing down her arm, down to the slope of her waist. Then I stop. By instinct, I spread my fingers wide on her lower stomach.

She turns to face me, and I wait.

'What if I can't have kids?' She whispers in the space between our mouths. 'What if it's cancer? What if they have to remove my womb?'

'It's not always the case, Ellie.'

'But, what if, Dion? What if it's bad?'

'Do you want to have children?' I ask.

'I don't know.' A soft smile ghosts her lips. 'Not now, but maybe someday? I want to be able to choose rather than have my body choose for me.'

I brush the strands of her hair away from her forehead. 'Then we'll deal with it.'

'We?'

'Yes, *we*. You asked me to give you everything I got.' I place her hand on my chest. 'This is everything I got, petal.'

She snuggles her face against my neck. Her breath blows into my skin, warm and damp. I hold her while she cries without any sound. Then she kisses me with her eyes closed, like she wants to imprint me into her other senses. I kiss her back, so hard, I can't think straight.

Then a phone rings.

It rings, and rings, and rings.

A nervous laugh spills out of me. There's only one person who would call her at this hour. Hats off to Lyla for having such impeccable timing.

'That's my executioner,' I say as I drop myself back on the bed and cover my eyes with my arm. I want to cover my whole body and hide—I'm a terribly shy person—but there's nothing I can use, so I lie there with nothing, acutely aware of Ellie's eyes on me.

'Hey. Yes, I'm at home.' Ellie uses the same voice she used on Aureli when her niece was whining in the car about watching TV, sympathetic but unyielding. 'Listen. I'm gonna turn off my phone now. No buts, Lyla. I'll see you tomorrow.'

After tossing her phone on the nightstand, she snuggles back to me.

'You can at least tell me how she plans to murder me,' I mumble without opening my eyes.

She's quiet. When I look at her, she's watching me with a thoughtful expression. 'My sister is not scary, you know. Wait until you get to know her. She's amazing.'

Her loyalty towards her family warms my heart. 'I heard *her sister* is also amazing.'

She pokes the side of my stomach and laughs. I hoist her on top of me, my legs and arms circling her as I rock us left and right, our breaths warming each other's face.

'What time do we need to go to the airport?' she asks.

'Not *we*. You sleep. I don't want you to see me leave.'

She smiles sadly at that but doesn't argue. 'Look at you,' she murmurs as she lowers her face to mine. 'Dr Dion Saputra, cardiologist.'

I put a hand over her mouth. 'Shush. Not yet.'

She licks my fingers, then feigns biting them. 'You're heading there.'

I picture my future in my mind. 'Yes, I'm going there.'

We stay quiet for a moment, each with our own thoughts. I mentally skim the momentous steps I need to take to arrive at that title. My dream title. *It's for you, Papi*, I tell it to a face that belongs to a memory of my father from when I was young. *I couldn't help you, but maybe I can help others.*

Ellie sighs into my neck. 'We have five hours and nine condoms left, just saying.'

'Is that a challenge?'

We laugh as one, without sound. Our limbs get tangled, it's hard to separate my own from hers. Then suddenly she stops laughing and stares down at my mouth. There's a storm behind her eyes and I feel the shift in me. At that moment, I hate myself. I hate that my fate always makes me leave the people I love behind.

'I don't want to go, Ellie.'

'Hey.' She frames my cheeks with her hands. 'I'm here until you get back.'

My chest is full, I can't breathe. The words tease my tongue again. This time, I'm forcing them out. 'I . . .' I try again, so hard my fists are clenched like steel. 'Ellie . . .'

She kisses me like I'm a fragile thing. In between our mouths, she murmurs, 'I love you too, doll-face.'

She holds me quietly as I feel every detonation in my body. From the corner of my eyes, I spot the blue box on her nightstand. I grab it and give it a shake. 'Challenge accepted,' I tell her.

She gives the box a glance, then me a comical arc of her eyebrows. We explode into another heap of gurgling laughter and snorts, boneless with mirth and silly tears.

Ever since our fight outside the Spring gymnasium, I re-learned that safety nets can take many, many forms. Wealth and power, definitely. But so is sharing birthday celebrations across two cities. So is welcoming a scared, angry boy into a loving home. So is swearing secrets about midnight snacks and TV binges. So is permission to choose your favourite dance team.

For Ellie and me, our first safety net is the ability to laugh in the face of everything together. We laugh because we can. We laugh because we're together, happy, and safe. I've laughed more in the months I was with her than my whole fifteen years of living here combined. Being with her makes me appreciate all the safety nets that are spread from left to right under my feet: my family, my Spring teachers, my *Wrecking Sea* crew, my ER buddies, my work—yes, including the ones I did with the helicopter, hands-on mothers. They've been there all along. I guess I've always known they were there, but not until recently did I recognize them as *what* they are. What Ellie said about me was right. *I am* privileged. I won't take who I have for granted.

Chapter 26

Ellie

'Look who's here.' Lyla says when I step into the busiest and loveliest part of their house: their dining room. At 8 a.m., the table is full of a combination of Western and Indonesian food: fried rice, scrambled egg, spinach soup, toast, sausages, and bacon. Orange juice for Lyla and coffee for Ferdinan. I pull a chair opposite my sister.

'Jetlag?' I ask as I snatch the crackers next to the fried rice bowl.

'We've been up all night,' says Ferdinan.

I notice his business attire. 'Are you off to work?'

'Yup, might as well,' he says. His phone dings. He looks down, then excuses himself from the table to take the call. With him gone, there's no more buffer between me and my sister. I dread the questions she's surely going to ask about my night.

'I have a few things for you from London,' Lyla says. 'Help me unpack?'

Glad for anything that doesn't remind me of Dion, I agree. Ferdinan walks back in, kisses his wife on the forehead, squeezes my shoulder, and leaves without a word. I'm struck by the normality of it. After not seeing them for six months, I realize it's the small things I miss the most. Ashley and Aureli must have felt this too.

Lyla's bedroom has so much stuff scattered on the floor. I have to watch my step, otherwise I'd sink into their exploding suitcases. Sliding to the floor at the feet of the bed, I watch Lyla sort her things.

'The girls and I used to have junk food parties here,' I confess.

'I know. They told me.'

I gasp. 'I told them it was a secret.'

'They wanted me to be a part of *your* secret. Aur always said, *don't tell Papa.* I'm sure she told him the same thing and warned him not to tell me.' Lyla chuckles. 'That girl doesn't understand the concept of secrets. So yes. I know all about your pizza party, about the time you guys dropped Coke on my bed, and when you played juggle with apples and my pillows.'

I laugh. 'Why didn't you stop us? Your instruction clearly stated no snacks and TV on school nights.'

'I was miles away. You were here. I trust you.'

For anyone else, it might not mean much. But I know my sister. Her speciality is micromanaging others. To have me run the show without her breathing down my neck is extraordinary. For both me and her.

'I love them, Lyla.'

'And they love you.'

Love.

I hug my knees and put my chin there. Time to come clean to my sister. 'I haven't made any progress with my resume. I'll do it soon, I promise.'

Lyla nods. 'You've been busy.'

I wait for her *but*, but it doesn't come. 'That's it? You're not mad?'

She shrugs. 'Well, you're here now. We can work on it as soon as I finish unpacking.'

Okay. Maybe not *that* soon.

'There's something else.' I take in a deep breath. 'I changed the PTA proposal. I'm sorry I didn't tell you sooner.'

Lyla folds a blouse and nods again. 'All right.'

'*All right*? You're not mad?' Who is this woman?

'Why should I be mad?'

'You told me not to change anything.' Just like that, I'm back at the first PTA meeting when I was just a clueless girl trying to be a grown-up. 'You know I'm incapable of handling that kind of stuff.'

'You think I see you as incapable?'

I know better than to answer that trap.

'I always believe everyone is capable of something if they put their mind to it.' A hint of mischief illuminates her eyes, making her look so much like Aureli. 'I admit there's also a little bit of an ego thing. I don't want other mothers to mess with my work.' She looks at me, expression dead serious. 'Maybe I shouldn't have done that. I coddle you like a little kid. Look at what you did on your own. Ibu Sylvia can't stop praising you.'

'Because they don't dare complain to you, Lyla.'

'Pshhh.'

She's back to organizing her stuff. It's therapeutic watching her hands move.

'Is he the one?' She finally addresses the elephant in the room. Her eyes unapologetically study me.

I don't know how to answer her. I woke up to an empty bed, the scent of him, and a note. *I'll call you when I land.* My heart can't patch the Dion-sized hole he left inside, so I hug my knees closer to my chest, hoping the pieces of my heart can glue themselves back together.

I don't hear Lyla move but a moment later her arms are around me.

'What can I do to make you feel better?'

'Him.'

'What's the closest thing to him that can make you feel better?' There's no mistaking the sarcasm in her tone. She must have rolled her eyes too.

I force my mind to stay in the present and to simply enjoy the company of my sister. I miss her. I miss the girls. If last night was before and after, this morning is another one: before and after as a live-in aunt. My chest constricts.

'Where does the school get their donuts from?' I can't believe I didn't ask my PTA teammates or Ibu Agatha this in the long six months I was there.

Lyla frowns as she thinks. 'I'm not sure but I can find out.'

A smile is forming on my lips. It feels unexpectedly nice. 'They have the best mochaccino. I'd love to order some.' I want to drown myself in them and imagine it's his mouth on me.

'Done.'

My chest still stings but I can breathe a little better. I rest my cheek on my knees.

'How about ice cream?' My sister is trying hard to cheer me up. My chest twists again with love for her. Talking about ice cream reminds me of that café where I found Dion napping.

'There's this gelato place inside the mall near the highway,' I say. 'It's an old coffee shop that's been upgraded to sell brunch and gelato. The girls would love it.'

Lyla chuckles. 'Done. You, me, Ash, and Aureli. I can use some sugar to fight off my jet lag.'

It's silly how much I long to hold the girls in my arms when hearing their names. I mean, they're still here in this house, most likely sleeping. I can still spend time with them whenever I want. But it won't be the same, I know it. Not that the change is bad. They have been mine for six adorable months. They will be mine forever.

'Lyla.' I lay my head on her shoulder. 'I need to see an OBGYN.'

The way she jerks away from me is comical.

'I'm not pregnant. Chill.'

The murderous look on her face reminds me to never *ever* cross my sister's bad side.

'I have very bad menstrual pain. It's getting worse every month,' I explain. My whole body tenses, bracing for the common responses I usually receive from other people.

Everyone gets period cramps. It's no big deal.

Are you sure you're not imagining it?

It'll pass.

I'm tired to have to defend what I experienced every time I skirt around the issue. But my sister doesn't say any of those things. She's alarmed, but remains calm. 'Since when?'

'Since forever. I've been postponing my doctor's visit because . . . I'm scared.' The admission surprisingly doesn't make me feel as powerless and small as I've often imagined it would.

'You're scared of seeing a doctor?'

'Well, it could be . . . bad, right?' I wipe a tear off the corner of my eye. A tear for my fear, for missing him, for my luck at having my number one supporter sitting next to me on the floor amidst piles of clothes and stuff. Lyla's body is erect like a stone. It should make leaning against her uncomfortable, but it's not. I love how unyielding Lyla is. Night or day, rain or shine, here or there, now or tomorrow, good or bad, PTA or rival moms, I know for certain that she'll be there for me. I'll do the same for her, no questions asked.

'Will you accompany me?' I ask her.

The touch on my skin before she envelopes my hand is soft. Her voice is even softer when she says, firmly and lovingly, 'Done.'

Six Months Later . . .

December

Epilogue

Dion

The travelling doctor job is my favourite, though perhaps I could do with less rain. Every now and then, the hospital will send their young doctors to remote villages. On a rainy day such as today, I'm grateful that the hospital has an old minivan that's used for these visits.

Six months into my job and I've already adjusted to the calmer pace of this quiet town. The hospital is small, but the staff and the doctors are the most caring and kind people I've ever met. After spending my entire life in a viciously ambitious, dog-eats-dog big city, the community here feels like a family. I welcome it, though I admit I miss the buzz and the chaotic life of Jakarta. Working at a much slower pace is nice, like having an overdue holiday, but deep down I know this place is not for me. I belong in the big cities.

I also miss Ellie a lot, so much that I've learned to live with the pinch in my chest whenever I think of her. And that's a lot of thinking. When I was out on those visits and had to spend the night in one of the villagers' houses, I missed her the most. Being in the middle of someone else's family opens up a longing so potent, my ribs feel like they're being cut open by an axe.

After collecting my medical bag and papers, I nod goodbye to the driver and enter the hospital through the ER side-door. My shoes are covered in mud. My white doctor's coat is partially wet and there are spots of dirt on the back.

Ira, the attending nurse for this afternoon shift, greets me with her usual chirpiness. 'You look filthy, doc.'

I drop the patient's records on her desk. One of the junior nurses takes the medical bag from me. 'Thanks,' I say. She mutters something under her breath and scurries away with her cheeks red. Even after six months, most nurses are still blushing around me. I mentioned it in passing to Ellie during one of our video calls. 'It's because you're juicy like apple juice.' She grinned as I made an *oh, please, not this again* face.

We don't talk every day, but we text constantly. Sometimes she sends me memes I don't understand, and some other times she posts Ashley and Aureli's pictures. The girls have switched from calling me Kak Dion to Uncle Dion, to match their Auntie Ellie. I feel like I'm the honorary member in their secret little club. Another safety net I cherish dearly.

'There's one walk-in patient in the waiting room,' Ira tells me. 'I wonder if you could take a look before you go?'

'Sure,' I say, 'I'll go clean up first.'

I take off the dirty coat before washing my face and hands. I rinse my glasses next. After I dry them with paper towel and put them back on, I step into the examination room, which is the only room we have beside the ER. The patient is sitting with her back facing the door. I make my way to my seat and stop dead in my tracks. I think I have a heart attack. My knees are failing me.

'*Ellie?*'

She looks exactly like the last time I saw her, lying in my arms in her bed: soft, pretty, and mine. Her face is free of makeup and a little sweaty. Her hair is in a low ponytail. She wears a white T-shirt and a pair of faded blue jeans. I recognize the black sport shoes she's wearing; those shoes scoured the Spring gym for months. It's her smile that steals my breath away. It's the kind that lights up the room—wide, genuine, and full of life. It's hard not to smile back and feel as if my entire soul is being lifted up to the sky. She's about to say something, but I pull her into my arms first.

'Oh my God. It's *you*! It's really, really you! I'm not dreaming.' I let her go for a second to make sure she doesn't disappear into smoke, then crush her into me again. We're laughing, or maybe I'm crying, shit, I don't know anymore. Six months! After only seeing her through the phone screen, she's here in the flesh.

She's really here in the flesh, isn't she? I hold her at arm's length. Then I pinch my own arm. It's always wise to be certain that I'm awake and not dreaming.

She grins, then spreads her arms to the sides. 'Surpri-i-i-se.'

I cup her face and kiss her. It's like drinking water for the first time after being stranded on a desert island for years. Her eyelids flutter close and her lips part. She kisses me back with the same amount of enthusiasm. My glasses become foggy from our breathing, so I take them off and keep them in my pocket.

'I can't believe it's you. What are you doing here? Holiday? Wait. Do they know?' I jerk my chin towards the door.

She leans against her chair, her lips swollen from my kiss, and says, 'Funny story, really.'

I raise my eyebrows. Everything is funny with Ellie.

'I was kind of winging it when I arrived. But then some of them recognized me. They said I'm the phone girl.'

Chuckling to myself, I show her my phone. The entire screen is Ellie's face from the gala night.

'Ah, that explains it,' she says. 'Anyway, I told them I came here to surprise you. Yada-yada-yada, your entire team helped, and . . .' She raises her arms and does a little pose. 'Surprise!'

I laugh and shake my head. 'Are you here until the weekend?'
Today is Thursday. I'm so hopeful, I'm counting the days already.

'There's this other thing.'

I narrow my eyes. 'What thing?'

She grins. 'You better sit down.'

'God, Ellie. Don't give me a heart attack twice in the span
of five minutes.' I run my hand through my hair. 'What is it? Is
it your . . .' My eyes drop to her stomach. Two months ago, she
underwent a minor surgery for her endometriosis. She still feels
her monthly discomfort, but luckily, it's not as severe as before.
One step at a time, I told myself. I was glad that she got it checked,
even when I couldn't be there with her during the procedure. Lyla
was kind enough to stay connected through the phone and update
me about the surgery.

'It's not bad news,' Ellie says, then pushes herself up from
her seat.

We stand so close together, I can't help it. I kiss her again.
'Okay, hit me.'

'You don't want to sit down?'

I close my eyes briefly. 'Ellie . . .'

'Okay, okay,' she says. 'So, I got a call back from a small
company I applied to a few months ago.' She holds my eyes. 'Me.
Not through Lyla's connections.'

I nod because I know how important that detail is for her.

'They didn't have anything in Jakarta at that time, but they
had a few projects outside Java. I casually mentioned your
hometown, and guess what? They were contracted to build some
market blocks in the East of Samarinda. Long story short. They
offered; I took the job. I'm one of their junior architects.' She
grips my upper arms. 'I'm here, Dion. I get to stay here with you
for the next six months!'

She waits for my response. I got none. My brain is running in
circles over the words *with you* and *six months*.

'Ellie. Don't joke about this. For the next six months? The whole six months?' My voice comes out weak, because my subconscious convinces me that this whole thing is a prank. I can't be this lucky.

'Until July. Oh wait, that's seven months. My math is not mathing.' She's excited, her voice is a little pitchy and her words run together. 'We can fly back to Jakarta together later. I promised my parents I'll stop by at home first though.' She throws an uncertain glance my way, looking almost shy. 'You can come with me if you want. They'd be thrilled to meet my *yada yada* in person.'

'*Yada yada*?' I slide my hand behind her neck and hold her close to me. Of course I'll go with her to meet her parents. 'Are they more like you or your sister? I need to mentally prepare myself.'

She laughs. 'You'll find out.'

Happiness and sadness have the same effects on our body: wobbling knees, racing pulse, star-filled vision. I've been forced to choose twice before. The first time was when I chose to leave my mom and live with my aunt and uncle. Second was the early morning when I left Ellie in her apartment. In those pre-dawn hours, I battled hard between selfishness and duty. I could've stayed with her; she was my new dream. But on the opposite side of her door was my old dream, my career dream, the one that's been patiently simmering for more than a decade. In the end, I couldn't pretend to be someone I wasn't. I was my uncle's son. I was raised by a man who taught me wisdom, humility, and responsibility. I left Ellie's studio with a full heart, knowing I'd be back without regrets. And now she shows up and tells me I can have both my dreams at the same time? Seeing her here already feels like winning a million-dollar lottery. Hearing her tell me she will stay for the next seven months is like winning a favour from God himself.

I proceed with caution. 'What does Lyla say? She's okay with you wasting your 3.8 GPA on a junior architect job in the small town?'

It took me a while to get myself used to addressing the formidable Spring chairwoman by her first name. Even after a few months, I still apologize whenever I call her Lyla, something both sisters find very amusing.

Ellie gives me a long look. 'Of course she prefers I accept her friend's offer. But she understands.' She takes my hands and gives them a little shake. 'Can you believe it? I got the job myself. My mom is very proud of me.'

My heart melts. My petal, my beautiful, adorable flower. 'I'm proud of you too. But Ellie, are you *sure*? It looks like you're setting yourself back.'

She puts a hand on my chest, like a warning. 'I know my privilege is showing here. But let me be clear. I'm not setting myself back for *anything*,' she says, carefully stressing each word with a quietness that makes me shudder. 'I'm sure about me stepping out of Lyla's shadow and doing things my way. And I'm sure about *you*.'

A punch to my solar plexus. A crack in my ribs. I have to bite my jaw to control my overwhelming affection. Her fiery eyes mellow, and she lays her palm tenderly against my cheek. 'Stay with me,' she murmurs.

I squeeze her in for another bear hug. 'I need to sit down,' I say after I release her from my arms. I'm unable to stop grinning at her like a doofus.

'Yes, me too,' she says, also grinning at me like a doofus.

I silently process the information I just received, grateful that she gives me the time I need.

'Where are your things?' I ask after a moment of silence, after my heartbeat slows down a little and my skin stops breaking into goosebumps.

'Ira hid them somewhere outside. I have something for you. Come on.' She jumps up from her seat, pulls my hand and drags me behind her. She jogs like a little kid, reminding me so much of that time when she sprinted with Ashley in the Spring hallway.

The moment we're out, Ira shouts, 'How did he take it?'

'Like a champ,' Ellie says with a familiarity that made it seem as if they were best friends and hadn't just met today.

'Don't do that again, please,' I plead. 'I nearly passed out.'

Ellie walks behind Ira's desk. A moment later she appears with a black duffel bag. She unzips it on the floor and pulls out two big white, square boxes. After putting them on Ira's desk, Ellie spends a few minutes concentrating on getting the boxes open. When she does, she takes a step back and smiles at me.

The smell hits me first. 'You brought mochaccino?' It's ridiculous how much power a donut has over me. My mouth waters.

'Two dozen,' Ellie says.

Each of the nurses and the hospital staff grabs one donut without being asked twice. We don't get many fancy-flavoured snacks around here.

'Oh, this is good.' Ira munches with her eyes closed. 'Thanks, Ellie.'

I lick my fingers after I shove the rest of the donut into my mouth. I grab my second one. 'I'm surprised you didn't bring cheese donuts with you.'

'Of course not,' she says. 'These mochaccinos are for you. You hate cheese donuts.'

'I don't hate them,' I say.

She looks puzzled and I don't blame her. Nobody knew the reason I hated cheese donuts, not even me at first. When my dad died, it felt a lot like a betrayal. I resented him for leaving us, even when I knew better that there was nothing anyone could do about it. I hated him the most for leaving my mom. She was devastated, still is, and I blamed him for it. I couldn't tell him I hated him, so I hated everything he liked instead. Cheese donuts were his favourite.

Ever since I arrived in my hometown, I'm seeing my childhood a little differently, from a point of view that's a little more detached and a little more forgiving. I've let my anger go piece-by-piece. I'm trying my best as my father's son to let him rest in peace. One day, I'll tell Ellie everything about him. I'll tell her that cheese donuts are most definitely not subpar.

'I have something else for you.' Ellie crouches again on the floor and rummages inside her bag.

'That's the only thing you brought?' I ask.

'She has two big suitcases,' Ira answers. 'We hid them in the ladies' toilet.'

That's more like it.

Ellie hands over a long cylinder tube to me. I carefully twist the cap and find a paper roll inside. As I unroll it, a few names catch my eye. Words and signatures are scribed on the white paper. I stop in the middle of rolling it out and stare. I don't know how long I stay silent until I feel Ellie's presence next to me.

'We feel bad for not being able to give you a proper send-off,' she starts, her voice quiet. 'We will give you a proper welcome when you're back. In the meantime, this is all that we can give you.'

I try to dissolve the lump in my throat. When I lift my head to look at her, my eyes are hot and my hands are trembling.

'It took three months to get everyone in Spring to sign it,' she says. 'From the students, the alumni, the teachers, your *Wrecking Sea* team, the parents, to the security guards. They all miss you.'

I take one hard swallow against the tightness in my throat and nod. Gently, I roll the paper and put it back inside the tube. I will dedicate a special time to read each and every comment later. They deserve my full and undivided attention.

'Do you like it?' Ellis asks, her eyes searching mine. She's looking both nervous and shy.

Do I like it? Oh boy, where do I even begin?

'I love you, petal. Thank you.' The words finally slip out of my mouth. I remember what my aunt said to me before. *The world won't stop turning just because you said them.*

Ellie beams at me like a blooming rose petal.

Ira insists I take the afternoon off to keep Ellie company. While we're waiting for the taxi to take us to Ellie's hotel, I show her around the hospital and introduce her to people I know. The two-storied building is old and simple with no fancy decorations or colourful, artistic materials. We have a small garden in the middle of the hospital, with a small fishpond and a smaller fountain. In the mornings, nurses bring out patients and babies here to soak in the sun. It's too hot during the day, but when it's cloudy like today, it's quite comfortable, romantic even, like living inside an old photograph in Sepia colours.

We sit on one of the wooden benches and face the fountain.

'You're thinner,' she says.

'I walk a lot,' I say. When I work in the villages, walking is the only mode of transportation.

She accepts my explanation without further questions, but she still studies me with concern.

'Aside from missing you, I'm happy here,' I assure her.

Her expression softens. 'I'm glad.' She threads our fingers together.

If we were alone, I'd kiss her until the fire that's raging inside me consumes us both. I chuckle, rub my eyes and mutter to myself, 'I'm trying hard not to do things that could get me fired.'

'Are they inappropriate things?'

I shoot her a look, and slowly, deliberately, lick my lips. It pleases me when her face flushes. We're quiet for the next few minutes. I assume both of us are trying to bring our naughty fantasies down to manageable proportions.

'When am I gonna meet your mother?' she says.

I've forgotten about my mother in the middle of this afternoon's excitement. My mom knows everything about Ellie since I can't stop talking about her. I nearly burst into confetti from the anticipation of having the two of them meet. My mom would be surprised. She'd be ecstatic. She'd insist on having Ellie stay with her for the next six, seven months.

'We can have dinner at her house tonight, if you're free,' I say.

Ellie touches her cheeks, turning to me with an over the top panicked expression. 'Ahhh! I'm meeting your mother. What should I wear? Jeans and sandals okay?'

'She'll love you no matter what you wear.' I lean closer and whisper conspiratorially into her ear. 'But first things first. I know a great restaurant that serves the best fried chicken skin. Crispy, oily, full of LDL cholesterol, and fucking delicious.'

Groaning, she punches my arm. 'Don't tease me, doctor. I haven't gotten any decent meals all day.'

'I know,' I say, grinning at her. 'So, you in?'

She smirks back at me, eyes twinkling with mischief. 'With you? *Always.*'

THE END

Book Club Questions

1. The argument about the best donut starts out as a meet-cute between our main characters. As the story progresses, the conversation about donuts is tied to the characters' arc. It reaches its climax when Dion's internal monologue says: 'Cheese donuts are most definitely not subpar.' How does Dion's realization about 'cheese donuts' help shape his and Ellie's relationship going forward?

2. When Ellie notices Dion's panic attacks, she does whatever she can to anchor him in the present. What does it say about Ellie's character? Is she the kind of person who will help other people unconditionally? What are her character traits that make you answer yes/no?

3. What are Ellie's and Dion's love languages towards each other? What's your favorite scene with Ellie and Dion together?

4. Can you relate to Ellie's choice of being silent about her menstrual pain? What can we do as a community to raise more awareness about chronic illnesses?

5. We witness how Dion crumbles under the weight of other people's kindness. Is too much kindness good for the recipient? Have you experienced a similar emotion?

6. Do you think there's sibling rivalry between Ellie and Lyla? If yes, at what point does it show in the book? If

no, what do you call the bond between the two sisters? Is it a healthy relationship or an imbalanced one?

7. Do you agree with Lyla's protectiveness of Ellie?

8. We live in a society that's obsessed with goals and conformity. Ellie's coping mechanism for this is letting other people's opinion about her define her. Dion does the opposite by proving to others that he's more than what they think of him. Can you see the reasons why Ellie and Dion react to their labels the way they do? How do we train our mind to separate other people's opinions of us from our own? Do you have any tips to share?

9. The women in PTA fight for power in one scene, then work harmoniously in another. Some would say that this is a portrayal of the real world; some would argue that this is an example of a toxic environment. What do you think?

10. Have you been to Indonesia? Is it on your travel wish list?

11. Name your Top Three Best Pastries. Go!

12. If you must sum up Ellie and Dion's relationship in one song, what would it be?

Acknowledgements

The idea of this story came to me in 2021 when the world was scary and uncertain. Maybe because I missed being with my friends and families so much, I created a fictional world where people could hang out and interact with each other without fear. Spring Academy was perfect for that. Please note that the school curriculum, medical study, the residency and internship in this book were simplified and modified to fit the plot.

I purposely wrote endometriosis into my story because I wanted to bring more awareness to this chronic illness. According to many medical studies, endometriosis is one of the most painful health conditions. The symptoms may vary from individual to individual, but the ones Ellie experienced here mirrored my own. If you're an endometriosis survivor, or currently struggling with it, know that you're not alone. Please consult your doctor and get help.

There are no truer words than: *it takes a village to write a book.*

Thank you to Penguin Random House SEA and its brilliant team for welcoming *Cheese Donuts* and me into their family. I'm grateful to each of you who work tirelessly to support my story and make it shine.

Swati, this book wouldn't be here without you. *I* wouldn't be here without you. You're an incredible mentor, a passionate editor, and a loving friend. You're forever my Petal.

I'm lucky to have writer friends long before I was a writer myself. Clarissa, your superpower is kindness. Never ever change. Tanya, love how we can go months (months!) without speaking to one another, then one day, one of us would drop an emoji without context and it would send us spiralling into laughter for days. Love you lots and lots.

My RWWB writing buddies. Thanks for the writing inspo, writing talks, writing meetups, and writing critiques. Boy, we had fun, didn't we?

Special shout out to Cynthia, my Ted Lasso partner in crime. I'm Beard to your Ted, Ted to your Beard, Roy to your Jamie, you name it. Football is life!

To my two kids who bring joy and brightness into my life. It's a blessing to watch you grow into amazing young adults. Don't give me that face. I'm your mother. I'm allowed to embarrass you every now and then.

To my other half, Robby, who is clueless about the publishing world but excited to hear me talk nonstop about it. Thanks for giving me space when I was deep in revisions and providing honest advice when I was lost. Most of all, thank you for believing in me and my little stories.

And lastly my readers. How can I ever thank you? Some of you have been with me for ten years. Every story I write is a love letter to you. This book is a romcom, yes, but it's also a story about family. To me, you're all family. Thanks for reading about Lea and Andrew, Ben and Kai, and Ellie and Dion. *I love you 3000* is never adequate to express how much I appreciate each and every one of you. Thank you, thank you, thank you.